SPICED TO DEATH

Also by Peter King:

The Gourmet Detective

Peter King

SPICED TO DEATH

St. Martin's Press ⚓ New York

Library of Congress Cataloging-in-Publication Data

King, Peter (Christopher Peter).
    Spiced to death / Peter King.
       p.   cm.
    ISBN 0-312-15661-8
    I. Title.
    PS3561.I4822S67   1997
    813'.54—dc21   97-8190
                                     CIP

First edition: July 1997

10 9 8 7 6 5 4 3 2 1

ACKNOWLEDGMENTS

My thanks are due to the following:

Dr. John B. Morrill of the Division of Natural Sciences at New College, University of South Florida, for his invaluable help in structuring the character of Ko Feng;

Joan Wasylik of Cargill Europe for an imposing array of data on the spices of the past; and

Donaleta Robinson of Magagnosc in the South of France for her tireless research into food and restaurants.

CHAPTER ONE

The food looked appetizing enough. It was the Styrofoam and the plastic wrap that spoiled the visual impact.

I opened the little package containing a knife, fork and spoon, a paper napkin, salt and pepper. It wasn't easy to open—why do they make the plastic so strong? Pulling out the fork, I broke one of the tines—why do they make the plastic so weak? But I wasn't here to make a critical survey of the plastics industry so I turned my attention back to the food.

The small salad wasn't too bad. The tomato slices were surprisingly tasty and the lettuce was reasonably crisp—not an easy achievement when it has been tightly wrapped for hours. The mustard greens and the endives were acceptable and the tiny croutons were crunchy. The dressing was too thick and too sweet for my preference but there was no pleasing every salad eater among the tens of thousands of airline passengers being served this same meal.

There was sufficient vinegar in the dressing—despite its sweetness—that I waited to finish before pouring the red Bordeaux into the plastic cup. Plastic is a terrible surrounding for any wine, especially a wine which is already struggling vainly against the disadvantaged background of being without a vintage—the vinous equivalent of being illegitimate.

CHAPTER TWO

I had first met Don Renshaw some years ago. I was living and working in London and he was visiting from his native Cornwall where he had a small boat-building business. His customers were mostly fishermen, who had been coming to him with increasing frequency asking how to get rid of their extra catches of lobster, crab, mussels and fish. A mutual acquaintance put us in touch with each other and I suggested that he start a soup cannery. I helped him do this and as the business prospered, Don sold the boat business and concentrated on canning.

My own business had been in existence for only a short period then. I sought out rare food ingredients, advised on the use of little-known food specialties, recommended new possibilities and marketing opportunities and put sellers in touch with buyers of exotic food products.

I had called myself a food-finder at first; then someone had dubbed me the "Gourmet Detective" and the name had stuck. I thought the title more suited to the flamboyancy of the advertising world than my humble enterprise but it was an aid in bringing in customers. The only disadvantage was that I had to keep explaining that I wasn't a detective at all in the usual sense of the word.

Some time passed before our paths crossed again. Don was in London and looked me up, enlisting my help in locating new markets for hawthorn, which was widely used in the Middle Ages for heart and blood problems. He told me that he had added an herb and spice operation and was planning on specializing in this area as the business was really thriving. When we had our concluding conversation, he told me that his wife, Peggy, had a brother who had emigrated to the States at an early age and done very well with a trucking business. At his instigation, Don had been persuaded to consider opening an American outlet.

Don called me once after that. He was back in England briefly after deciding to move permanently to the States. In New York, his Spice Warehouse, catering to a rapidly expanding demand for herbs and spices, was doing phenomenally well. I had not heard from him then for some years. Then came the phone call . . .

After we had exchanged greetings, statements of health, interchanges of how long it had been and so on, Don asked, "How busy are you?"

"Things are ticking over," I told him.

"Quiet, huh?"

"I have been busier," I admitted. "You know how it is— up and down."

"How about helping me out with a small job?"

"I probably could," I said, not wanting to sound too anxious.

"You'd have to come over here."

"For how long? I have to give evidence in Scotland next week. Some poaching is going on in the trout streams—"

"I prefer them grilled myself."

"This is the other kind. I have to give evidence on whether I consider that the trout that were caught are the property of a certain laird or whether they are free souls, blithely independent, owing allegiance to no one."

"Like the poacher."

"He's innocent until caught with a rod in his hand and a trout on the line."

"Well," Don said, "this job won't interfere with that. It'll only take a couple of days, three at the most. Besides, it's one you won't be able to resist."

I knew Don well enough to know that if he said that, it must be something out of the ordinary.

"How long since you were over here last?" he went on.

"Some years," I admitted.

"And I recall you saying that New York was one of your favorite cities?"

"Don—your sales pitch has worked. What's the job?"

He chuckled. "I managed to get a contract to authenticate a shipment coming into New York from Asia. I did a job for this outfit once before and he threw this one my way. The thing is—" He hesitated.

"Go on," I urged. "What is the thing?"

"Because of the importance of this shipment, the buyer insists on having two referees. He's prepared to accept my recommendation on the second referee and I thought of you."

"Authenticate a shipment, you say?"

"Right."

"Like in examine it, smell it, test it, taste it, whatever else?"

"You've got it."

"Our choice on methods?"

"Yes."

"Then declare that to the best of our knowledge, et cetera, et cetera . . ."

"Right."

"Or not—as the case may be."

"Absolutely."

"Well," I said, "sounds straightforward enough to me. And—Don, you're right, I would like to see the Big Apple again."

"It has been some years since you were here, hasn't it? We call it the Big Bagel now. I can count you in, then?"

"What's the fee?"

"Five hundred a day—dollars, that is. First-class travel and accommodation. Two days, maybe three. You'll be back in time for your fish."

"Sounds good. What's the shipment?"

There was a couple of seconds hesitation, which should have given me some kind of a clue . . .

"You know about my Spice Warehouse, don't you?" he asked.

"You mentioned that's what you were going into when I talked to you last."

"Yes, well, I've disposed of all the other activities and am really building this business up."

"Fine. How's it going?"

"Tremendous. Planning on expanding again. In fact"—he paused and there was a flatness in his tone that sounded peculiar—"after this job, I'll be able to really expand."

"And this is a spice shipment that's coming in? They're usually pretty easy, emphasis on aroma and taste, difficult to substitute—"

"This one won't be that easy."

He paused.

"Go on," I urged. "What's the problem? Which spice?"

"It's Ko Feng," he said and I almost dropped the phone.

CHAPTER THREE

That conversation had taken place thirty-six hours earlier. I finished the salad and cut into the steak, which was reasonably succulent, and poured some more Bordeaux. The pepper on the steak activated the tannin in the wine and gave its powers of self-assertion a much-needed boost.

The rest of our telephone conversation had been taken up with a discussion of Ko Feng, which was something like playing a game of tennis without a ball. In my business, I often handle spices so I know something of them and am aware of their long history and the vital part they have played in the annals of food.

The ancient world had many famous spices. The earliest of these was what today we refer to as "ordinary" black pepper but two to three thousand years ago, it was anything but ordinary. In fact, it was so valuable that it was sold by the individual peppercorn. All the early trading caravans carried huge quantities of it as they tracked across the deserts of the Middle East, and fortunes were made from a string of camels and a great deal of risk and hardship.

The reason for pepper's value was simple. The diet of those days was coarse, monotonous and unpalatable by modern standards. Food spoiled quickly. Pepper—and later other spices—served two purposes. Not only did they add flavor but their antioxidant qualities retarded spoilage, particularly of meat.

Other spices included ginger, nutmeg, cloves, cinnamon and many others which are lost to us today. These others were used for drug and medicinal purposes and extraordinary claims were made for them. The Code of Hammurabi stipulated that a surgeon was to have his hands cut off if a patient died under his care so it is understandable that the use of drugs was extensive.

One papyrus found in China listed eight hundred herbs and spices with medicinal value and when the Magi brought their gifts to Bethlehem, myrrh was rated next in value to gold. Myrrh was also the biggest selling commodity in the little spice shop in Mecca run by Mohammed before he became the prophet of Islam.

All these thoughts were tumbling through my mind as Don and I exchanged information. He reminded me that silphium was a much sought-after drug in the ancient world and was exchanged on a weight-for-weight basis with silver. It was already extinct by the end of the first century.

But the most famous of all was Ko Feng, known as the Celestial Spice.

"It's been unknown now for—how long? Four hundred years? Five hundred?" I asked Don.

"Something like that. Maybe more."

"And now somebody's found some?"

"Right."

"Or say they have."

"That's where you and I come in," he said cheerfully but I was feeling a slight chill.

"This is some authentication job," I said grimly.

"Want to back out?"

"How could I? This may be one of the most exciting moments in the history of food since Nicolas Appert discovered how to preserve it in cans."

"Okay, then you and I are going to have some Ko Feng in our hands next Tuesday."

"Or not—as the case may be."

"Pessimist."

"Maybe, but it's hard to believe."

"True. I guess I've had a little longer to adjust to it," Don had said.

I finished the steak and unwrapped the cheese. It needed to sit exposed to the air for a short time so that it could recover some taste after its incarceration in aluminum foil and plastic.

Don and I had concluded our conversation with details on how, where and when. I had called him back with flight information and he had given me hotel reservation numbers. He would like to meet me at JFK, he said, but the buyer of the Ko Feng wanted a last-minute meeting with him. Don's wife, Peggy, would be taking care of the Spice Warehouse so she couldn't come either. I assured him that I could easily find my own way to the hotel in Manhattan.

Sunlight glinted off the silver wing outside my window. This time tomorrow I would be looking at some Ko Feng, the miraculous spice from thousands of years ago. I tingled with impatience. It was like anticipating a date with Cleopatra.

CHAPTER FOUR

Reeger," said the cab driver, jerking a thumb toward his chest. He had a slight stubble and tired eyes, and he wore a cap that was more nautical than automotive. He didn't handle the cab like a true professional and I presumed he was new at it, perhaps forced to switch jobs by the recession. Evidently he wanted me to know that his name was Reeger but I was looking at the identification tag fastened to the dashboard. It said that his name was Janis Rezekne and his photo looked worse than he did.

He told me a lot about himself with the plexiglass slide between us pulled open—another sign that his cab-driving experience was not only recent but downright contemporary. At least, I supposed he was telling me about himself. I could only understand about one word in ten and wondered if I had been away from New York too long. But no, that couldn't be the reason because just last week I had watched an Al Pacino movie on television and understood every other word.

I didn't want to uphold my end of the conversation with too much conviction as I was afraid I might distract him from his driving, which needed a lot more practice. So I managed an occasional nod or look of comprehension. By concentrating on his words, I learned that he was a Latvian and from Riga, which was what he had been proudly trying to tell me. He had only been here six months. I would have believed six days but didn't press the point as he used fingers to illustrate the number and that didn't leave any hands for the wheel. America was a wonderful country, he told me, and we embroidered on that theme all the way in to Manhattan, making full use of our joint vocabulary, which eventually stretched to about two dozen words.

New York hadn't changed that much, I noted. Traffic was just as thick and the cars seemed so much bigger as they always do. The streets were a little dirtier and more untidy but then, on returning to London after a spell away, that was noticeable there too. People looked more polyglot as they now look in all big cities.

When the cabby dropped me at the Courtney Park Hotel, it was like the parting of two old friends. He clapped me on the back and let me lift my own bags out of the cab.

The lobby was stunning with a tinkling fountain in the center and a chandelier above it that would have had the Phantom gnashing his teeth in envy. Shops and boutiques ran off along small streets in all directions from the fountain and the sign said that the display of life-size sculpture was changed every week. Don Renshaw had meant it when he said that accommodation would be first class.

There were lines waiting at each of the four check-in desks and though I switched a couple of times, I was still in the longest when I signed in. I was handed a note from Don saying that he and his wife, Peggy, would pick me up at 7:30 for dinner.

This was my home away from home, the brochure in the room assured me, but they obviously didn't know that my apartment in Hammersmith in West London could fit into the bathroom here. From the window I could see a corner of Central Park. I had a long and leisurely shower, then watched some television.

This was something that had changed in the country since I was here last. Television's emphasis was no longer on entertainment but on exploitation. I watched in near disbelief as first a black woman was encouraging a studio audience to applaud couples consisting of men and women who had stolen their best friend's spouse; then a Puerto Rican gentleman was investigating homosexuality in mental institutions; and then an Asian interviewer was telling how she used promises of confidentiality to persuade guests on her show to divulge scurrilous opinions of famous people, then blabbed them on the air. I skimmed through the channels but Bugs Bunny seemed to be the nearest I could get to entertainment.

I dressed and went downstairs. The shops and boutiques were full of fabulous merchandise at what, by London standards, were extremely low prices. I made a second tour and then sat by the fountain until Don and Peggy arrived.

They didn't look a lot different, possibly a little fatter and more affluent. Don was stocky, of medium height with fair, thinning hair and a ruddy complexion. He greeted me effusively, then Peggy and I exchanged hugs. She was light blond with a smooth English complexion and eyes that always looked happy.

The short taxi ride to the restaurant was taken up with exchanges of information on mutual acquaintances, their progress and problems. It was not until we were seated that I was able to get to the questions that had been burning in my brain ever since Don's phone call.

"Sorry to talk business so soon, Peggy," I said, "but this is the most exciting thing that's happened in the food business since an innovative caveman found that meat tasted better cooked than raw. Finding a crop of Ko Feng—it's amazing!"

Don smiled. "I know. I felt the same way at first. I've had some time to get used to the idea so I'm finally beginning to accept it. It certainly sounded incredible when I first heard about it."

"I take care of the Spice Warehouse when Don's away, buying or whatever," Peggy said, "so I'm just as enthusiastic as you. I must admit I hadn't heard of Ko Feng before this, though."

"It's been extinct for centuries, so not many people know it," Don said. "Folks in the trade have heard of it, of course, just as many have heard of Melegueta peppers."

"Known as the Grains of Paradise," I contributed. "Nobody expects to hear of either of them cropping up today, though."

"Nice choice of a verb," commented Don.

"Sorry—it was accidental. But how *did* somebody find it? And who was it? Was he looking for it? How did he know it was there?"

The wine waiter arrived and introduced himself. This is a practice which is creeping into the London restaurant scene but hasn't made significant headway yet. Under some circumstances, I respond with "I'm the Gourmet Detective and I'll be your customer tonight" but my head was spinning with questions and anyway Don was the host.

If America is a melting pot, then New York is a cooking pot. Surely no city in the world has so many eating places and such an enormous variety of ethnic cultures on which they are based. There cannot be any cuisine in the world which is not represented in New York.

We were in the Mondragon, one of Manhattan's newer eating establishments. The canopied entrance was in soft French blue with gold lettering. Inside, the stained-glass ceiling panels, the elegant mahogany-railed curving staircase leading to the upper dining level and the luxurious leaf-patterned carpet made a sumptuous background. Don caught me looking around.

"Don't worry—the food's as good as the decor."

He ordered a bottle of champagne by way of celebration—it was the Dom Ruinart Brut Blanc de Blancs.

"Well, that tells me one thing about the buyer of the Ko Feng—he's paying well for this job," I said, knowing that the price tag would be close to $100 for the bottle.

Don nodded. "You were asking about him. Name's Alexander Marvell. He was in the restaurant business for many years, then went into the food importing field here in New York. When I first opened the Spice Warehouse, he bought some turmeric from me. It was from Alleppey in India—the very best kind as you know. I've sold him a couple of other shipments since then but that's all. I was surprised when he picked me for this assignment."

"Willard recommended you, that's why Marvell picked you," said Peggy.

"Willard Cartwright is Marvell's right-hand man," Don explained.

"Nobody better qualified than you, surely," I said. "The Spice Warehouse must have put you in the forefront of spice experts."

"It'll work the other way too," Peggy added. "There's a lot of prestige involved here—should boost business in the warehouse by a few percent."

The wine waiter brought the champagne and opened it expertly, enough of a pop to satisfy but not enough to make heads turn. It bubbled perfectly into the glasses and we drank and studied the menus.

Don and I both decided on the Oysters Rockefeller while Peggy chose the crab meat with avocado and lemon grass with a red pepper coulis. For the main course, Peggy and Don had the rack of lamb while I ordered the *Jarret de Veau à l'Italienne*— a refined French version of osso buco, one of my favorite dishes.

We finished the champagne and Don ordered a Diamond Creek Cabernet Sauvignon. The appetizers were excellent and so were the main courses. Don and Peggy's rack of lamb was rosy red and oozing with taste, they told me. My slowly cooked veal shank had been sprinkled with gremolata, that wonderful blend of garlic, parsley and lemon zest, and it was slightly dry rather than being drenched in braising juices, a common fault with this dish. The imaginative accompaniment was a purée of white beans.

The waiters were prompt and attentive, and Don and I compared service in New York restaurants with their counterparts in London.

"Many's the time I've had to wait thirty minutes for a check in London," Don said, "even in the West End. Some restaurants seem to have a positive aversion to bringing it."

"English middle-class disdain for any dealings with money," said Peggy. "Anyway, waiting for the check never bothered you—you'd just order another bottle of wine."

"Isn't that out of character for a nation of shopkeepers?" I asked.

"We never were," Peggy said. "That was just Napoleon's way of showing his contempt."

"Or his ignorance," added Don.

We sipped the wine.

"Meanwhile," I said, "back at the Spice Ranch with the Ko Feng . . ."

Don laughed. "The way it was found, you mean? Alexander Marvell was in Saigon negotiating a contract for rice—that's one of his biggest commodities. One of the men he was talking to mentioned a cinnamon plantation that he thought Marvell ought to take a look at. Marvell doesn't handle that many spices so he was reluctant, but he couldn't get a flight out right away so he went.

Well, the way Marvell tells it, they were driving along and from the jeep, Marvell looked down into a valley where he saw a strange-looking crop. He said it glowed in the setting sun and he asked what it was. The answer was 'Just weeds.' "

The waiter brought dessert menus and I reluctantly tore myself away from Don's fascinating story. The specialty was a *mascarpone* sorbet with wild strawberries and all three of us ordered it. Don continued.

"Marvell said he couldn't get the image of that peculiar crop out of his mind. He felt there was something about it that was far out of the ordinary. He went back again the next day and took a sample and went into Saigon to the university."

"I have to chip in here," Peggy said. "If Alexander Marvell didn't have an import business, he might be running a religion. He's an extraordinary man—I can just picture him standing there, looking down into that purple valley and having an unshakable conviction that there was something magical about it."

Don nodded in agreement. "It's true, that's how he is. Anyway, the people at Saigon University were puzzled. It was no weed they recognized—or plant, for that matter. So Marvell changed his flight plan back to New York. Instead of going via Bombay and London, he booked in the opposite direction so as to stop off in San Francisco"—he broke off and looked at me—"I'm sure you can guess why San Francisco . . ."

"Probably because that's where the Mecklenburg Botanical Institute is. They're number one in that kind of study."

"Right. He even stayed in a nearby hotel and pressured them into going to work on the investigation right away. Once they had started, they got really interested and—to cut a long story short—they eventually concluded that it must be Ko Feng."

"Which presumably didn't mean much to Marvell at that point. I mean, not being a spice specialist, there would be no reason for him to even know the name—"

"He didn't. Once he read up on it, though, he became really excited."

"I hate to ask such a crass commercial question," I said, "but how much do you suppose Ko Feng is worth on today's market?"

Don grinned. "It's okay to ask the question. You're in the U.S. of A. now—commercialism comes with the territory. This wouldn't be the country it is without commerce. Money lubricates the wheels of progress."

"We still want to know how much," Peggy said, tapping a spoon on the table for emphasis. "I was asking you this question the other day and I never did get an answer."

Don spread his hands. "It's so hard to say. How can you value something like this? It's worth whatever someone wants to pay."

"Sort of like the *Mona Lisa?*" Peggy asked.

"In a way, yes."

"Or that Van Gogh that a Japanese bought for thirty million dollars?"

"They'll do as examples. What's the Van Gogh worth? Wood, paint and canvas—total twenty dollars. The *Mona Lisa?* Maybe less, the materials are older."

"There is a difference, though," I pointed out. "When a million visitors to the Louvre have looked at the *Mona Lisa,* another million can come and look at it. When this spice has all been eaten up—then what?"

"The scarcity makes it all the more valuable," Don said.

Peggy looked at Don. "Hasn't Marvell said anything about value?"

"I haven't been able to get any clue from him as to what he's going to sell it for."

"Will we get some?" Peggy wanted to know.

"Doubt it. I told him I'd like some, though."

"What does saffron sell for now?" I asked. "It's the most valuable spice there is today."

"At the point of retail sale—about $200 an ounce," Don replied.

"Ko Feng must be worth far more than that. Like ten times more?" I pressed.

"More, probably."

"And the shipment is—what did you say, Don—about forty kilograms?"

"About that."

Peggy was doing quick sums on the tablecloth with a fork. "That's two to three million dollars," she said softly.

We sat silent for a moment, all of us awestruck at the thought of such wealth in such a simple form. The dessert arrived to end our reverie.

It was superb. The piquancy of the wild strawberries contrasted perfectly with the smoothness of the *mascarpone,* which is one of the newer arrivals on the dessert scene though long a popular cheese in Italy.

Peggy ordered tea, Don and I coffee. Before it came, I had already asked the big question.

"About tomorrow. How do we go about authenticating a spice that has been unknown for centuries?"

We sat over coffee discussing it until the waiter came by for the second time to ask if we wanted more coffee or anything further.

"Big day tomorrow," Don said, examining the check. "Pick you about eight o'clock. There'll be some formalities to go through before the flight gets in at ten forty-five."

"I can hardly wait," I said, and I really meant it.

CHAPTER FIVE

It was cold with a blustery wind and there was the threat of rain from a gray sky. The yawning expanse of the cargo area at JFK added to the bleak aspect of the morning but I was tingling with anticipation. It was a rare occasion and I was going to enjoy every minute of it.

At the entrance, we had shown our identification and signed in. The security man assigned to the hangar we were heading for was waiting and he joined us. He was a rugged-looking young man with a determined no-nonsense air about him. His name was Karl Eberhard and he had a slight but unmistakable German accent.

Don followed his directions and we pulled up in front of a large hangar with BLS 12 painted on the side in red letters. A cargo tow truck stood near it with a flatbed trailer. We walked into the hangar. It was cold and the bare concrete floor made it even colder. Voices echoed several times before becoming lost in the cavernous ceiling.

Along the length of one wall of the hangar, several bays were separated by partitions. Each bay had desks, chairs, benches, tables. In the first one, half a dozen men sat playing cards. The second had several men and benches and tables that were littered with equipment. Karl Eberhard led us toward this second bay and I noticed that the third bay was empty except for a big black car. Three or four men were talking in the fourth bay and two more bays were empty. A closed pickup truck sat in front of the first bay, a gray van was at the entrance to our bay, and there was a shiny new rental van by the fourth bay.

Don held out his hand toward one of the men in the bay we entered.

"Hello, Willard, didn't expect to see you here. Where's the boss?"

"Something vital came up. He can't make it. He asked me to take care of it. It's just formalities here anyway."

Don took my arm and introduced me. Then to me, he said, "This is Willard Cartwright, Alexander Marvell's assistant."

We shook hands. He was lean and spare, light on his feet and lively in his movements. His face was older than his body, creased and worn, but the faded blue eyes were quick and intelligent. He introduced Don and me to the others.

Arthur Appleton of FarEast Air Freightlines was balding and shivering in a lightweight suit. "Coldest building in the airport," he said. "Good for your spice, I guess, but it's not very friendly to humans."

Sam Rong was a Cambodian representing the sellers, who had a series of Asian names which I promptly forgot. He was short and had one of those smooth and unlined faces which was probably twenty years younger than his birth certificate.

Coming from the first bay was Michael Simpson, who introduced himself as Customs and Excise. He was heavily built, getting close to retirement age. He wheezed as he spoke. "Hear you're from London. Spent three weeks over there last year—loved it—hope we can go back next year."

Cartwright explained that two other high security shipments were coming in on the same flight as the Ko Feng and all would be processed in this hangar. The men playing cards in the first bay were bringing in some experimental computer circuit boards from their parent, Sushimoto Electronics. The fourth bay was handling a crate of ivory carvings destined for the Chicago Museum of Oriental Art.

"I hear the other people canceled out," said Eberhard, nodding toward the empty third bay.

"Yes," said Appleton. "We didn't know until the aircraft had taken off from Bangkok."

All of them were to handle the formalities for all three shipments but there would be no delays, Appleton assured us. He excused himself to answer a call on his belt phone, which seemed to concern a flight arriving in the afternoon from Taiwan.

Karl Eberhard went for a stroll and seemed to be surveying the bare walls. I couldn't see anything to look at but maybe that was the way security people did it. Simpson wandered off to talk to the Chicago Museum people and I took the opportunity to study the bay we were in.

Briefcases, papers, folders, a metal file box and a phone were on the desks, but it was the benches on either side of the stainless steel sink and drainboard that caught my attention. All kinds of laboratory equipment were on them and I looked at Don.

"Did you arrange for all this?"

"Yes. I told Cartwright what we wanted and he rented it for a couple of days. We checked it all out yesterday."

Appleton's phone buzzed again.

"That's flight 227," he said, snapping the instrument back into place. "Airport radar has picked it up. It's being cleared for landing."

"Flight 227 is ours," Willard Cartwright said. He looked tense enough to start chewing his fingernails.

Appleton walked to the next bay to give them the news and it effectively broke up the card game. Voices were raised over who owed how much. Eberhard came back, then walked off again. I moved to Sam Rong's side. It was a good chance to find out more about the Celestial Spice.

"I'm curious about the Ko Feng crop, "I said.

He smiled, apparently pleased at my curiosity. "Ah, yes."

"I wondered how much of the crop you harvested?"

"Almost all," said Rong, still smiling.

"Will there be another crop next year?"

His smile broadened. "Must wait and see next year."

"You mean there may not be another crop?" I said, surprised.

"Don't think so. Must remember we know nothing of this crop. We think it is weeds."

"How long has it been growing? After all, it was supposed to be extinct centuries ago."

"Maybe grow a long time. We think it is weeds, pay no attention."

"Hadn't you noticed the haze?"

For the first time, his smile ebbed. "Please?"

"Marvell saw a glow over the field . . ."

"Ah, yes—glow. No one else sees this."

"But you did when Marvell pointed it out."

Sam Rong shook his head firmly. "No. No one else sees it."

"What processing have you carried out so far?"

"We follow Mr. Marvell's instructions. Pull stamens out of flowers." He paused and repeated the word, proud of knowing it. "Stamen—is like a stalk. End produces pollen. This work can be done only in early morning when flower opens to greet new day." His wide grin came back.

"Very poetic," I complimented, then wondered if he understood me.

"Poetic," he said. "Poetic, yes." I still wasn't sure.

"Need thirty thousand stamens—make one ounce Ko Feng," Sam Rong went on. "Foundation in San Francisco say so."

Don came back from talking to Arthur Appleton, and Willard Cartwright asked Sam Rong something about documents.

"Learning all about Ko Feng?" Don asked me.

"I learned that it takes thirty thousand stamens to yield an ounce of it," I said. "I hate to ask how long it takes to collect them."

"Now you know why it's already the most expensive spice in the world," Don said. "How about a cup of coffee?"

Two large vacuum jugs stood on the table and as we sipped, I noticed that Karl Eberhard was still patrolling. Michael Simpson returned from the Chicago Museum bay and went to talk briefly with the Sushimoto Electronics people. All was in order apparently and he came back to us and struck up a conversation with Don and me about London.

A phone buzzed again. Arthur Appleton unhooked his and answered. When he put it back, he came over to us.

"Two-twenty-seven's been cleared for landing. Want to watch her come in? She'll be on runway 31."

He walked off to give the same information to the men in the other two bays. We all went outside. An Air India freighter was just lifting off the ground and the shattering noise drowned any conversation. The sky was still gray but cloud cover was high enough that we could see the lights twinkling on a distant aircraft. On an adjacent runway, a four-engine plane with a high tail was taxiing for takeoff. I couldn't make out what it was but Arthur Appleton waited until the Air India freighter was dwindling out of sight and said, "Tupolev—Russian—we call it the Vodka Express."

A breeze blew across the field, augmented by jet engine slipstreams and dust and papers billowed. The lights on the incoming aircraft grew stronger and we stood in scattered groups, watching.

The 747 came in trailing streamers of vapor. The motors thumped rhythmically in the humid air. The plane loomed larger, then it was touching down with spurts of burning rubber. The thrust reversers cut in and the motors snarled mutinously. The plane came rolling down the runway, slower and slower until it turned off and came toward us, stopping about fifty yards away.

Our eager clusters of onlookers stood there as the underbelly of the huge craft hinged down and a slide emerged. The motors were down to an idling whisper. I heard Karl Eberhard behind me saying, "Our three shipments will be unloaded here. The aircraft will go on then for normal unloading."

He went over to the tow truck and started it up. Arthur Appleton was on the phone again, this time to the crew chief in the aircraft. Someone from the Chicago Museum asked him a question and he nodded. "We do it this way with high-security shipments. Minimize the number of persons involved."

Two crewmen emerged from the aircraft and the slide was positioned. Down it came a wooden case, a teak chest and an aluminum case bound with reinforcing strips. Eberhard revved up the tow truck and came slowly back toward us. Over a dozen pairs of anxious eyes watched as the truck came nearer.

Michael Simpson pushed a button to open the vertical sliding door and Eberhard drove in. We all followed. Eberhard went first to the Sushimoto bay where two of their people lifted down their wooden crate. Simpson and Appleton joined them. Eberhard drove on to ours where Cartwright and Sam Rong took off the teak chest and then he went on to deliver the Chicago Museum's aluminum case full of ivory carvings.

But those of us in our small group had already lost interest in the vehicle for our attention was fully on the chest before us. The teak seemed strangely out-of-date compared with the smart wooden crate and the aluminum case carrying the other two shipments. Cartwright and Rong set the chest by the back of the gray truck. Sam Rong came forward, smiling still. He had a small briefcase and took from it a bunch of keys. He selected one and unlocked the padlock. Cartwright lifted the lid and we crowded closer.

Cartwright pulled out a sack of gray coarsely woven canvas and Don brought a two-wheeled trolley from inside our bay.

The sack didn't look heavy but Cartwright put it on the trolley and brought it in to stand it by a bench.

"Go ahead," Don told him.

Cartwright opened the sack, which was tied at the neck with thin rope. Inside was another sack of the same material. He opened that too.

The fabled Ko Feng didn't look like much. Stringy pieces of blackish gray stuff with a dull texture that wouldn't merit a second glance ordinarily. The aroma though—ah, that was a different matter entirely. It came as a fragrance like cloves at first, then it seemed to be more like cinnamon but no, more like cardamom. A mustard odor lurked behind it but that was too harsh a judgment—it was closer to the licorice component of fennel.

"Anise," said Don huskily. "Chervil too but then there are hints of orange and a fragrant tobacco—but then . . ."

We became aware that Cartwright and Rong had stepped back. Don and I probably sounded to them as if we were running through the gamut of smells and would soon be arriving at kerosene and week-old tennis socks.

Sam Rong smiled, noting our return to reality after moments of rapture—but maybe that was just another version of his perpetual smile. I thought not though—I believed he genuinely understood how we had been temporarily carried away.

"Is wonderful aroma. Not like any other."

We agreed with him. Willard Cartwright pushed forward.

"Aroma," he said. "You're satisfied, then?"

"I know I've said this before" said Don, "but if this is Ko Feng, it has been lost for centuries. We have no standards to judge it by. We don't know what it did smell like and we can't—"

"I know," Cartwright said brusquely. "I know all that. But you're happy with the aroma?"

Don looked at me. I nodded.

"We see no reason to doubt but we've only just—"

"Okay," said Cartwright. "What next?"

Don went to one of the benches and brought back a pair of tweezers and a glass flask. He took a few stamens and carefully dropped them into the flask. He took the flask over to the bench and poured in some alcohol. He shook it and held it up to one of the fluorescent lights.

From the next bay came the sounds of splintering wood—presumably they were removing the lid of the wooden crate to examine the circuit boards. Don shook the flask and held it up again. Cartwright started to say something but Don shushed him with an angry wave of his hand. He turned to get a better light behind it and motioned for me to take a look.

Arthur Appleton walked in. "All clear with Sushimoto," he announced breezily. "The merchandise is as advertised and conforms to the documentation. How are you doing in here?"

Cartwright glowered at him, and Don gave a look of annoyance at being interrupted. Sam Rong's smile had been reduced to its minimum dimension. I tried to look neutral.

"We're doing some sensitive testing," I told Appleton, hoping he'd read me. He didn't.

"Looks a lot more fascinating than those dreary circuit boards," he said. He peered into the open sack. "So that's the fabled lost spice, is it? Paperwork okay?"

We had all been so excited that we hadn't given it a thought. Sam Rong walked out of the bay and pulled away the plastic folder fastened to the outside of the crate. He brought it back in and Appleton gave us an amused smile but said nothing. He took the papers and spread them out on the bench. Don shook the flask and stared intently at it again.

"Well?" asked Cartwright impatiently.

"We could probably do this better if you didn't keep interrupting," said Don in what I thought was a tolerant tone of voice.

"I want to know what's happening," Cartwright said, and his voice grated.

"Every minute?"

"Yes," said Cartwright, "every minute."

"Tempers become warm when big decisions hang in balance," Sam Rong said. It sounded like a line from a Charlie Chan B movie. He went on, sensibly enough, "Perhaps Mr. Renshaw could tell us briefly what is purpose of each test and what is result. This way, not necessary to ask questions."

He smiled urbanely at Cartwright, who glared back. Arthur Appleton had momentarily shifted his interest from the papers before him to the minicrisis here and he tried his hand at smoothing the waters.

"I'm only a bystander at this stage, I know, but I'd be interested too in knowing—in layman's terms—what you're doing. After all, each of us is involved in this to some degree."

"I think we can do that, can't we, Don." I put it as a statement rather than a question.

He shrugged. "Sure. Want to tell them what we just did?" He sounded slightly irritated but the unique nature of the moment was bound to be raising tensions and his irritation was exceeded only by Cartwright's impatience.

"Don put the Ko Feng into alcohol because it will dissolve any adulterants or coloring agents that might have been added," I explained. "No color is visible in the alcohol."

Don was already busy with the next test.

"He's now soaking a stamen in distilled water—" I caught a puzzled look from Appleton. "Stamen is a common term with botanists—it's the male reproductive organ of a plant where pollination takes place. Now he's rolling it between two sheets of absorbent paper. Any water-soluble contaminants will show up at this stage . . . No, there aren't any."

The commentary seemed to be working. Cartwright looked

marginally more composed but I realized how great a strain he must be under. Simpson was walking by. He called in cheerily, "Making progress with the ivory. Be with you in a while." He went on to the Sushimoto bay.

Don was now switching on the microscope. He gave me a nod to say he would take over. I nodded back, glad his humor was restored.

"I'm looking at the stamen at a hundred magnifications . . ." He waved to us to approach and we crowded round to look at the screen. "Now I'm zooming to five hundred . . . looks normal . . . this is a thousand."

There was a silence while the watchers wondered exactly what they were looking at. Don went on, "It looks just like a plant stamen. Of course, we have no way of knowing what a Ko Feng stamen looks like. All I can say is there is no reason to suppose that this is not Ko Feng."

He looked at me. The others followed suit. "I agree," I said.

Don took one more of the stamens with tweezers and laid it on a plastic board.

"He's cutting a cross-section so as to look at the internal structure of the stem. It might be possible to breed a hybrid which would look different from any plant we know and thus it might be passed off as Ko Feng . . ." The significance of what I was saying suddenly occurred to me and I turned to give Sam Rong an apologetic grin. He interpreted it with impeccable intuition and widened his smile in understanding.

". . . but a cross-section reveals the botanical structure and would be almost impossible to change."

Don was unrolling a chart showing graphic illustrations of sections of various plants. He ran through them, frequently stopping to compare with the image on the screen. Finally, he nodded.

"Looks good."

A few exhalations of breath might have been sighs of relief

all around. Arthur Appleton excused himself. "Better go check on the ivory carvings. More exciting here, though." He walked off and his voice could be heard echoing as he hailed the museum people.

Karl Eberhard came in. I had forgotten him. He looked curiously at the microscope screen but said nothing. He seemed to have temporarily concluded his security patrols and he stood and waited to see what was happening next.

Don now took a ceramic crucible and dropped a couple of stamens into it. He placed the crucible into an infrared heating coil and turned the switch. The digital readout flickered, numbers climbing. Don adjusted the switch to slow the heating rate and we both sniffed, then sniffed again.

"No obvious aromas that shouldn't be present," I reported.

Don pulled over another piece of equipment. A hood mounted on a pedestal fitted over the crucible and a duct led to a square black box. Several dials on the front of the box showed zero. Don turned switches and a red light glowed.

"This is a smoke-analyzing probe," I explained. "It's being used here first, to look for constituents that shouldn't be here, and second, to see what constituents are present that would indicate a specific botanical family or group."

"Looks good," Don said again. He activated an adjoining device which clattered and then spat out a sheet of paper. "A readout for the records."

Even Cartwright looked more relaxed now and Don continued with the testing. Occasionally, he explained what he was doing and when he didn't, I took over. Eberhard walked off briskly, as if he were going somewhere vital but it was probably another of his patrols. Simpson came back and stood watching. At a lull in the proceedings, he said apologetically, "None of my business but some of the special goods that come through customs have to be accompanied by an analysis. They use a piece of equipment called a quantometer which does it real fast. I was wondering—"

"No," Don said. "You can't analyze plants that way. They contain mostly the same elements and in the same approximate percentages. An analysis would tell us nothing."

"Sorry," murmured Simpson. "Just a thought . . ."

"What we do have, though, is this," Don went on, patting an instrument that looked like a small hi-fi unit. It bristled with gauges, needles, knobs and digital readout displays, and was connected to a computer next to it.

"It's called an HPLC. That's high pressure liquid chromatograph. It can separate the components of the plant, some of which fluoresce. It exposes this fluorescence to a light beam which . . . well, you'll see in a minute."

Don took the sample in the alcohol flask and carefully set it in an opening in the machine. He pushed a button and a shutter snapped closed as the sample disappeared. He twisted a couple of knobs, pushed some buttons and a pattern flickered into view on the computer screen. It looked like a seismograph—all peaks and valleys.

"There," Don said. "That's the pattern which represents this sample. Now, we superimpose"—he pushed more buttons—"the pattern of the plant that the Mecklenburg Institute examined."

Everyone crowded closer for a better look.

"As you can see, they're almost identical."

One or two sighs sounded, a blend of relief and approval.

Arthur Appleton rejoined us with a Did-I-miss-anything? look but no one moved to enlighten him.

Don had recovered his usual good spirits and he went through the remaining tests with just enough comments. At last, looking around like a lecturer, he said, "Now, Ko Feng could easily become the most valuable food flavoring ever used by man. So it's important that we establish now"—he spread his hands—"how does it taste?"

He brought over a sealed container and set it on the infrared heater, adjusting the temperature. He removed the lid and looked at us with a half smile.

"Looks like spaghetti," muttered Arthur Appleton.

Karl Eberhard came into the bay, sniffing. "Something burning," he said. "Hasn't triggered the smoke alarms, though . . ." A couple of grins must have informed him because he looked at the crucible and the heater and nodded acceptance.

Don was chopping a few of the stamens in a portable blender. He squeezed the button and the machine whirred. Over the gentle noise, Don said, "The trick is to use only a very tiny quantity. Many of the spices we use today are like this—you need to use only a minimal amount to generate the maximum taste, use more and it will taste bitter. Saffron, cardamom, ginger, cayenne and the chile spices are all examples."

He shook out a little finely ground powder, separated a microscopic quantity and sprinkled it carefully into the now steaming spaghetti.

"Pasta is a suitable medium as it's bland and acts only as a means for carrying the taste," he explained. He stirred a few times.

"Most spices and flavorings need to be cooked for some time to generate their taste," I added. "We can investigate that later—right now, we just want to confirm the identity of the Ko Feng."

"True," Don agreed. "If this is really Ko Feng and if it is the wondrous spice that myth, legend and history say—then tasting will put the crowning seal of verification on it."

I added a comment. "Testing equipment keeps getting more and more sophisticated but human taste is still amazingly sensitive. The tongue can detect a flavor in a solution of more than a million times its volume."

With all three of the JFK officials back with us now, we must have been a strange sight—seven men all eagerly dipping plastic forks into a bowl of pasta. Some went back for another forkful but Don and I were still moving that first one around in our mouths.

Arthur Appleton was the first to comment.

"Beats anything I've ever tasted," he said, adding hastily, "not that I'm a connoisseur."

Sam Rong and Karl Eberhard looked at each other and nodded enthusiastically. Willard Cartwright was savoring a mouthful. He raised his eyebrows to me questioningly.

"Magnificent," I said. "Not like anything I've ever tasted before. Don, don't you agree?"

"Wonderful," he nodded, his eyes bright. He looked at Cartwright. "I believe we can say that as far as we can determine—this is truly Ko Feng."

Something like a subdued cheer arose. It was also a vast sigh of relief, and the tension that had existed before went down like the temperature when going from a hot kitchen into a walk-in deep-freeze.

Sam Rong clapped Michael Simpson on the back and his smile reached record dimensions. Arthur Appleton pumped Cartwright's hand and told him he was delighted. Cartwright still looked tight-lipped but a hint of a smile was there. Don beamed at Karl Eberhard, who simply nodded his satisfaction and hitched up his military belt as if to say he was glad that job was out of the way and what was the next one.

Cartwright retied the inner sack and then the outer one.

"Our property now," he said to Sam Rong, who beamed and handed him the keys. Cartwright put the sack on to the two-wheeled trolley and took it to the van. He unlocked the back door, rolled it up, carefully set the sack inside the chest and we watched him lock it and then the van.

"We complete documents now?" Sam Rong asked.

"Sure," said Appleton. He spread out what looked like the air waybill, the bill of sale and a couple of other documents.

Simpson took out his customs documents and contributed to the paper chase.

"Certificate of authentication," said Appleton and held out a pen for Don and me to sign.

A squawk sounded from the bench. We all looked for the source. It was a timer that Don had been using during the testing. He pushed a button to silence it. "Sorry. Must have forgotten to shut it off."

Printed forms moved to and fro, some blue, some yellow, some white. Duplicates and triplicates were torn off and distributed. Papers begat more papers. Signatures were applied and dates added. Appleton and Simpson worked smoothly, making it clear that they did this kind of thing every day.

All went well until—

"Hold everything!" said Michael Simpson. He was staring at the form in front of him. "This is wrong!"

CHAPTER SIX

Everyone froze. Then we crowded around the desk where Simpson was tapping his finger on the thick Customs and Excise manual, which listed every conceivable product and gave its commodity code. Alongside the manual, the receiving documents were opened at a page where the code number was ringed in red.

"They're different," Simpson said. "See, we're classifying Ko Feng as 'Spice, Oriental, Code 174.67,' but on your receiving document, you've got the code as 176.47."

"Clerical error," said Arthur Appleton dismissively. A voice shouted his name from the Chicago Museum bay and he excused himself and walked off. Simpson went into a discussion with Cartwright and Sam Rong. They found another minor discrepancy which prompted further debate but the points were finally resolved to everyone's relief.

Papers packed, hands shaken, farewells said, we prepared to leave. Don had told me that we had to go to the New York and Asian Bank in Manhattan, which had provided the financing and was handling the escrow. Cartwright climbed into the driver's seat of the van, telling us he didn't trust anyone else to drive, not even a professional. The vehicle had been modified so that it had an extra row of seats. Sam Rong sat with Cartwright, and Don and I sat behind.

Love it or hate it, people say about New York. Its detractors say that Peter Minuit was robbed when he paid $24 for it but that's unfair. Most—and especially European visitors—think it's a fabulous city and so do I. But one facet of it appeals to no-body, and that's the traffic. We crawled along the Long Island Expressway through the Queens Midtown Tunnel, then out into the creeping mass of cars, buses and trucks that edged through green lights and stood at red lights, fuming with impa-tience and the occasional faulty exhaust.

Noise always seems louder in New York but there is that indefinable crackle of excitement that is almost tangible. Cartwright's driving was expert and we made reasonable time down toward the financial district. Cartwright glanced anxiously in his rearview mirror every time we stopped at a light or signal but finally we turned into a ramp on the Avenue of the Amer-icas. We went down a darkened tunnel where a guard stopped us. He had been alerted by phone that we were approaching and he promptly raised the barrier and directed us ahead.

We went down another ramp and emerged into an area that was little more than a concrete box, not a lot larger than the van. Two bank guards appeared and stood guard by the van while we went inside.

The conference room was lined with mahogany panels and portraits of former bank presidents, all Asians. Amber ceiling lights cast a mellow glow, which was reflected in the shiny top of the large table. Five of the bank staff were present, but the one who did all the talking was Ben Thuy, a wiry little man with a commanding presence.

"We have everything prepared for you," he said. He didn't even have to snap his fingers before an aide came forward with a folder. Cartwright and Sam Rong produced their documents and they had a great time, shuffling and signing.

Ben Thuy looked at Don and me. "You gentlemen have examined this Ko Feng," he said, eyeing us intently. "You are satisfied that it is genuine."

"We have no way of establishing with utter certainty that this is Ko Feng," said Don. He had told me how he had rehearsed various ways of saying this. "No one has seen or smelled or tasted any for at least five hundred years. But we have conducted as many meaningful tests as we can conceive and to the best of our expertise and experience, we can say that it has passed all of these."

Ben Thuy picked up a sheet of paper and studied it. "You are both considered as experts, I see. You have wide knowledge in this field."

I wondered what the paper said and who had written it but Don nodded, so I did too. I put on what I supposed was an expert look.

"So to the best of your professional ability, you verify that the spice is truly Ko Feng." He eyed us sharply as he said it.

"I do," Don said.

"I do," I said.

One of Ben Thuy's staff murmured something in an Asian language and slid a sheet of paper across the smooth desktop. It was a statement of authenticity. Don and I read it a couple of times, then signed it.

Ben Thuy beamed. Cartwright produced his check and Sam Rong brought out the bill of sale. A few more signatures and it was all over. Ben Thuy leaned forward.

"This must be very exciting for you," he said to Cartwright.

"Very" he agreed. Weariness showed in his face. Now that it was all over, he was probably feeling down after the tension.

"It is exciting for me too," said Ben Thuy. "You see, I was born not too far from the region where the Ko Feng was found."

Sam Rong arched his sparse eyebrows. "I did not know this."

"Oh, yes. And so—it is from a personal viewpoint that I ask this—can I see this Celestial Spice?"

Sam Rong looked at Cartwright. "Is now property of Mr. Cartwright. I do not object."

Cartwright hesitated but the five eager faces across the table were hard to resist. Ben Thuy faced him, eye to eye. Cartwright grimaced but managed to turn it into a smile.

"Of course."

Papers were loaded into briefcases and we went back to the underground parking area. The two guards stiffened—Ben Thuy was evidently a martinet for discipline and efficiency.

Cartwright unlocked the back door of the van and slid it open. There was a low gasp of awe from a couple of Ben Thuy's aides at the impressive sight of the teak case. Cartwright unfastened the padlock and lifted the lid with a proud flourish. Ben Thuy craned his neck to stare inside and his aides squeezed closer. Ben Thuy turned to look at Cartwright, who had a frozen expression on his face.

Don and I took a step forward.

The case was empty. The Ko Feng was gone.

CHAPTER SEVEN

Ben Thuy must have carried a lot of clout in New York City. It couldn't have been more than three minutes before two uniformed policemen came in, evidently called while on patrol in the neighborhood. It took them no time at all to decide that they were out of their depth and one of them promptly called the Wall Street precinct.

We all sat at the big conference table. The lights didn't look so mellow anymore. They were menacing and sinister. I was stunned and Don looked the same. Cartwright was haggard and even Sam Rong's smile had gone. Ben Thuy moved as if he were wrapped in a thundercloud, furious that such a thing could happen under his roof. His aides walked softly and quietly, fearing his wrath. The two guards had the air of men about to walk down Death Row.

A few miserable attempts at conversation died at birth. An uneasy silence still prevailed when a tough-looking black man came into the room. He wore a dark suit that didn't fit very well. He had a clumsy way of moving that suggested it would not be a good idea to get in his way. His small black mustache had bristles rather than hairs and his face was in a grimace which changed all the time—and never for the better. It looked as though we were in for a rough ride.

"Lieutenant Gaines," he said in a dry, gritty voice. "Detective, Unusual Crimes Unit. All I got so far is a report about a missing sack of stuff." He looked around the table and turned to Don who was nearest. "You first—who are you?"

Gaines didn't take notes but his frequent and unexpected interruptions showed that he had an alert and intelligent mind. Listening to our stories, I thought them weak and unconvincing. I could only wonder uneasily what Lieutenant Gaines was thinking.

When we had all finished outlining, he started on Don again.

"Spice Warehouse? Spices—you mean that's all you sell?"

"We sell spices and herbs," Don said.

"And this spice—this what do you call it? Ko Fang?"

"Ko Feng."

"Whatever . . . that's all that was in this sack?"

"That's right."

"All that's missing is just this sack of stuff? The one sack?"

"It's a very rare spice. It's been lost for centuries."

"And now it's lost again . . ."

Don was tight-lipped but I thought his self-control was admirable as he told the detective about the background of Ko Feng.

"So all you did was see if you thought this Ko Fang was the real McCoy?"

"I was hired to authenticate it," Don said stiffly.

Gaines turned to Cartwright. "And you're the guy who bought this stuff, right?"

"Yes."

"This stuff worth a million dollars," he repeated, determined to get it right.

"Round figures," grunted Cartwright, not willing to debate a million or two.

The detective's attention moved to Sam Rong.

"And you—you're the guy who sold it?"

Sam wasn't smiling anymore but he was amiable. When that interrogation was finished, the detective's face contorted in a series of chewing motions. Some of them looked like they might be skepticism.

He directed his attention to me.

"You're from England—right?"

I agreed.

"You came all this way just to smell and taste this spice?"

"Not just that," I said. "Don Renshaw was asked by the buyer to get another referee to authenticate the Ko Feng and he proposed me. The sellers agreed. We tested the spice in a number of ways before declaring it genuine."

"Genuine . . ." He chewed the word, making it rhyme with *wine*. "You declared it genuinely worth a million dollars?"

"That wasn't part of my assignment—to estimate its value," I said, "only to assess its authenticity."

"Assess its authenticity." He was probably mimicking my accent but it didn't sound anything like me so I wasn't bothered by it. Whatever his shortcomings as a mimic, he was extremely good at his job.

"Let me run through it the way I see it. This spice was never unattended, never out of sight except during the drive here from JFK. The van never stopped, there were no incidents on the way, no opportunity for anyone to open the back door—"

"It was locked. I had the key," said Cartwright. He was still shaking his head in disbelief. "The door was locked the whole time."

Gaines studied the two bank guards. "No one came in to that parking area while the signing was going on in here?"

"No, Lieutenant." One of the guards was a beefy man with bulging biceps. He was perspiring and stubbornly determined in his attitude. "Nobody came in. Del and me just stood there the whole time."

Gaines pierced him with an unbelieving look and the guard smiled uneasily. "Well," he amended, "we strolled around a bit, stretched our legs—but," he went on firmly, "we never left the area."

The detective's gaze switched to the other guard, who was older, with graying hair and the weatherbeaten face of an old sailor.

"No, sir. Neither of us."

"You went out for a smoke, to the john . . ."

Both shook their heads.

"One at a time maybe . . ."

They shook their heads again.

Gaines continued his interrogation but learned nothing further. The two men were unshakable in their stories. One of Ben Thuy's aides described the geography of the bank building. The way we had come in from the closed parking area led to this conference room in one direction and into bank offices in the other. A stairway went up to the ground level and into the part where everyday, off-the-street banking was done. It didn't sound as if anyone could have gone through there carrying a sack and not been noticed.

The detective rubbed his chin, scratching the stubble as if he was wondering how it got there. He went back to Sam Rong and interrogated him about the spice, how it had been found, how it came to be sold to Marvell—all the way up to its disappearance. Sam brought all of his Asian stoicism into play, not letting the detective's hectoring manner upset him.

A pretty young Thai woman came in with a tray holding a thermos of coffee and some cups. Gaines eyed it and Don pushed it over to him. Cartwright was nearest the cups but didn't even glance at them and Gaines had to get his own. He sipped the coffee and his face contorted as if it tasted awful.

"Not bad coffee," he said. He sipped again.

"You guys are lucky," he told us. "I don't have much on right now so I can spend all my time on this case." He twisted his face, rubbed his cheek. "We're gonna be seeing a lot of each other."

"Gosh, that's wonderful news, Lieutenant" would have been a fine response but nobody said it. He drank more coffee and his sour expression deepened. I realized now what it was and my guess was confirmed a minute late when he took out a plastic tube, shook a pill into his hand and swallowed it with coffee. He was dyspeptic. His facial contortions were genuine pain—gen-u-wine—and if I had needed further corroboration, it came quickly.

"I'm a burger-and-fries man myself," he announced. "Pizza sometimes—with the works. I love chili dogs, lotsa hot mustard. Black coffee by the gallon—though this brew here beats the stuff we get at the station."

He paused. He might have been waiting for comment but nobody really thought he was.

"So you can see how the idea of a sack of pepper being worth a million dollars kinda sticks in my craw," he went on. A thought struck him and he looked at the assembly. "Say, how would it be on pizza—this Ko Fang?"

Our combined expertise was not up to the question. We didn't even have to exchange glances. He nodded as if we had confirmed his opinion.

"Wouldn't help it none, huh? Well, you know your business, I guess," he said, although his tone clearly said that he wasn't convinced of that.

"Now," he resumed, invigorated by the coffee, "let's go over all this again and this time, let's see if we can make some sense out of it."

The interrogation was repeated. Cartwright controlled his tongue admirably, though a couple of times it was a near thing. Sam Rong had recovered his smile but soon lost it. Don was terse with his answers but kept remembering that he had to give them to help find the Ko Feng. I found the whole experience interesting even if it did get a little boring after going over the same points several times.

In fact, it was only about this time that the bottom line was finally sinking in. Who had taken the Ko Feng? And how? It was impossible.

"My sergeant is talking to all the bank people and getting statements right now," said Gaines. He pushed his chair back from the table. "Now I'm going to see them and the sergeant is going to come in here and talk to you. You can go over it all again, maybe remember things you forgot."

The loud groan that went up was unmistakable in implication. Cartwright looked distinctly unhappy. I had no doubt that he wanted the Ko Feng recovered but his dislike for Gaines was obvious and it wasn't hard to surmise that he didn't have a great deal of faith in the detective's ability to recover it. Don was squirming with suppressed sarcasm and Sam Rong was clinging valiantly to the frayed ends of his dignity.

And what did we have to look forward to when the sergeant came in? More of the same—maybe worse. Another devotee of Ronald McDonald and Wendy or perhaps a loyal subject of the Burger King.

Lieutenant Gaines left. There was no time to compare thoughts before the sergeant entered.

CHAPTER EIGHT

They were called interviews but they were really interrogations. The lieutenant had evidently wanted all of us to be present when telling our stories so that he could catch us out in contradicting one another. The sergeant arranged to talk to us individually and we all sat in the conference room, waiting to be called into a smaller room. Cartwright went first, then Sam Rong and then Don. None of them came back but I tried not to read anything sinister into that. When my call came, the sergeant wasn't at all what I expected.

After asking me to sit facing her across the small table in a room that was a smaller copy of the larger one, she introduced herself.

"Gabriella Rossini, Detective Sergeant."

She was about thirty and looked as Italian as her name. Her accent was strictly New York so she had most likely been born here of Italian parents. Certainly her looks were classical Italian. A strong nose, firm cheekbones and large expressive eyes gave her more the look of a budding actress than a detective. She had lustrous short dark hair but it was cut a little shorter than she would perhaps have preferred in order to conform to police convention. She probably had a lovely smile and even white teeth but her formal, almost severe manner prevented me from seeing either feature.

She regarded my card and said in a disapproving tone, "I see you're a detective. May I see your license?"

"I'm not," I explained, "I don't have one. What I do is—

I seek out rare food ingredients, recommend markets for exotic and uncommon foods, advise on food and wine, things like that. Somebody nicknamed me the Gourmet Detective and it stuck. It's good for business and so—though I don't like it—I keep using it."

"Hm," she commented. She had some notes in front of her, written in a squiggly speedwriting in a black, spiral-bound notebook.

"Donald Renshaw brought you over here from England."

It didn't sound like a question so I didn't say anything.

She looked up sharply. "Did he or not?"

"Yes, that's right," I said hastily. "Yes, two referees were needed and Don suggested me."

"You know each other well?"

"We had business contacts a few times over several years."

"You are friends?"

"Business acquaintances." I wasn't sure how much detail she wanted but she apparently wanted more. She nodded for me to continue and her shiny dark hair bobbed up and down. I described the times we had worked together and how we had done it.

"You were never partners? Never in the same business?"

I could see what she was driving at—she was trying to determine if we were a team in the theft of the Ko Feng.

"No. We have never been partners, never in the same business."

She glanced at her notes again.

"You came over here strictly to do this—" She looked for the word and I supplied it.

"Authentication. Yes."

"Don't we have any people in this country qualified to do it?"

"Oh, yes. In this case, Don—representing the buyer—suggested me and the sellers agreed. The old adage of an expert being nothing more than an ordinary fellow a long way from home probably applies. In England, we often call in American experts."

"So how long did you intend to stay?"

Her use of the past tense wasn't encouraging. "Two or three days was the arrangement. I have a flight booked for tomorrow on British Airways."

She might be a member of the police department but she took considerable pains with her appearance. Italian women's eyebrows tend to be thick but hers were expertly tweezed and beautifully shaped. I noticed this because she had raised them while asking her question. I also noticed the gray, silky blouse which was all I could see of her clothes.

"I might have added another day," I said, "and done a bit of sightseeing. I love New York and haven't been here for some years."

She seemed to reach some kind of decision. She leaned back and half pushed the notebook away in a gesture that might be meaningful. The police interrogation aura eased and she became almost friendly. More likely it was a technique, but she was very attractive and I didn't want her thinking I was the kind of man who would steal Ko Feng.

"What do you think happened to it?" she asked me.

The world of music owes more to the Italians than to any other country and it has bestowed upon them more musical voices—a blessing which has spilled over into speaking voices too. Certainly, Gabriella Rossini had the kind of voice that was a delight to listen to and then there was that name . . .

After these musings, I almost asked, "What was the question?" but I didn't want to appear flip so I pulled it out of my memory and said, "I'm completely baffled. I don't see how it can have happened. The chest was never out of our sight—"

"What about during the drive from JFK to the bank here?"

"True, we couldn't see it but the back was locked. We

made no stops except for traffic lights and no one could have forced the back without us feeling or hearing it."

"Other than Donald Renshaw, you had never met any of the others before?"

"None of them, no."

"Did you know this bank?"

"No."

"Do you know anyone here?"

"No, no one."

"You have a very interesting job," she stated and if it was technique, she certainly knew how to move around.

"I love it."

"It must have been an exciting moment when you tasted the Ko Feng. How long has it been lost?"

"About five hundred years, maybe more."

She leaned forward and I thought I caught a whiff of perfume but perhaps not. That would really undermine the image of the NYPD.

"What did it taste like?"

"Indescribable, really. At first, there were hints of other spice tastes, then I felt I was mistaken and that it wasn't similar to any other spice. It was unique and somehow powerful, yet subtle at the same time."

"Spices can be hard to describe, can't they?"

"Very. We have lots of ways of describing how wines taste but the language seems inadequate for spices."

"My parents have a restaurant in Greenwich Village." Her tone was bordering on the friendly now but I kept myself ready for another of her shifts of emphasis. "I grew up there, so I love food. The idea of this Ko Feng fascinates me."

"Why do I think it's an Italian restaurant that your parents have?" I asked.

I had made the breakthrough after all. She smiled slightly and I had been right—she did have a lovely smile and even white teeth.

"La Perla di Napoli it's called. Open every day except Sunday. The specialties are *scaloppine* with mushrooms, *saltimbocca* and *gamberi con aglio*. Of course, they make all their own pasta."

"No *piccione?* What a shame!" I said.

"In New York?" She raised those eyebrows again. "Pigeons are considered a menace not a food."

"I'll have to eat there. Good *saltimbocca* is getting hard to find."

She nodded and the police persona returned. "Inspector Gaines wants you to stay in the city for a few more days."

"In that case, my address is going to change. My fee was on a daily basis and it's not likely to continue so I can't stay at the Courtney Park any longer."

"Here's my card," she said. "Let me know what your new address and phone number are as soon as you move."

"I will. At least, staying in New York a little longer will give me a chance to sample more of the wonderful cooking."

"Of all kinds. Naturally I'm prejudiced in favor of Italian. And I will need to talk to you again."

"Tell me," I asked, "is evidence obtained while under the influence of minestrone admissible in court?"

She smiled charmingly.

"I mean, it doesn't come under the Carmen Miranda act or anything like that, does it?" I asked.

"There isn't anything like that," she assured me. She closed her notebook. "You can go," she said.

"You want me to go?"

"You can go," she repeated and I told myself that she was making that careful differentiation.

CHAPTER NINE

I awoke the next morning before eight, jet lag notwithstanding. I called room service and ordered a half grapefruit, scrambled eggs with ham, and coffee. I remembered that Americans specify the bread they prefer and asked for whole wheat. The hotel brochure promised room service within fifteen minutes. Then I called Don.

We went over the events of the day before and agreed that it was hard to believe the theft had really happened, When would we hear about the Celestial Spice next? Don had a theory. "Do you recall what Peggy said when we were discussing the value of Ko Feng? She said putting a value on it was like putting one on the *Mona Lisa*."

"So?"

"If the *Mona Lisa* were to be stolen, what could the thief do with it? There's the old story about a recluse millionaire living in seclusion on a mountaintop and stealing it so that he, and he alone, can enjoy looking at it—but nobody buys that anymore. No—a more probable reason is ransom."

It did make sense. "Do you think we'll be hearing from the kidnappers soon?"

"It's the best guess I can come up with," Don said. "And kidnapping the Ko Feng seems like a better idea than kidnapping a rich man's daughter or a champion racehorse."

"You may be right there," I admitted. "You don't have to feed the Ko Feng. Have you told Lieutenant Gaines about this theory?"

"What do you think?" It was rhetorical.

"I can just see his face if you did. He'd look as if he'd drunk a bottle of soy sauce."

"He's the detective," Don said. "If he hasn't thought of the ransom idea, then he ought not to be running the Unusual Crimes Unit. They must get all kinds of weirdo crimes and bizarre motives. Ransom's bound to be among them."

"Tell me something. Did anybody contact you once you had agreed to take on this job?"

"No. But I wouldn't be surprised if they do now."

"Neither would I. The two of us are prime suspects."

We chatted on for a while then I said, "I don't suppose Marvell is going to want to pay me my expenses any longer. This hotel is $285 a night."

"I don't suppose he will. He isn't the easiest of men to get along with—I certainly wouldn't want to be in Cartwright's shoes. Marvell's probably got him in the roasting pan right now and is turning up the temperature."

"His opinion of us isn't likely to be much higher," I added.

"Well, at least we declared the Ko Feng genuine," said Don. "He must be thankful to us for that."

"And then it was stolen from under our noses. He won't thank us for *that.*"

"We weren't hired as security guards," Don argued.

"Is he reasonable enough to take that into account?"

"Aye, there's the rub. Reasonable is not one of the first adjectives to come to mind when you're dealing with Alexander Marvell. You'll soon find that out when you talk to him."

"I have to, I suppose?"

"No way you'll be able to avoid it. I expect to hear from him any minute—literally. You'll probably be included in the invitation—if you can call it that. In the meantime though, back to your question . . . The answer is no, I don't think he'll spring for any more nights at the Courtney Park." He paused, thinking. "Listen, there's a place over on West Seventy-third Street, not far off Central Park. I've put visitors in there a few times when they weren't on a first-class expense account. It's okay and reasonable. It's called the Framingham Hotel. It's one of those conversions from an old apartment building."

"It sounds good," I told him. "Inspector Gaines told me to stay around a few days so I hope it isn't any longer than that."

"And that cute sergeant? What did she tell you? The two of you seemed to be getting on very well when you came out of that interrogation."

"I always try to cooperate fully with the police," I said virtuously.

"Especially when they're policewomen . . . Is she interrogating you again today?"

"We don't have any plans for it. I keep seeing these posters about this International Food Fair and I thought I'd go take a look."

"I was thinking of putting in an hour or two there myself, but I can't. I've got a visitor this morning and another this afternoon. Give me a call later."

I had a shower while waiting for breakfast and was astonished to find that the powerful aroma of the Ko Feng was still on my hands. After thirty minutes, the breakfast had not arrived and I called room service.

More than forty-five minutes had elapsed before the meal did arrive. Service in New York had deteriorated since my last visit. At $285 a night, I expected better than that and I said so when I checked out. The clerk apologized and said it was because they had a lot of guests. I suggested that as this was a hotel, they should expect guests. My transatlantic sarcasm went over her head as she was too busy adding to my bill 8.25 percent sales tax, 6 percent city occupancy tax, 5 percent state occupancy tax and $6 for delivering breakfast. So not only was service down, but prices were up. Frank Sinatra might sing of the city that doesn't sleep but anyone who did sleep certainly paid dearly for it.

I took a cab to the Framingham and checked in. The room was half the size and about half the price, and I got a 15 percent discount by taking the room for a week. I took out some business cards and wrote the address and phone number of the Framingham on the back. Then I took a cab to the Javits Center and the International Food Fair.

CHAPTER TEN

It had only been open a few minutes but already it was fairly crowded. I skimmed through the catalog and picked out a few names that were familiar. The nearest pavilions were those of Japan and the West Indies and I chose to start with the latter.

Many of the islands were represented, the biggest and most colorful booth being that of Jamaica. Tables were set out under palm-fronded roofs and a realistic stand of sugar cane swayed in the breeze from hidden fans. Music from steel bands throbbed softly and despite the early hour, a bar was dispensing rum drinks. A snack bar and a restaurant were preparing typical Jamaican specialties and tempting aromas were drifting out.

There were strips of curried goat for the more adventurous American eater, Jerk Chicken for the lovers of the hot and spicy, beef patties and spareribs for those who wanted more familiar food. The national dish, Salt Fish and Ackee, was on display— the salted cod was mixed with red and green peppers and ackee, a Jamaican fruit. Slices of pawpaw, pineapple and mango were on most tables and it all looked irresistible. But I managed to resist and moved on to the Middle East pavilion.

Persia had a large display. As food disdains political boundaries, the change in name to Iran was ignored. In any case, the home country played little part in mounting this display, which was put on by American establishments. Lamb tongues simmered in a rich sauce under the eye of a swarthy chef in a clever duplication of a Persian kitchen. I asked him what was in the sauce.

"Advieh," he told me. "A spice mixture containing cumin, coriander, cardamom and cinnamon plus secret ingredient."

"And what is the secret ingredient?" His grin widened. "If I tell you—is no secret. No, I tell you—is rose petals."

"Aren't they lost with all those other spicy ingredients? Don't they overwhelm it?"

"No, no, they give it fragrance."

He may have been right. Certainly the aroma was different and I knew that the Persians had traditionally used rose petals in many of their dishes.

The next stand was a spectacular reproduction of a restaurant front in the Middle East and had an eye-catching sign: PHOENICIA. Beneath it, another sign said FOOD IN THE STYLE OF THE ANCIENT WORLD. The front was half cut away so that the visitor could walk in, and the interior was half restaurant and half kitchen. I was admiring the ingenuity of the layout when a woman came out of the kitchen, saw me and walked toward me.

She had a bold, hip-swinging gait that emphasized her voluptuous figure and long legs. She had jet black hair held in a golden band and her skin was a pale olive color which almost shone. Full red lips and a bold nose were noticeable only after you had looked at her eyes. I had heard eyes referred to as "almond" but had never before seen any that truly deserved that description. They were long and brilliant as jewels, and their color was extraordinary.

"Welcome to Phoenicia. My name is Ayesha."

Her voice had an indolent, purring quality and I could hardly wait for her to go on talking. She wore a blouse and a flowing skirt, both in reds and greens with a wide belt of gold mesh. Bare ankles led to high-heeled sandals with gold straps.

"Food in the ancient style," I said. "What does that mean exactly?"

She shrugged carelessly. "Everybody cooks modern food but there is an awakening of interest in what those of the ancient world ate and drank. I use the same cooking tools and the same methods of preparation that my ancestors used two thousand years ago."

"The same ingredients too?" I asked.

"As far as possible—though that can be more difficult. The herbs and spices, for example, used in earlier days are not easy to find."

I was unable to look anywhere but deep into those gorgeous eyes and I realized that her words were uncannily intuitive. It was as if she were reading my mind.

A voice called from nearby, petulant, demanding, but it was in a language I didn't understand. I presumed it was addressing her but she ignored it.

"I see from your face that you know something of spices. Come inside. I will show you Phoenicia."

She moved as gracefully as a ballet dancer but with a cat-like deliberation. I was relieved to escape from her spell but I couldn't wait to be enveloped in it again.

The kitchen where we went first was a remarkably faithful-appearing replica of the real thing. Copper caldrons stood along-side wicker baskets of fruit and vegetables. A stone mortar and pestle were near a wood-burning stove. Ayesha pointed to a stack of thick green leaves. "Those are our plates."

In a wooden tray was cutlery—two-pronged forks and bone-handled knives. Earthenware pots and bowls could easily have been a thousand years old. Flat stones were scratched and worn. "Those are our chopping blocks," she said musically. The walls of the adjoining restaurant area looked like the interior of a tent and the floor was at different levels, each carpeted differently in bright colors.

"We are featuring lamb today," this exotic creature told me as she pointed a slim elegant hand with purple nails and several jeweled rings. She gave a tinkling laugh. "You are thinking this is not a costume for cooking or serving. You are right but America is show business, is it not? Hype and razzle-dazzle."

"I'm sure the food is as good as the presentation," I said.

The lamb was in large pieces and turned slowly over a spit in an alcove like a fireplace. Other pieces hung on chains.

"We burn only olive wood—it does not smoke," she told me, then she indicated a heap of flat cakes of bread, thin enough to be sheets. "We call this *petlah* bread. It is unleavened, and it is thin so it serves also as a table napkin—you can wipe your mouth with it and then eat it. The poor people buy these on the streets from vendors and fill them with vegetables."

"It's fascinating," I said. "You've done a remarkable job of reproducing the ancient styles of cooking and eating."

"Thank you, kind sir." She gave me a curtsy. Her eyes mocked her action but her smile was full.

"You mentioned spices. What spices do you use?"

Her expression changed, became serious.

"Yes, you are very interested in spices—no, more than that, involved even. Is it not so?"

I was debating an answer, not sure how much to tell her.

"Who are you?" she asked softly.

I handed her a card. She took it in long slender fingers and her wonderful eyes turned to me.

"You are one who tasted the Ko Feng," she said, and her voice was as reverent as if she had referred to an audience with the Dalai Lama.

I nodded.

"Let us go over here and talk." She led the way to a table. The restaurant was still empty. It was early for people to be eating, though the streams of visitors passing by were thickening.

We sat then she rose abruptly. "Let me get something."

She was back with porcelain cups and a steaming brass vessel shaped like a samovar. She poured from it and set down a tray of delicious-looking cookies. "Rose-hip tea and those are almond paste—we call them *sanbuniya*. Now tell me about the Ko Feng."

Her imperious tone didn't offer me any alternative but it didn't matter because I would have seized any opportunity to have this glorious creature hanging on my every word. I told her all I knew.

When I told her of the disappearance of the Ko Feng, she frowned.

"It is not possible! How could this happen?"

"I wish I knew."

"The East is a place of magic and illusion—but here, in New York . . ." She shook her head in bewilderment and I was ready to speculate just to keep the conversation going when there was an interruption. The same petulant voice that I had heard before called out loudly, then a man came in through a curtain at the back.

He had a head of tight black curls and dark, darting eyes. He wore a white silk shirt and black matador pants with a belt of decorated leather and calf-length black boots. He showed white teeth but it wasn't a smile.

Ayesha didn't seem inclined to introduce him. She gave him an annoyed half glance.

"What is it, Lennie?" she asked impatiently.

He wasn't going to be dismissed that easily. His gaze held mine. He looked at the samovar and the tray of cookies.

"I'm Lennie Rifkin," he said. "Are you selling something?"

"No," I said and let it go at that.

He was about to address me again but he turned abruptly to Ayesha. "Haven't the figs arrived yet?"

"Not yet," she said without looking at him and as if they were of no importance.

"You did order them?" he said accusingly.

"Of course."

He hesitated, then turned to walk away. As he did so, he tossed a parting comment over his shoulder. "My wife often forgets." He exited through the same curtain with a flourish.

Ayesha resumed her conversation with me as if there had been no interruption.

"We would have been one of the many restaurants that wanted some Ko Feng."

A thought struck me. "Had you contracted to buy any?"

"No. I don't know that any contracts were issued although many people knew of it. I presume you are trying to get the Ko Feng back—after all, you are a detective."

"Actually, I'm not—a detective, that is." I explained but she didn't look convinced. "I am trying to recover the Ko Feng, though, "I added, anxious to maintain my status in her eyes. I wasn't sure if I did that or not.

"You might want to talk to some of the other restaurant owners in the city. Several of them are here."

"That would be very helpful. Who do you suggest?"

She ticked them off on brilliant fingernails. "Selim Osman is here—he has the Topkapi Castle; Abe Kefalik is in the next pavilion with his Himalaya restaurant; then there's Louis Alacourt of the Duke of Gascony; Jim Keillor of the Hunters' Lodge—oh, and you might see Mike Earhart, he's planning on reopening Tony Pastor's. Others who aren't here at the fair are sure to be wanting some Ko Feng—Robert De Niro's Tribeca Grill; Mandarin Court; '21'; Lutèce; even Lespinasse and La Caravelle . . ." She waved a hand in a glittering arc. "What chef would not want to have the Celestial Spice!"

"That's a lot of competition."

She shrugged, disdainful as Nefertiti on hearing that another pyramid had collapsed.

"This is New York. Competition is what makes this city. But we are not like all the others. Topkapi Castle is Turkish, Himalaya offers food from all those countries surrounding the mountain range—my intention at Phoenicia is not only to serve the foods of the ancient world but also to cook them in the ancient style—to be authentic in every way."

She gave me a long look from those beautiful eyes. "You must come and taste for yourself. We are limited here, as you can see."

"I will," I promised.

A couple drifted in and sat down. A family with strong Southern accents came in, staring at the cooking pots.

"I'd better go," I said.

"Yes. Go and find the Ko Feng. It is very important." Her voice was earnest, almost pleading.

I was almost outside when she called to me.

"Ex-wife."

Out in the madding crowds, it was becoming harder and harder to move around. Most of the stands and booths were doing a good business. Barbara's Breakfasts were obviously popular and I paused to eye in amazement the enormous amounts of food being consumed. It all looked good too—thick buttermilk flapjacks, creamy scrambled eggs, fat brown sausages, slabs of succulent ham, crusted hash-brown potatoes, red-golden tomatoes, plump mushrooms, crispy bacon . . .

The fast food stands were lining customers up already—hamburgers, hot dogs, pizza, tacos, burritos, Orange Julius, Coke, beer, root beer. . . . Chicken in a dozen ways sizzled and smoked—fried, Southern fried, baked, roasted, broasted, grilled, char-grilled plus every state's variation from Kentucky Fried to Rhode Island Roasted.

I found the Himalaya first. An artist's depiction of the majestic sweep of the world's mightiest mountain range was a mural that was really eye-catching. A few people were already seated and appetizing aromas were drifting among the tables.

Abraham Kefalik, the owner, was easy to find. A huge, barrel-chested man with a bushy black beard and a deep, booming voice that came from the very bottom of that barrel, he was arguing with an unfortunate fellow delivering a crate of rolls. The disagreement ended in Kefalik's victory—an outcome that was never in doubt. He looked at me quizzically from under beetling black brows.

I told him who I was and gave him a card. I added that I had just come from Phoenicia.

His reaction was cool. "What do you want?"

"To talk to you for a few minutes."

"I'm very busy here, as you can see."

He didn't look that busy.

"Ayesha said I should come and talk to you."

His face split into a big grin. "Ayesha! Ah, what a magnificent woman! Why didn't you say so? I thought that miserable, no-good Lebanese bandit sent you!"

"Lennie Rifkin? No. I saw him for a few seconds but he had other things to do than talk to me. He's a very lucky man to have such a wife."

"They are divorced," Kefalik said with a booming laugh. "Good thing, too—for her, anyway."

"But they work together in the restaurant, don't they?"

"She does all the work."

"What's he—head chef?"

"Poof! He is nothing. An entrepreneur before he met her. What she saw in him, nobody knows." He tapped the side of his nose. "Women! They are wonderful, are they not? But sometimes, they do crazy things—" He stopped and gave me a questioning look. "You said you wanted to talk to me—what about?"

"About Ko Feng."

His demeanor changed sharply. "You had better come in." He dropped the bread crate he had been holding and bellowed for a kitchen helper to come and take it. He led the way to a corner table.

The Himalayan motif had been carried throughout and a snow-capped peak met the eye wherever you looked, either singular or in ranges. On the walls were a multistringed lyre, a farm yoke with leather strapping, a long curved sword with a bronze handle and a lot of other items that looked either useful, deadly or just strange.

A few tables were occupied. People were drinking thick black coffee and eating gooey buns dripping honey. Kefalik sent his voice booming in the direction of the kitchen and a young girl with doelike eyes and a voluminous dress scurried away to return quickly with a silver pot and china cups. She poured coffee like congealing tar and smiled shyly.

"Is good coffee, is it not?" Kefalik asked. He was watching me drink. He chuckled and it sounded like a boiler overheating. "You drink this before, I can tell."

"In my business, I eat and drink a lot of things from a lot of countries. I like this coffee. Is it Kenyan?"

"From Ethiopia—the home of coffee, many say. It is hard to get now." He looked at my card again. "So you tasted the Ko Feng—was it wonderful?"

"Word gets around fast in the restaurant trade."

Kefalik laughed. "Faster even than the hairdressing business."

"Yes, it was wonderful. Hard to describe, too. Hints of other spices yet not really like any of them."

"And then you lost it."

"Yes," I said ruefully.

"And now you are trying to get it back."

"Yes. Well, not just me, "I added hastily. I didn't want Lieutenant Gaines to hear that I was doing some investigating. "The police are working on it. I was just here at this food fair and was talking to Ayesha—"

He squinted at my card once more. "But you are a detective . . ."

Perhaps I should get some different cards. "Not exactly." I explained what I did and he nodded.

"Like I said, you want to get it back."

"Were you planning on buying some?" I asked him.

"Every chef in New York would want some. The romance of it alone—imagine! lost for centuries, then it is found! And it is probably the most famed of all the old spices. Even more than silphium—you know about silphium?"

"I know something about it."

"It was not only a spice but a valued drug—it was bought with silver. Did you know that?"

"Yes, I knew it." Was he avoiding my question? I tried again.

"Were you offered any Ko Feng?"

He poured more coffee.

"Before Alexander Marvell decided to buy it, you think he let news of it slip out? No, someone else would have stepped in." He laughed his booming laugh once more, alarming a couple in shorts and Hawaiian shirts. "We are good fellows in this business," he said earnestly. "Most of us—no, nearly all of us. But there are one or two—maybe a few more than that—who would do anything."

"Such as steal the Ko Feng?"

"Including that."

"And then what would they do with it?"

He nodded slowly. "I see what you are saying. It is so special that it is worth nothing unless it is known for what it is. To sell it announces that the seller is the one who stole it."

"Something like that."

He grinned. "You have a problem, my friend." He stood up and held out a hand. "Good luck with it—and please, come and dine at the Himalaya. You like grilled yak?"

"I've eaten a lot of different foods but I don't recall ever eating yak," I said cautiously.

"Call me a couple of days ahead. It needs marinating."

I didn't doubt it. Scampering up and down the Himalayas

would develop a lot of muscle that would need tenderizing.

Farther down the aisle was the Armenian stand. Armenia no longer exists as a separate country but its traditions and customs endure and its food is still eaten with enthusiasm by millions in the region. Many of these foods were on sale—Armenian sausages, which are not quite like any other sausage; *lavish*—thin bread like crackers; *lehmejun*—the small meat pieces that are sold on every corner stand in the Middle East; plus many items not readily found but common in Armenian cooking, such as pine nuts and *mahleb,* a fennel-like flavoring.

Half a dozen spits rotated, kebabs oozing fat as sharp-bladed knives sliced off thin strips. *Kufta,* small meatballs, sizzled on a grill wafting scents of mint, basil and cinnamon. Huge bowls of rice were in profusion—the indispensable accompaniment to any Middle Eastern dish.

My glands were salivating as I reached the Topkapi Castle, "where all the jewels are food" according to the board outside. The restaurant in the Murray Hill district of Manhattan was the home of this exhibit and the smells promised well to anyone liking the cuisines of Istanbul and the Anatolian provinces.

The Turks haughtily assimilated any good cooking they encountered in their wars, making Turkish cooking today a fascinating mixture of Greek, Jewish, Central Asian and Arab influences. The decor was pleasant but not gaudy—often a good sign that the emphasis is on the food. Tables were in sunken areas and a long mezzanine stretched along one wall. Ceramic, glass and copper utensils hung on the walls and the waiters were all dressed impeccably in white.

Selim Osman was of medium height, with thinning hair, slick and black. He had piercing black eyes and a trim little black mustache. Energetic and resplendent in a white suit, he received me politely but with a reserve that hinted I wasn't going to learn very much.

"I know about the Ko Feng, of course," he told me. "In our business, it's today's topic of conversation." He shrugged. "Tomorrow, who knows?"

"Do you see any place for it in your cooking?"

"I suppose any chef would want to try it. It is not just a spice—it is history."

"Have you been offered any?"

He pondered the question for a minute. Early diners were already in place. A dish of pan-fried squid, golden and with a bowl of garlic dipping sauce, went by on a waiter's arm. Swordfish kebabs with rice dotted with currants and flecks of spinach swished past. Bottles of Turkish beer clanked on another tray.

"I wouldn't say 'offered.' "

"What would you say?" I countered and he smiled suavely.

"A commodity like a spice that has been lost for centuries requires a different marketing approach from a trailer load of potatoes. Anyone possessing it might not even know precisely how he intended to market it—but how could any man decline such an opportunity?"

His speech was carefully metered. The thoughts behind the words were, I felt, significant. He was telling me something. His English was flawless and wherever he had learned it, I would bet it was a tough environment. I thought he could handle a frontal assault.

"Who do you think stole the Ko Feng?"

He didn't bat an eyelid. He said nothing for a few seconds but I wasn't hopeful that he was going to reel off a list of suspects.

"I don't know."

"Care to make a guess?"

He smiled. "Slander can be expensive. We are sue-happy in New York and we have spread the habit all over the country. I wouldn't want to risk a lawsuit."

"So you might suggest a name if you weren't afraid of legal action?"

"We must talk again." He was being politely dismissive. "You should come and eat at the Topkapi Castle."

"I'd like that. Here's my card. Call me if you hear anything that might help me get the Ko Feng back."

He took it. I added quickly, "After you've told the police, naturally."

He nodded and watched me leave.

I was some distance away when I heard a call from behind.

I turned to see a man approaching me at a brisk pace and waving an imperious hand. He was a military-looking character with a small mustache and an erect bearing, and he was wearing a Nehru-type jacket that I hadn't seen since the Margaret Thatcher era.

"Caught a little of your conversation back there," he said in a voice that must have served well on a parade ground. "Name's Nelson Keyhoe—I'm Keyhoe Chemicals, we're in the Fortune 500."

"Congratulations," I said. "That's a nice place to be."

"Been there for the past five years and one way we stay there is by keeping up with trends and developments."

"What sort of chemicals?" I asked.

"Our current product list has about eight thousand of them on it—so we're in a great many markets," he said proudly.

"And what's your connection with food?"

"We make additives, coloring agents, sugar substitutes . . ."

"Flavor enhancers?" I asked.

He nodded. "Yes, we make those too."

I pondered my next question for a split second, then I decided that, what the heck, I hadn't been getting very far anyway—so what if I upset somebody?

"It must have been a relief to you when the Ko Feng was stolen," I said in a chatty tone.

He frowned. "Why do you say that?"

"It would take away a lot of your business, wouldn't it? Ko Feng is probably many times more effective than any of the flavor enhancers that you produce."

"We're accustomed to competition from all directions," he said. His face suggested that if he'd had me in his battalion, I'd have been locked up by now and with no likelihood of release.

"On the other hand, you might welcome Ko Feng—if you could get hold of any, that is. If it's such a powerful flavor enhancer, then it could be much more valuable than any your lab makes."

His expression changed to what in someone else might have been almost a smile.

"Well, now, if we could get hold of some of this Ko Feng, our laboratory boys could make a comparison and see if that's really true."

"When it's recovered, you may have a chance to do just that."

"Getting close, is it? That recovery?"

"The police are confident," I told him. "Good luck with the comparison."

I walked away without waiting to be dismissed.

CHAPTER ELEVEN

I wasn't sure if Selim Osman knew anything or if he suspected someone. Even the thumbscrews and the racks of his ancestors wouldn't get any information out of him so I didn't expect to. Still, it was a lead—even if I didn't know what to do with it. The question wasn't only what he knew but how he knew it. He might be unwilling to divulge the former but the latter might be easier to uncover.

Not that I had any intention of investigating the theft, of course—that was strictly the affair of the police as Lieutenant Gaines had pointed out. Still, I *was* involved. I knew I had been brought here only to authenticate the Ko Feng but I felt that my professional integrity had been sullied when the spice had been taken from under my very nose.

I went outside to cross to the next pavilion. I was assailed by powerful aromas that I would have been able to grab by the handful if they had been only a fraction stronger. SAY CHEESE was the name of the stand, and they were all there—from Arrigny to Vendôme, from soft to hard, from mild to extra sharp, from aperitif to dessert, and in every color—blue, yellow, red, green, white. There were slabs and slices, bars and hunks, wheels that would barely fit through a doorway.

It was an aggressive stand and it didn't require any signs pointing in its direction. A board inside carried the thought that "Cheese is milk striving toward immortality." The most valuable item mentioned in the will of François Villon, the French vagabond poet, had been the contents of his cheese cellar and the throngs at this stand indicated that cheese had lost none of its pull.

I passed through Kosher Canyon where the most amusing sign said JEWISH TEX-MEX. Ingenuity and humor abounded in the entire exhibition, and I walked on past NOTHING BUT THE WURST where the perspiring staff was having a hard time handling the flow of sausages of all styles and sizes. Mustard was being supplied by the bucketful, a German band oompahed in brassy bursts, and girls in Bavarian dress hurried between tables with trays of foaming steins.

It was a problem to know where to eat.

I finally decided on a Magyar cafe in the Hungarian quarter and ordered the smoked tongue, a dish I had not eaten in a long time. The way it is cooked in its home country is to boil the whole tongue until it is tender, dredge it in eggs and flour and then pan-fry and slice it. A few dumplings and a piece of black pumpernickel spread with Liptauer, a cheese flavored with paprika and caraway, made a very satisfying lunch. A glass of Hungarian Riesling was my choice of a wine. The famous Bull's Blood was not easy to resist but it is a little heavy for midday drinking. A popular Hungarian dessert, crepes with chocolate syrup, got a second glance but only out of professional interest.

Such exhibitions are tiring but I set out again on a tour of some of the other attractions. I admired a replica of a Hong Kong riverboat restaurant with a menu that would take as long to read as it did to eat. The Napa Valley vineyards had a big spread and I browsed and chatted. Morocco's stand was a brilliantly decorated affair and the food looked and smelled so good that I almost wished I had waited.

By now, it was late afternoon. The crowds were thicker still. Many were eating and drinking as they walked between stands. One speaker was trickling out the dainty music of Schubert's "Trout" Quintet while another across the way had the Ink Spots singing "The Java Jive." Aromas were now becoming indistinguishable as I found a phone booth and called Don.

He sounded strangely uncommunicative.

"Is something wrong?" I asked.

"No, no, everything's fine," he said quickly.

"A problem with the business?"

"No, it's not that . . ."

"Is someone with you and you can't talk? I can call you later."

I would have thought he would want to discuss the theft of the Ko Feng, in fact, be anxious to do so. Between us perhaps we could conceive some approach for finding out where it was and what the thief's intentions were.

"No, there's no one here,"

"I was thinking of coming over."

"Look," he said hurriedly. "Could you come over in the morning?"

"Sure. I'm anxious to see your warehouse and we can—"

"Okay," he cut in. "See you in the morning."

I plunged back into the throng, puzzling over what could be the problem. Was it something connected with the Ko Feng? That was the uppermost subject in my mind and it must be in Don's too. But it looked as if I had to wait until tomorrow to find out what it was.

I took a cab back to the Framingham Hotel, stopping to buy some essential supplies. I watched television for a few minutes while drinking a vodka and tonic. A hair salon was advertising "follicle nutrition" with panther urine and on the news, a man was perched on the ledge of a tall building in Manhattan threatening to jump if the Mets didn't end their eleven-game losing streak. I fell asleep during a Doris Day movie and it was ten o'clock before I awoke. I made smoked salmon sandwiches, ate them accompanied by another vodka and tonic and went back to sleep.

CHAPTER TWELVE

The Spice Warehouse was a place of spectacular aromas. Some could be isolated but the mingling of so many different herbs and spices resulted in an exotic atmosphere that was both heady and mysterious.

Both the retail and the wholesale were catered for and it looked like a botanical wonderland. I couldn't see either Don or Peggy so I picked up a current copy of the newsletter from the stack of literature by the door and looked around.

It had really been a warehouse and had high ceilings with air vents and windows, ideal conditions for its present purpose. The retail section was laid out like a supermarket with herbs and spices in open boxes and trays—each marked with its country of origin and giving a description of its uses and characteristics.

Chervil from Belgium, poppy seeds from Poland, nutmeg from Grenada, juniper berries from Italy—the extent of the stock was amazing. Glamorous names from all over the globe sprang out everywhere—Madagascar, Cyprus, Zanzibar, Bahamas, Ecuador, Egypt . . . It was like walking through a minijungle.

Peggy was just concluding the sale of some lemon grass when I found her.

"Don's in his office talking to somebody," she said. "I don't know how long he'll be."

"That's all right," I said. "I could browse here for hours. Wonderful place you've got—you must be very proud of what you've done here."

Her face lit up. "We are. So glad you like it."

"Is Don okay?" I asked casually, examining some sage, the herb whose smoke was used to protect against the black plague.

"Yes," she said and looked at me quickly.

"He sounded preoccupied, worried even, when I phoned yesterday. I thought maybe something was wrong."

Alarm was beginning to show in her eyes and I hastened to placate her. "It was probably just worry about this Ko Feng business."

"He is very concerned about it. It's the strangest thing . . . I could hardly believe it when he told me . . ."

We discussed it for a few minutes, then an assistant in a trim green uniform came over to ask her help.

"Go ahead and browse," she told me. "I've got a perplexed customer here."

A pile of ugly, dirty-brown plants that looked like knobby clubs caught my eye. They were stacked high on a shelf and I went to take a closer look. I was reaching for one of them to feel its texture when a hand touched mine. A very attractive woman in a light blue wool suit turned to smile at me.

"Sorry," she said. "You were first."

"No, go ahead. I'm only looking."

"So am I. It's a curious plant, isn't it?"

"It is. A lover of ginger, are you?"

She looked at me perplexed, then at the label.

"Yes," I said, "ginger, that's what it is."

She examined the unpleasant-looking sticks with a look of surprise on her face. Finely chiseled features, light chestnut-brown hair and a pretty smile made her well worth looking at and there was a firmness in her brown eyes that gave her character and suggested plenty of determination.

"I've seen it before but never in such large pieces."

"It's probably African," I said, searching for the tag. "Yes, it is. Most people consider the Jamaican variety as the best but recently, more and more has been coming from Africa. It's much larger and many like the flavor even better."

"I must admit I usually use the shaker," she said, tilting her head to one side in a charming gesture.

"A lot of people like to chop the plant. They find the taste of the fresh ginger different from that of the dried powder. You need two to three times as much of it, though—when it's dried, the taste becomes really concentrated."

"You sound as if you know a lot about it."

"Don Renshaw's the man to talk to. He owns this place. He can tell you all about any of these spices and herbs."

"You know him well?" she asked.

"We've done a little business together over the years."

"You're English, aren't you?" Her brown eyes appraised me frankly.

"Yes. So's Don. I knew him in England, then he came over here to expand his business. He decided he liked it so much he wanted to stay."

"It's a fascinating business. I had no idea that so many of these herbs and spices came from so far away."

"The history of spice trading was written in blood a few hundred years ago. Nations went to war with each other for control of the pepper trade. The price of pepper was the standard for trade in all commodities. Like the way we're on the gold standard today, it was the pepper standard then."

Her brown eyes widened. "That's amazing."

"Perhaps we could have lunch together. We can talk spices and eat spices."

She frowned. "Lunch is usually difficult . . ."

"Dinner, then?"

"I'd better tell you—I'm here to talk to Mr. Renshaw."

"Really?" I put an inflexion on the word that invited further explanation.

"But I have a scheduling problem. I wanted to talk to him but he's tied up and now I'm running late for another appointment. I'll have to come back."

"I hope I'm here—" was all I could get out before she was hurrying away.

"I do too," she tossed over her shoulder.

I went in search of Peggy and was in time to catch her coming from another section of the building. She waved when she saw me.

"Those are our storage rooms," she said. "We have a lot of our own stock in there and we store herbs, spices, plants, aromatics for others. This was a very expensive installation for us. It has control of temperature, humidity, particle size of foreign bodies, and it kills insects and bugs of all kinds. There are separate compartments for items that are sensitive to other aromas."

"You're really well equipped" I said admiringly. "You and Don have done a terrific job here."

"Like to take a look inside?"

"I certainly would."

"Let me get the keys—" She broke off as a woman in jodhpurs approached her asking where she could find pomegranate seeds.

"I'll be back in a minute," Peggy said and led the woman across the floor.

I wandered around, looking at rare and bizarre plants, unusual herbs and strange-looking spices. Peggy finally came back.

"I can't imagine why Don's taking so long," she said. "He knows you're here. Let's go see how much longer he's going to be."

We walked across to a small office with a glass-paneled door. Inside, the phone was ringing. Peggy rapped on the glass panel. There was no answer. She rapped again.

"That's funny," she said. "Why doesn't he answer it?"

The phone continued to ring. She rapped a third time, then opened the door.

She let out a gasp of horror and I pushed the door farther open.

Don lay there on the floor. He was on his back and blood was dribbling from a hole in his chest. I put my fingertips against his left carotid artery.

I could feel nothing. He was dead.

CHAPTER THIRTEEN

In response to my call, Lieutenant Gaines and Sergeant Rossini arrived together, siren shrieking. I had had Peggy lock the front door and had asked the customers to remain for just a few minutes. They grumbled and protested but I was lucky. I expected New Yorkers to be more vociferous in their demands to be allowed to leave but maybe eating spices made people meeker. Certainly, none of them objected very strongly and one or two expressed interest as to what would happen next, possibly seeing themselves as playing supporting roles in a cops and robbers TV drama.

One customer, a very pleasant elderly lady from Queens, was a regular and knew Peggy. She said she was with a support group and although I wasn't sure what that meant, it evidently was something to do with people who banded together to battle a common misfortune. This lady had a lot of experience with this organization and was consoling Peggy.

Gaines's face was screwed up as if he was in agony. The pretty Italian sergeant was moderately friendly but her attitude clearly said that a murder right after a major theft was too much. Gaines didn't wait for me to read his attitude. He let me have it right between the eyes.

"How come you're always on the scene when these things happen?" he growled.

"Lieutenant, I know this looks bad but I had nothing to do with it. Not with the theft either, for that matter."

He hit me with a barrage of questions. I answered them with what seemed to me straight responses.

"As for an alibi, I was standing talking to a woman just before Peggy and I went to the office," I added.

"What makes you think you need an alibi?" he asked accusingly.

"Well, the questions you're asking—"

"Which woman is it who'll alibi you?"

"She—er, she isn't here."

"What's her name?"

"I don't know."

He squinted at me in disbelief. "You call that an alibi? You could have shot Renshaw any time and then come out here and pretend to find the body. Nobody heard a shot—the gun was obviously silenced."

"No," I protested. "Whoever was with him must have shot him and then gone out of the other door from the office—the door that goes directly out into the parking lot."

"How long have you been here?" the sergeant asked, her voice calm.

"About forty, forty-five minutes."

"Did you talk to anyone else besides this woman?"

"No."

"Why did you talk to her?"

"We were both at the ginger stand. We talked about ginger."

The lieutenant's eyes were on me while she was asking the questions and I could see his skeptical look. Talking about ginger was not a credible action in his book.

"Tell us again what she said."

I did. Technicians began to come in and there was a steady flow of men and women, cameras, plastic bags and various pieces of equipment.

The sergeant turned to me. "You say you had no idea who was with Renshaw in his office?"

"No. I called him yesterday to ask if it was all right to come over but he said it was better to make it this morning. His wife said there was someone with him but she didn't know who it was and I didn't either. The woman I was talking to said she had an appointment to talk to him but couldn't wait."

"I don't need to state the obvious," Gaines growled. "This must have some connection with that pepper of yours . . ."

"I can't imagine what connection but I have to admit it seems likely."

"Tell me somep'n—when you both tested the stuff at JFK, you said it was genuine . . ." He let the rest of his sentence trail away in an uncertain manner that was not typical of him.

"To the best of our knowledge, it was."

"Both of you?" he pressed.

"Yes."

"Stuff's worth more'n a million, you say? If it's genuine?"

"That's right."

"What's it worth if it's phony?"

He rapped it out fast before I could see where he was going.

"Well, nothing . . . but it can't be phony . . . we both—" I broke off. "Ah, I see what you're saying. Don Renshaw and I could be in cahoots."

I didn't know if the word was still current but it was expressive. The lieutenant seemed to have no trouble recognizing it. His nod suggested that he not only recognized it but approved of it—the very word he wanted.

"Is there another variable?" the winsome sergeant asked. "Could the spice have been phony *and* you said it was genuine?" She no longer looked quite as winsome.

"I suppose we could come up with handfuls of theories if we tried hard enough," I said bitterly. "The truth is that we both considered the Ko Feng to be genuine and we declared it genuine."

The sergeant scribbled in her notebook. Gaines looked skeptical although the look was nearly lost in some facial contortions.

"By the way," I added, "Don Renshaw had a theory."

Neither of them showed any interest. I wasn't invited to contribute to the pool of ideas but I went ahead anyway. When I had finished, Gaines chewed it over, then shook his head.

"Ransom, yeah, we thought about that but it doesn't show up very high on our hit parade."

A sallow young man with hair in what looked suspiciously like braids came up and said something to the lieutenant, who nodded.

"We're fingerprinting. Got most of the people here, we need yours. Any objection?" His tone suggested that he hoped I did object.

"None at all," I said promptly.

"Also, we need you to stop by the station—the sergeant will give you the address."

"You'll want a statement. All right."

"And we'll want you to leave your passport."

"I've got to stay?"

The shock of the crime had occupied my mind to the extent that I hadn't considered this possibility. The lieutenant nodded, his face muscles moving as if he were chewing invisible gum.

"Yeah, you gotta stay. It was a major theft before—now it's murder. You gotta stay, all right."

Now that the idea had sunk in, I didn't mind. In fact, I wanted to stay. I had to clear myself, find out who stole the Ko Feng and who killed Don Renshaw, and get the Celestial Spice back. It was an ambitious program.

I didn't imagine that Gaines and the sergeant would look too kindly on the idea of my investigating the two crimes but that was what I was going to do whether they liked it or not. I hoped I could convince them that I was only doing my duty and helping them.

I put on a look of annoyed aggravation.

"Well, if I have to stay . . ." I said with all the reluctance I could muster.

CHAPTER FOURTEEN

I had plenty to think about on the cab ride back to the Framingham Hotel. I had talked briefly with Peggy. She was distraught but controlled. The very helpful support lady said that the full significance of Don's murder hadn't hit Peggy yet. Her sister-in-law was on the way over and though the Spice Warehouse would remain closed for the rest of the day, Peggy was determined that she would open tomorrow as usual. The support lady said she would come by and she agreed that it was best for Peggy to have a lot of work to do.

I changed my mind about going directly to the hotel and told the driver to drop me at a good Irish pub. I wasn't that hungry but it would be better to eat now so I had a corned beef sandwich on rye bread and a bottle of Guinness. Nowhere in the world are there such delicious corned beef sandwiches as in the Irish pubs in New York.

I was able to spot a few sights on the ride from the pub to the hotel although my heart wasn't in it. But then the Empire State Building loomed up on the right. I remembered that it had been unchallenged as the tallest building in the world when I had first seen it. The cabby was staying to the west of Broadway, presumably to avoid the thicker traffic. We went by the newly opened Woody Allen Theater and, in the next block, the massive billboard advertising the latest Sondheim–Lloyd Webber blockbuster musical about World War I—*Trenches*. Soon after we passed Lincoln Center we were at the Framingham.

I was asking for my key when a uniformed man appeared at my side.

"Would you please accompany me, sir?" His tone was frigidly polite but the "please" and the "sir" sounded superfluous, as if it didn't matter what my answer was going to be.

He had a large, round face and was big and burly. His uniform was neat and crisp, dark gray with black leather cuffs and epaulettes. His cap was flat and straight on his head and his boots were shiny black. He looked threatening without even trying.

"Where to?"

"Just a short ride."

"What's it about?"

"I'm really not able to say, sir."

Under normal circumstances, I would have asked more questions but Don Renshaw's murder had left me in a careless mood.

"All right," I said. "Why not?"

Outside, a long limousine, sleek and shiny, stood at the curb. The chauffeur gave the uniformed hotel man a bank note for keeping such a prime spot for him.

We headed south. The driver was a real professional and despite the traffic, the ride was smooth. He offered no conversation and didn't open the glass window that separated us. I presumed there was an intercom but I couldn't see it. The soft leather interior was luxurious and there was a TV and a minibar.

When the twin towers of the World Trade Center cast the street into shadow, we turned and a few minutes later stopped before a smaller building—a mere forty stories or so. The chauffeur took me into a busy lobby with half a dozen receptionists. He spoke a few words to one of them and I was taken to an elevator. He pushed a button and left me.

At the thirty-first floor, a man was waiting for me. He was young, thin, dark and Latin looking.

"This way please."

He led me through a waiting area where several men with briefcases sat reading magazines. We went on until we stopped before a heavy, smoked glass door. He knocked, opened the door and ushered me in.

I knew who the man sitting behind the large desk was— the name of the Marvell Corporation was emblazoned on the wall outside in large letters. He was of stocky build with a bald head and pugnacious features. He was signing a pile of papers and had no intention of acknowledging my presence until he had finished. I wasn't going to stand there that long so I sat in one of the several chairs opposite him. The office was comfortable but not large or elaborate. A couple of Matisse prints were on the walls and an enlarged photograph of a jungle river. Outside the window, adjacent skyscraper buildings climbed up and out of sight.

He finished signing, pushed the pile away and examined me from under bushy eyebrows, which contrasted with his bald head. It wasn't a very friendly appraisal.

"This is a hell of a mess," he said authoritatively.

I couldn't argue with that statement so I didn't. He eyed me, waiting for a comment. When I didn't produce one, his tone grew angrier.

"I was so furious when Cartwright told me about the Ko Feng disappearing that I could have torn this building down with my bare hands. I couldn't believe it. I still can't. How could it disappear like that?"

"I wish I knew," I said sincerely. "It's unbelievable, I agree. It wasn't possible for it to happen that way—but it did."

He sat for a moment. "I can't put into words what an extraordinary moment that was," he said, and I thought he was referring to the theft but he went on. "We came around that bend and I looked down across the valley. The glow over that field was magical. It was like an aura. The Cambodians in the jeep didn't see it. Even when I pointed it out to them, they didn't see it."

He paused. "Don't think I'm crazy," he warned.

"No, not at all," I said. Whatever else I thought about him, I didn't think he was crazy.

"I didn't know what it meant. I'd never seen anything like it before. People might say it was a trick of the lighting or something reflecting in the setting sun. But I knew it had a meaning. I knew there was something special about that field—something extraordinary. I would have gone to any lengths to find out what it was. And I found it—I found the Ko Feng!"

His words bordered on the fanatical but there was nothing of the fanatic in his manner. Other than the mystic awe with which he regarded the Ko Feng and the way he had found it, here was a hard-headed businessman who had had an extremely valuable commodity snatched from under his nose.

"I'm telling you this so that you can understand why I nearly went through the roof when I was told about the theft," he continued. "And I'll tell you this—my first reaction was that you and Renshaw were responsible for it. And then I get this phone call from the police. Renshaw's dead—murdered."

"I know," I said. "I was there."

"So you can see why I got you up here right away."

"When I say I was there—I mean, I was in the Spice Warehouse. I was talking to a customer, left her and met Renshaw's wife on the way to his office. When we got there we found him dead."

He gave me a chilly look. "Leaves you in a hell of a spot, doesn't it?"

It wasn't much of a question, more of an accusation.

"I had done a little business with Renshaw—not much," he said. "He seemed honest to me, that's why I picked him for this job. Plus he knows as much about spices as anybody in the business. So what does his murder have to do with this theft of the Ko Feng?"

"I wish I knew. Seems like there must be a connection but how, I don't know."

"Lucky for you that you were talking to a customer at the time of the murder, otherwise you'd be a prime suspect," he said, looking at me from under those bushy eyebrows.

It wasn't a good time to be specific about the sequence of events so I didn't correct him.

"I'm a blunt person," Marvell said. "I say what I think. I'm doing that now. Even if you couldn't have committed the murder, you're still top of my list for suspicion in the disappearance of the Ko Feng."

"It's unfortunate that you feel that way. All I can say is that I assure you I had nothing whatever to do with it."

He didn't look assured in the least. I tried harder.

"You can check with Scotland Yard if you want a character reference. I've worked with them on some cases and they'll vouch for me."

That glanced off him without leaving a mark. "Doesn't change my mind," he grunted.

"Not only that but I'm going to stay here in New York and help find out the truth—about the theft and the murder both." I put all the determination into the words that I could.

He didn't look impressed in the least. The same skeptical expression remained. The face blended into the bald head in a monolithic whole, unmoving, unchanged.

"One thing you can tell me that might help . . ." I said.

He might have nodded imperceptibly but probably not. I continued regardless.

"What were your intentions once you had the Ko Feng?"

"Sell it to people who wanted to buy it, of course. That's my business, brokering food and food products."

"Who specifically?"

"I'm not going to be specific. You're asking me for my customer list. I'm not going to give it to you. Wouldn't give it to anybody."

"It might help to—"

"You're not working for me. There's no reason why I should help you."

"I should think getting the Ko Feng back would be a good enough reason. Another would be to find Don Renshaw's killer."

"I've already made it clear that I don't have any faith in you doing that. The police are working on it and if necessary I'll hire a private firm. Besides, when I've told you I suspect you of being involved, you can't expect any help from me."

His tone was growing increasingly belligerent. He was a tough cookie and no mistake. Any progress I made was not likely to be the result of any assistance from Alexander Marvell.

I've always suffered from the disadvantage of being able to see other people's point of view. I wished I had Marvell's single-minded, tunnel vision but I didn't. I could readily see how—from his position—I was a top suspect.

In fact, if I didn't know myself so well, I'd think I was guilty too.

CHAPTER FIFTEEN

I bid him a curt "Good day," just out of politeness, and walked out of his office. He didn't attempt to match my politeness.

The reception room was still busy as I walked through it. Normal business manners would have meant that the big chauffeur was there to take me back to my hotel but that was too much to expect from a man who thought I had stolen his Ko Feng.

A young man in leather, carrying a motorcycle helmet, elbowed past me on his way to speak to the receptionist.

"Taking these papers to the lab," he told her, holding up a slim dispatch case. "Anything else to go?"

She searched under her desk. "There's something here . . . where . . . ? oh, here, this package. Don't leave it, though. Give it personally to Joe Malenkowski. Oh, and drop these off on your way." She handed him two large envelopes.

He looked at the addresses in disgust. "On my way . . ." he muttered.

I watched him take the parcel and the envelopes and leave. An idea was stirring as I saw the rack on the wall. Adjacent to the rack full of magazines was a prominent heading—THE MARVELL CORPORATION. I picked out a colored brochure and sat down to read it.

The corporation didn't issue annual reports as it was privately owned, I learned. This brochure gave many of the salient facts about the corporation, though, and I skimmed through them, looking for information on the laboratories.

They couldn't be far away if the young man was going there

on a motorcycle. They weren't; they were in Leonia, New Jersey, and an insert map showed that to be just across the Hudson River from the northern part of Manhattan.

I took the elevator down and walked a couple of blocks until I found a drugstore. I bought a box of envelopes and a roll of wrapping paper. I made a parcel out of them and the girl at the checkout desk gave me a couple of pieces of Scotch tape from her dispenser after I told her that my girlfriend would be furious if I forgot her birthday. When she gave me change from three dollars and saw what I had bought, she threw me a contemptuous look that plainly said she didn't consider me the big spender of the week.

The cabs here in the financial district looked to be in better shape than some other parts of New York and the driver was a pleasant Jamaican who explained to me that going out of Manhattan entailed a surcharge.

From the upper level of the George Washington Bridge, I had a fine view of the Manhattan skyline and then we were passing through wooded countryside before turning into a research park. Most of the companies in it were chemical- or electronics-oriented. The cabby got directions from the guard and dropped me at a brick and glass building with grassy slopes on one side and benches under shady trees.

"Parcel for Joe Malenkowski," I told the young woman with chocolate-colored skin and big brown eyes sitting behind the reception desk. I said it slowly and tried to talk through my nose. It wouldn't have worked at an audition for *On the Waterfront* but she merely said, "I'll give it him" and held out a hand.

The motorcyclist evidently hadn't arrived so I breathed easier and said, "My instructions are to give it to him personally."

The phone rang to divert her attention and she waved me to a double door.

"Know where he is?" she asked.

I nodded confidently and moved to the door.

"Got a badge?" she called out.

I turned to her, patted my chest and nodded again. She went back to the phone and I went on through.

Offices took up the first part of the corridor. Computers, fax machines, copy machines and other equipment that I didn't recognize outnumbered people. Machines were spewing out coiled yards of paper while other machines were taking in full sheets and filling plastic barrels with shredded strips. A man came out of a doorway and stepped in front of me.

"Looking for something?"

He was heavyset with prominent veins in a red face. I had a vague feeling that I had seen him before but maybe not.

"Got a package for Malenkowski."

"Who?"

"Malenkowski," I said in an Everybody-knows-him tone. "Joe," I added to emphasize how well I knew him.

"Where's he work?"

"In the lab." It suddenly struck me that this building was all labs and I expected him to ask me which one but he didn't. He motioned me down the corridor.

I walked on, looking for labs.

I soon found them. White-coated workers were watching screens, tinkering with glass equipment and peering into the backs of instrument panels. A pungent acid smell hung in the air. Somewhere, an automatic washer clanked glass in metal trays. I picked out a skinny, fluffy-haired girl standing tapping a pencil against her teeth and asked for Joe.

"He's out today. Kid's sick. Other car's in the garage for a new transmission."

"Sorry to hear that. Who works with him?"

She pointed with her pencil. "You might try Anton."

He was an earnest Ukrainian, with sparse light hair and a quiet demeanor. I commented on his accent but he didn't even notice mine—he was too engrossed in telling me of his horrible time in a government laboratory in Odessa and how lucky he had been to get out and come to the United States.

"Is Joe a Ukrainian too?"

He was and had been very helpful to Anton when he first arrived. That was my chance.

"I was hoping you'd be helpful to me," I told him. "I'm trying to find out about the Ko Feng that you tested."

"Ko Feng?" He looked puzzled.

"A spice. You must have tested it for FDA approval."

Anton shook his head. "I don't know. Let's take a look."

It wasn't easy to find but he did find it. It was known to the lab as AM 51—Marvell had used his initials. Anton was able to identify it only after I mentioned the Mecklenburg Institute in San Francisco.

"What work did you do on it?"

He studied the file. "We submitted to the FDA a proposal to establish nontoxic and noncarcinogenic properties, also that it was suitable for human consumption."

"You did all that and no problems?"

He looked again, nodded his head. "Just routine."

"What else did you do?"

"Nothing."

"Mass spectrograph? Submicroscopic molecular pattern? Any other testing?"

Anton frowned, puzzled. "No. Why should we? What would we be looking for?"

"I was just wondering," I told him. "You have so much equipment here—you must enjoy using it all."

That prompted laments about the lab in Ukraine and contrasts with his surroundings here. I thanked him and he looked queryingly at me.

"I haven't seen you here before. What department are you in?"

"I'm new here. They told me I ought to get around some of the other areas. See what you guys who do all the work are up to."

He smiled, pleased. I shook his hand and left quickly. I walked with the air of a man who knows exactly where he's going but the fact was, I didn't have any idea of which way to go. It was inevitable that I should find myself trying to go through a locked safety door.

A man appeared. "Hey, you can't go through there! You'll set off the alarms!"

He was the same heavyset character I had just encountered. He gave me a second look. "It's you again!"

I gave him a disarming smile. "Sorry, wasn't thinking. Got a lot on my mind."

He frowned and I thought he might be noticing my accent but with Anton and Joe here, there were probably lots of funny accents on the premises. The only possibility was that there was an alert out for an accent like mine.

"Still looking for what's-his-name?"

"Joe. Yes."

Down the corridor, I could see a sign. It pointed one way to what was called the PROTOPHYLLOSCOPIC LABORATORY. I didn't know what it meant and wasn't even sure I could say it so I read out the name pointing in the other direction.

"I think he's in the Environmental Laboratory."

"See that sign down there?"

"No," I said. "Where?"

He stabbed a finger, exasperated.

"There—right there!"

"Oh, thanks, yes."

I was getting a lot of practice at making fast escapes. I did it again, my fastest yet.

Determined not to look back, I kept going where the sign pointed. There was a notice hanging on the door handle but I ignored it and went in. The door slammed behind me with a sucking sound, probably a sealing system of some kind. The door sounded as if it weighed a ton.

There was no one there and I was going to go through until I realized that I was in a closed room. The walls were stark white and all that was in the room were two large tables. Both were completely covered with trays, dishes, bowls and boxes, all glass or plastic. All had labels with code numbers and all contained what looked like heaps of rice, grain, sugar, bread crumbs and other foodstuffs. Several had liquid that looked like water. They were evidently test substances and I wondered what they were testing for.

I spent a minute or two examining the room casually so as to give the man who had stopped me time to go on about his business. As there was no other way out of the room, I didn't want to run into him again. When I judged it was safe, I went back to the heavy door. It wouldn't open.

I struggled with the handle. It wouldn't move. There was some self-locking mechanism—unless it had been locked from the outside. Set into the longer wall was a horizontal window, about waist level to eye level. It was thick glass and double glazed. I banged on it but there was no sound. Two men walked by and then a woman but none of them paid any attention to me. I tried the door handle again. It wouldn't move.

My throat felt dry. Nerves, that was silly. What could happen to me in here? I coughed. The sound echoed eerily. It was then that I noticed a couple of gauges set into the wall near the door. My subconscious had registered them before but now I saw that a needle on one of them was moving. "Atmospheric pressure," the gauge said. The needle was falling steadily.

I looked for a phone but there wasn't one. I had never experienced claustrophobia before but I did now. I felt like a rat in a trap.

My head was buzzing. I didn't know whether it was the decreasing pressure or my nerves. My ears were playing tricks on me and I could hear a high-pitched buzz. I coughed again—and again. It was hard to get my breath . . .

I stumbled over to the window. A girl in a yellow dress walked by. I thumped with my fist but even I couldn't hear the sound. She didn't even notice me. I spread my hands flat against the glass and pressed my face to it. My heart leapt with joy as a couple of women came along and one of them looked my way. She nudged her companion and pointed. They both laughed, waved and walked on.

I couldn't believe it. They had seen me—why hadn't they—then it struck me. A nose squashed against a pane of glass merely looks funny—from the other side . . .

A man in a white lab coat came in the other direction, carrying a box. He looked at me and I grabbed my throat with both hands and made strangling motions. The man smiled, shifted the box under his left arm. He put his right forefinger to his temple and pulled an imaginary trigger. Still smiling, he passed out of sight. The corridor was empty.

My breath was coming in gulps. I refused to look at the gauge but found I couldn't resist. It was very low and still going down. I banged futilely on the glass.

Another man came into sight. He was tall and lean and I was certain I knew him. Surely it was Willard Cartwright! Or was I delirious? It could be him, he worked for the corporation. I thought he was looking at me but he made no sign of recognition. It probably wasn't him and anyway he was gone.

My eyes hurt. They felt as if they would burst out of my head. I didn't have much longer. If I was to get out of here alive, I had to act and act fast.

I searched the room, looking for something I could use as a tool. I could find nothing. The room was empty except for the two tables and all the glass and plastic vessels on them. I couldn't move one of the tables even if I weren't weak and dizzy.

I felt through my pockets, forcing myself to breathe slowly. All I could find was a ballpoint pen. It had a metal body. I looked up at the ceiling but the lighting was all sunken behind plastic panels. By the entrance door, though, was a light switch. I placed the end of the pen against the plastic cover and hammered it with my fist. Nothing happened. I snatched a jar off the table and used it. The plastic cover of the switch cracked, then a piece broke off and I levered the remainder away.

I picked up the bowl which had the most liquid in it, knocking over several others in my haste. I threw the contents into the light switch cavity. There was a dazzling flash and a sizzling noise as the lights went out. I staggered to the gauge. It was almost down to zero now—and still falling. The pressure pump must be on a different circuit from the lights.

A fog was gathering around me but I was aware of motion. At the window, a face looked like it was in a fishbowl and arms were waving. I dragged myself over there. A man was pointing at the ceiling and making gestures. In my befuddled state, I couldn't understand at first, then I realized he was asking me why I was there in the semidarkness. I pointed urgently at the door and made opening signs.

I didn't pass out but I was in a stupor as the door swung open and I was carried outside. For a few minutes, I sat on the floor learning to breathe all over again.

People gathered, asking what had happened. Had I had a heart attack? Had there been an accident? Where were the medics? Were we making a movie? When would it be shown? Alarm bells were clanging and their echoes were bouncing around inside my skull.

I must still have been oxygen-deprived. I thought that in the crowd around me was the face of the girl I had talked to in the Spice Warehouse just before Don Renshaw's murder . . .

Fortunately, no one around me seemed to be in any position of authority as no one asked who I was or what I was doing there. I continued to groan and look drowsy even after I had re-covered. One young man peered into the room and his an-guished look told me that I had ruined his experiments. The face I expected to see—that of the heavyset, red-faced man—was nowhere in sight.

Finally, I got to my feet, said I was much better and began to walk away. There were protests and I was told to wait for the first-aid people but I said I would go to them.

The young woman at the reception desk was already phon-ing for a cab for one of the waiting visitors and I told her to make it two. They pulled up in front within minutes and I just going out thankfully when a voice shouted, "Hey, wait a minute—you there!"

For a second, I contemplated making a dash for the taxi but I couldn't be sure the driver would aid and abet my escape. I stopped and turned.

The young man with the roomful of ruined experiments was hurrying toward me.

"You forgot this," he said and thrust the box of envelopes into my hands.

CHAPTER SIXTEEN

A warm bath relaxed and restored me to near normality. The phone rang. It was Sergeant Gabriella Rossini.

"You were supposed to bring us your passport," she said accusingly.

"I haven't forgotten," I told her, "but I was summoned into the presence of Alexander Marvell. I just got back."

I had decided not to mention my brush with extinction at the Marvell Laboratories. I was not certain whether it had been a true accident or whether it had a more sinister meaning. Until I learned more, I didn't see any reason to tell the police about it.

"There are a few aspects of the case we should talk about," she said. "I can get your passport from you at the same time."

Did I detect a hint of conciliation in her voice. I thought so . . .

"What time is it now?"

"Nearly five o'clock."

"I was just taking a bath—hey, I have an idea. Why don't we have a bite to eat? You'll be off duty shortly, won't you?"

"Well . . ." She hesitated just the right length of time. "As a matter of fact, I promised to go see a former roommate of mine who just opened a restaurant—you know, lend some moral support." As if she had just thought of it, she went on, "This is right in your line of business, isn't it—you could probably offer some tips."

"Sounds good," I said and meant it. It was much better than being suspected of murder.

"It's not a terribly gourmet place," she cautioned. "I mean, don't expect too much—it isn't another Four Seasons or anything."

"Sounds fine," I insisted even though she hadn't told me a thing about it.

"It should be fun," she said and I wondered what she meant by that but I didn't ask.

We discussed arrangements. She lived in Brooklyn near Prospect Park and the restaurant was on the northern edge of Greenwich Village so we agreed to meet there.

CHAPTER SEVENTEEN

Americans love clever and catchy names and slogans. Bumper stickers abound and are an outlet for some of the more ingenious of these and those brave hopefuls who venture into the restaurant business believe that one way to plaster their establishment's name onto the public consciousness is to give it an original—and if possible, unique—name.

THE BULL MOOSE said the glaring red neon sign where the cab dropped me. I didn't know exactly where I was other than bordering on Greenwich Village, but it looked safe enough, despite all that I had heard about the physical dangers of New York City. I remembered, though, that Don Renshaw had been killed only yards away from where I had been standing so complacency was to be avoided.

The name of the restaurant was not as scintillating as some of those in New York. The Quilted Giraffe is a popular and expensive restaurant that I had heard of but never visited. The Monkey Bar and Smith and Wollensky and 8 1/2 are all names that stick in the memory. Mad 61 is the address as well as the name of a popular New York Italian restaurant whose fame was widespread—number 61 Madison Avenue. One If By Land, Two If By Sea is unwieldy but undeniably patriotic and, I understood, a fine combination of American and Continental cooking.

But if The Bull Moose wasn't the wittiest name in the city, its subtitle, in pulsating electric blue lights, came close. It was described as NEW YORK'S FIRST SASKATCHEWAN RESTAURANT.

"Jean has been wanting to do this for a long time," Gabriella told me. She was wearing a smart blue plaid jacket over a cream-colored blouse and a short blue skirt. She looked very trim and appealing and anything but a detective sergeant—as I told her.

"I wasn't always one," she said.

"Now don't tell me you had several careers before joining the force."

"I went to acting school and had a few minor roles, including a couple Off Broadway."

I was impressed and told her so. "Why did you give it up?"

"I didn't really feel it was my calling. I enjoyed it but I realized that I didn't have the talent for major success and I wasn't willing to settle for a life of uncertainty and small, occasional roles."

"And backstage didn't interest you?"

"No. It was acting or nothing. Then one day, I was in a market when this kid held up the owner. He managed to sound the alarm at a station which was only a block away. A police-woman came, talked the kid out of pulling the trigger and took away his gun. I was so impressed that I decided there and then that I wanted to join the force."

"And you did and now you're a sergeant."

She smiled a charming smile that lit up her eyes and her entire face.

"And loving it—especially since I became a detective."

"So you knew your friend Jean during your acting days?"

"We shared an apartment. Jean wanted to act too."

"You became a cop and Jean went into the restaurant business?"

"Not just like that. An aunt of Jean's died and left quite a lot of money. Jean was the principal heir."

"Ah," I said, "I was wondering about that. I know how much money it takes to open a restaurant in London. It must cost even more here."

It was easy to see why Gabriella had used the word *fun* in relation to the restaurant. A plastic-encased review reprinted from *New York* magazine on the occasion of the opening summed it up well—"Highly irreverent—geared to a youthful sensibility that enjoys a large helping of craziness. It is at the same time a museum of trivia, kitsch and nostalgia." The rest of the review had been overscored with a thick black pen.

A couple of massive fireplaces were molded in brown plastic. Hollow plastic logs glowed from red bulbs inside them. Beams crisscrossing the ceiling were unashamedly plastic and from them hung the illumination—wagon wheels with electric candles. The walls were almost hidden by bullfight and old movie posters, copper fry-pans, farm tools with what looked like earth still clinging to them, the head of a cross-eyed reindeer, a papier-mâché Santa Claus, a cuckoo clock big enough to house an ostrich . . .

I caught Gabriella watching me as I stared around in goggle-eyed disbelief. She was trying not to laugh but couldn't hold it in any longer. Her giggles were infectious and I had to join in.

"What do you think?" she asked when she had regained control.

"Really classy," I assured her. "Did Jean spend a lot of time and most of the inheritance at Sotheby's getting hold of these art treasures?"

"Ask him yourself," she answered and I realized that the name should be spelled Gene. He was slim and dark-haired, very good-looking and moved like a ballet dancer. He and Gabriella hugged each other like—was it like old friends or was it more than that?

After she had introduced me, they exchanged compliments on each other's appearance, asked about mutual friends and then hugged again.

Business was good, he told me when I managed to cut in and end the hugging. He had a melodious voice and had probably been a very sensitive actor. A voice called from across the room and he sighed apologetically. "My partner—excuse me—he's got a problem. I'll send a waiter over."

The tables were vinyl-topped with a pattern of red and white squares. The chairs were all different, some wood, some metal, some ex-Salvation Army. On the wall behind us, Ronald Reagan in a cowboy outfit wore a sheriff's badge and held a six-shooter. A WANTED DEAD OR ALIVE poster had been stuck above it. A Polynesian mask and a wooden airplane propeller were on either side of it. A waiter came up and put down two glasses of sparkling liquid.

"Compliments of the management," he said with a grin. He pushed aside the quart-sized ketchup bottle and the rusty salt and pepper shakers, making space for a basket of appetizers.

"Here's to success," I toasted Gabriella.

She nodded. "Success to the Bull Moose, to your visit to New York and to the investigation."

"And our better acquaintance," I added.

"That too."

We drank. It was a good cocktail in the best tradition of New York, the home of the cocktail. It tasted like vodka, orange juice, orange Curaçao and some sparkling water. I didn't want to ask what it was called.

I reached into my jacket pocket and handed her my passport. "There, now I'm your prisoner."

She opened it, looked at my picture and looked at me. "I've seen worse."

"In police lineups?"

"No, it's not that bad. Well, considering that there is no such thing as a good passport photo."

She sipped her drink and looked at me speculatively.

"Go ahead," I urged.

She smiled. "I got a fax today. It was about you—from Scotland Yard."

"I expected you to check on me. Present at a major theft, then at a murder—naturally I'm a suspect."

"They give you a glowing testimonial," she said carefully.

"I worked with them on a couple of cases," I explained. "Scotland Yard has a Food Squad—it gets involved whenever there's a crime involving food or drink or the businesses surrounding them."

"You worked in Smithfield Market in London in your teens, then got a job as an apprentice chef at—Kettner's, wasn't it?"

"That's right. One of the best in London. I had a wonderful training there."

She nodded. "Then you were a chef on cruise ships. Both coasts of the U.S., Australia, South America, Europe, Africa—that must be how you learned so much about foreign foods."

"Scotland Yard really are a bunch of blabbermouths, aren't they? I'm appalled that they told you all this. Do they spread my innermost secrets all over the world?"

"You've no idea—that girl in Rio, for instance . . ."

"What!"

The twinkle in her eyes gave her away but if she had wanted to conceal it, I was sure she could have done so.

"They withheld that part of the file. Then after that, you went into the food-finding business, which led to your present job—which I understand a little more clearly now."

"Food finding was interesting and very educational. I tracked down unusual food items and ingredients, looked for substitutes for rare products, advised on markets."

"This doesn't mean that you are incapable of committing a crime, of course." Her face was stern.

"Of course not."

Then the face relaxed into a delightful smile. "However, I have dismissed you as a suspect."

"Thank you," I said. "It's not pleasant having people suspect you of murder."

She nodded in understanding. The waiter came with menus, massive documents as large as a newspaper.

"And what about Lieutenant Gaines?" I asked. "Does he still think I did it?"

"Hal is a man you need to get to know. It takes a long time. But I'll tell you one thing—there isn't a better cop in all of New York City."

"So he does still think I did it."

"One of the reasons we make such a good team is that he operates on facts and reasoning. I go on hunches and intuition."

"But you can't persuade him over to your point of view that I'm innocent."

"As a matter of fact, I have managed to convince him . . ." She paused, an impish look on her face.

"Go on."

"That we should use you to help us."

"That's great," I said enthusiastically.

"And that I should be the contact."

"Even better."

"It's logical too. We may be the Unusual Crimes Unit but we're not gourmets, either Hal or I."

I looked slowly and meaningfully around the Bull Moose. "I can't believe that."

She laughed, a tinkly laugh that I was really beginning to like.

"But you were raised in a restaurant."

"This case goes far beyond a knowledge of restaurants. Hal and I both agree that we are going to need some genuine expertise to crack it. Which, incidentally, we are going to have to do very soon."

"Why is that?"

"In Unusual Crimes, we have a rule. It's solvable in ten days or not at all."

"Surely that's a bit unreasonable."

"It may sound that way but the chances of solving it after that period of time decline rapidly. We can't put manpower on the investigation any longer so we have to drop it. The only likely way of solving it beyond the ten days is a fluke or a tipoff, so it comes off the active list and we go on to something else."

"That must mean that you have to really concentrate on it during those ten days."

"We do. And that's all the more reason for bringing in all the help we can get."

"Well," I told her, "as far as available help is concerned, here I am."

"I should tell you," she said after draining her glass, "that Hal Gaines has another reason for wanting to have you work with us."

I was about to ask what it was when it struck me. "Makes it easier for you to keep an eye on me."

"Right."

She seemed pleased at the way I was taking it.

"I'm supposed to be back to do a job in Scotland," I said. "I'll fax them some data instead."

"What kind of a job?"

I told her of the salmon poaching incidents and my anticipated appearance in court to give testimony.

"Interesting," she commented.

"So's this," I said grimly. "And a lot more serious. Have you learned anything that I ought to know about?"

"Renshaw was killed with a seven-millimeter bullet, fired from an automatic pistol, probably a Russian Tokharev or a Japanese ripoff. No prints in the office that are of any help. No witnesses out in the parking lot, no clues of any kind otherwise."

"This is a wild shot," I said, "but I suppose you have considered checking on Sam Rong? He couldn't have taken the Ko Feng back with him to the East, could he?"

"We checked him thoroughly. We had his luggage searched when he arrived back in Bangkok. We checked him out there too. Nothing."

"I didn't think so but I had to mention it."

"That's okay. Shall we look at the menu?"

The menus were written in a jokey style that fitted with the theme of the Bull Moose. Typical entries were:

Alaskan Salmon Salad
Tell us whether you want the small can or the large can

Hudson Bay Hawk
It tastes just like chicken, in fact, we cook it with tomatoes, onions and mushrooms so that you can't tell the difference

New Brunswick Stew
Don't ask what's in it—believe us, you don't want to know

Yukon Sole
Remember Charlie Chaplin eating "sole" in *The Gold Rush?* Well, ours may not be that tender but it's cheap

Gabriella and I were chuckling over every item. We worked our way through the menu. It had Quebec Quail—shot down while escaping to America; Great Lake Bear Steaks, Prince Edward Potatoes, Chased Goose and a long list of other humorous dishes.

The wine list was not nearly as long. There were beers of many nationalities but the wine list declared, "You're in luck— we have Baffin Bay Burgundy and Calgary Chardonnay—yes, both of them!"

Gene came back to take our order himself. I ordered the

Caribou Steak, about which the menu stated, "You can't tell it from beef" and Gabriella went for the New Brunswick Stew. First, though, she interrogated Gene as efficiently as if he were a witness to a holdup.

"The traditional Brunswick Stew used squirrel meat," I reminded her and Gene replied, "We can't get squirrels in New York so we have to use cats." Finally, he broke down and admitted that they used only the finest sirloin of beef. He was about to leave when Gabriella asked him, "Any celebrities in here tonight, Gene?"

He glanced around. "Sure, there's Springsteen over there."

Gabriella half rose out of her seat.

"Where? Where?"

Gene pointed. Gabriella frowned.

"That's not Bruce Springsteen."

"Sam Springsteen. Comes in here all the time. Has a laundromat down on—"

Gabriella gave him a slap with her napkin. "No, seriously . . ."

"Okay," Gene said, "let me see—well, there's Betty over there—"

"Bacall?" asked Gabriella excitedly.

"No, Betty Barker, she's assistant manager at the blue movie theater down the block—"

"Get out of here!"

When he had left, I said, "Gene must have been a lot of fun to live with—he has an unquenchable sense of humor."

"He sees the funny side of life no matter how grim it gets."

"How many of you were in that flat?" I asked.

"Just Gene and I. We were together a little more than a year."

"Why'd you break up?"

"That was when Gene met Terry. They decided to go into partnership in this place. That's him over there"—she pointed to a tubby fair-haired man of about Gene's age who was active at the cash register. "That was also the time that I got promoted to sergeant and could afford an apartment of my own. So I moved out and Terry moved in."

"You mean they wanted to live together and work together?" I was asking curiously when I saw the glance that Gabriella darted at me.

"Oh, you didn't know Gene was like that?" she asked. She stopped as the waiter came with the food and a carafe of Canada's finest wine from Baffin Bay. When he had gone, she went on, "That's why sharing an apartment with him was such a good arrangement. He had no interest in me—except as a friend, I mean."

"Ah" I said, relieved. The thought had been nagging at me.

The burgundy proved to be an excellent California variety, merely masquerading as Canadian. Gabriella pronounced the stew almost as good as her father's *cassoeula,* adding that the pig's feet her father used gave it a different flavor. The menu proved to be right and my Caribou steak was as good as beef. That's because it was beef, a tender juicy porterhouse.

When I had finished it, I asked her, "You spoke about having me help in the investigation. What perilous assignment do you have in mind?"

"My, my," she mocked. "The burgundy must be strong. It's making you reckless, isn't it?"

"Before it does that, it has to make me brave."

"What! After all those daring exploits with Scotland Yard?"

"I'm a coward really," I insisted. "After all, I'm not really a detective, you know. I'm a—"

"I know. You told me. Don't worry, we won't send you out into the dangerous New York underworld without a bulletproof jacket and a SWAT team for protection."

"I do want to do what I can," I told her earnestly. "I want

to help find Don Renshaw's killer. I didn't know him that well but we were in this Ko Feng thing together. Send me anywhere."

I hoped I would be able to behave as intrepidly as I sounded. The kiss she gave me when we parted would have inspired Sir Galahad but he had the advantage of a suit of armor.

CHAPTER EIGHTEEN

Breakfast at the Framingham Hotel was served downstairs only as there was no room service. The facilities were a long way short of the luxury at the Courtney Park Hotel but then so was the tariff. I didn't like the look of the food they were serving so I walked north and watched for something better. No city in the world has more places to eat than New York and I found a diner on the next block.

When Walt Scott opened the first diner in Providence, Rhode Island, in 1872, he had no idea what he was starting. It was a humble establishment—a wooden wagon with holes in the sides. Scott handed out chicken sandwiches through the holes to the night shift workers, his initiative being prompted by the fact that nothing in Providence was open at night. Fifteen years later, the first walk-in diner opened in Worcester, Massachusetts, and customers sat on stools and ate sandwiches, pies and cakes, and drank coffee.

Diners shot up all over the country and became an integral part of the eating experience. They survived for decades but in recent years the diner has been emulating the dinosaur and the few that are left are rarities.

Like this one. However they fared during the rest of the day, this place put on a breakfast that would provide endurance for hours. Eggs, bacon, ham, sausage, waffles, tomatoes, mushrooms, hash-brown potatoes with lots of toast and coffee were the standard breakfast here but there were a dozen or more side dishes to add if you were hungry. I had forgotten too how speedy and efficient the service is in eating places like this.

I was on my way to see Peggy at the Spice Warehouse and after paying the very modest bill for my ham and scrambled eggs, I set off toward the subway station. This wasn't entirely for economical reasons. I had always had a sentimental affection for the subway and longed to try it again and see how much of the affection remained. Its reputation had declined owing to muggings and vandalism, I knew, but this was past the commuter hour and I wasn't going to be deterred by the media. I had a map of the city which I had bought at the airport and knew that there was a station at the Museum of Natural History nearby and it was a direct line.

There was only a moderate flow of passengers going down the steps and I bought my token and went to my platform. It was fairly quiet, some graffiti, a few candy wrappers blowing but not as bad as I had expected. Down at the far end of the platform, I could see a uniformed policeman. Nearer to me, two women were discussing the price of shoes at Bergdorf-Goodman, a studious-looking youth was immersed in a large paperback, a man in a black suit and a black hat was reading a newspaper and two girls were in a giggly conversation. All was very safe and normal.

A distant rumble gave notice of an approaching train. Time was eroded second by second then the push of air from out of the tunnel swept along the platform and the awaiting passengers shuffled positions. The sound of the train mounted in volume. Everyone took an impatient step or two forward and the train came out of the tunnel like a roaring lion.

Brakes hissed and metal squealed on metal. The train was still moving at a fair speed and it loomed larger. It came closer—and I felt a strong push in the middle of the back. Arms flailing, I fell from the platform and all I could see was the front of the train, growing enormous, filling my entire vision.

The next thing I knew I was standing on the platform, heart

racing. The man in the black suit and hat who had dragged me back still had one strong hand on my shoulder. He was bearded and had thick glasses. The two women gave me curious looks, the youth was still immersed in his paperback and the girls were still giggling. All of them boarded the train after a few people got off.

"Thanks," I said weakly.

"New York is dangerous place," the man said in an accent that I didn't recognize. His voice was thick as if he had throat trouble. "Is necessary to be friendly—to be helpful. If you are asked, you should respond."

I didn't understand but I was too concerned getting my nerves under control to think about it. The doors clashed and the train pulled out, rumbling and rattling as candy wrappers flew like mad butterflies. The platform cleared and quieted. The policeman was nowhere in sight. There were just the two of us. It was only then that the thought hit me. The same hand that had dragged me back must have been the same one that had pushed me.

I tried to see what the man looked like but the thick glasses with heavy rims, the beard and the black hat pulled down made it impossible. He spoke again.

"When you are asked to cooperate, you must do so. When questioned, you must answer. Withhold nothing. Tell what you know. You will be wise to do this—next time when there is a push, there may not be a helping hand to save you." His accent had evaporated. He turned and walked down the platform. The policeman reappeared and the man walked straight past him. I had a momentary idea of calling out but there seemed no point.

I gathered my wits as I waited for the next train. The policeman gave me a searching look as he passed me but it must have been only because I was still on the platform when everyone else had left.

I was musing over the warning I had received—if that's what it was.

Be friendly, helpful and respond, he had told me. Cooperate, answer and tell what I knew. There was an echo there of Marvell's words when he had told me that he didn't believe my protestations of innocence. Someone else was going to pressure me to tell them where the Ko Feng was. But was it someone else? Or had Marvell himself sent an emissary to do it?

There had been something about that accent that had bothered me—but what? Was it one I remembered? Passengers drifted onto the platform. I eyed them all suspiciously, picked a place to stand near the wall and when the next train came, I boarded it in the middle of a group of Japanese tourists. When I alighted, it was in the middle of another group of Japanese tourists.

The Spice Warehouse was doing a roaring trade. Some of it was undoubtedly sensation-seekers but a good number of previous customers had come to offer their condolences and ask what they could do to help.

"There can't be any more generous people in the world than here," Peggy said, her mouth twitching with emotion. "They're wonderful, they really are. Even ones I don't know by name but have only seen here in the warehouse a few times—even they want to do what they can."

Her sister-in-law was there and learning the business fast. The line at the checkout was long but—strangely for New York—no one was complaining.

"I'm trying to get the office in order," Peggy told me. "It's coming along well but there are a couple of things Don was doing that don't make sense. I wonder if you'd mind . . ."

I helped her to straighten out a shipment that was overdue from the Philippines and promised to find a source of chile pequins, a small but fiery member of the chile pepper family. Mexico is virtually the only source but unusually severe weather conditions last winter had caused a shortage. It was possible that one of the smaller supplying countries might be able to fill the gap.

She was already in the warehouse and busy catching up on

orders. I encouraged her to keep as busy as she could and told her to call me if there was anything at all I could do. She assured me she would.

"And if you think of anything that might be helpful—no matter what it is or how irrelevant it may seem—be sure and call me, will you?"

"I will," she said. She seemed to hesitate.

"Go on," I urged. "Is there something?"

"It can't have any meaning . . ." she said slowly.

"Tell me."

"When you called the evening before—well, before Don was killed, you said he sounded strange. He went out right after that and said he was going to the library."

"Go on, Peggy," I urged. "Was that unusual?"

"Well, yes, it was—especially at that time of the evening."

"He didn't say anything about why he was going?"

"Not a word. Just that he didn't know how long he'd be."

"Is there a library near you?"

"Yes, there is."

"Do you think he went there or to the main library?"

"He must have gone to this one. He wasn't gone long enough to go much further."

I asked her for its location and she gave it to me.

"Does it mean anything?" she asked tremulously.

"I don't know but if it does, I'll find it," I said firmly. "Now, one more thing—did Don ever prepare any King's Balm?"

"Yes, he did. He had quite a devoted following for it among the regular customers."

"What did he put in it? Do you know?"

"Fumitory and gentian. He'd tried variations on that combination but found those two to be the most effective by far."

"Can you let me have some?"

That transaction completed, I told her again to call me if

there was anything at all I could do. She nodded and then was called upon to help with the lengthening line at the checkout where even the sympathetic New Yorkers were getting impatient. I headed off for the library.

A friendly lady with a pronounced Scottish accent was in charge of the reference desk and after we had exchanged vital data on place of birth, how long we had been here, what we were doing here, her acquaintance with London and mine with Scotland, we got down to business.

I described Don and she remembered him at once.

"He wanted to see copies of the *New York Times* from five years ago."

"The *New York Times?* Did you have them?"

"Five years ago? Och, that's easy."

"Can I see them?"

"All of them?"

"Do you have an idea which issues he was particularly interested in?"

Half an hour later, I wasn't much wiser. I had been through every page of every issue for the first three weeks of the month of May, which it seemed were the ones that Don had zeroed in on, and I could find nothing to suggest what Don might have been interested in. I ploughed on doggedly and my persistence was rewarded—during the last few days of the month, there had been a theft at JFK.

There were a couple of reports on progress in the investigation that followed and I went into newspaper copies for the month of June to see if there was any further information but could find nothing. The Scottish lady showed me where the copy machine was, changed some coins for me and I copied all the relevant paragraphs.

There wasn't a great deal to the story. At first, it had received a full treatment because it had been mysterious. The aircraft had landed, been unloaded, the shipment had been examined by customs and cleared. It had been loaded onto a vehicle bound for a New York warehouse—but when the vehicle arrived, the shipment was gone.

The shipment had consisted of birds' nests.

I could see why Don had been interested in the story. It was a very close parallel to the disappearance of the Ko Feng. But what had made him look for it in the back issues of the *Times?* Had he known it was there? He must have—he was able to find it. I took the copies, thanked the lady and headed for the subway station. Then I thought better of it and chose a busy intersection to hail a cab back to the hotel.

There was a message for me at the desk. I was to call Dr. Li at a Manhattan number. I went up to the room but first I called my favorite New York police person. She was out in the field, I was told. I explained who I was and added that it was important I talk to her in connection with one of her current investigations. I was told to wait and within a few minutes, she came on the line. It was an exceptionally noisy one and Gabriella said, "I'm at Kennedy airport. You can probably hear all the planes and trucks. You'll have to speak louder. Is it important?"

"It is," I said. "An attempt was made on my life this morning."

There was a shocked silence, then "What!"

"Well, sort of . . ."

She sighed, an exasperated sigh that I heard clearly despite the bellow of a climbing jet. "Look, if this is some kind of gag just to get to talk to me, I don't find it—"

"No, it isn't. Listen, Gabriella—this is what happened . . ." I described the incident on the subway platform as briefly as possible, not omitting anything and repeating the dialogue almost verbatim.

"Hm," she said thoughtfully when I had finished. "Sorry I was suspicious of your motives."

"No, no, you were right to be suspicious. It just so happens that they have no connection with this incident."

"You say the man had an accent?"

"I thought so at first although it wasn't one I recognized. Then it faded away. At the end, I didn't notice one at all."

"A phony," she said promptly. "It's not that easy to maintain an accent—I know, I used to be an actress, remember?"

"I remember and I wish I'd been around to see you on the boards. But in the meantime, there's the matter of the threat to my life."

"Oh, that!" she said dismissively, then laughed. "You didn't recognize the man?"

"No, should I have recognized him?"

"Well, it sounds as if he were in a disguise—you say a beard, thick glasses with heavy rims, black hat pulled down—and nothing about him seemed familiar?"

"No. Nothing."

"And he not only pushed you in front of the train—he pulled you back. He's trying to frighten you."

"He's doing a great job," I said fervently.

"He's going to ask you where you've hidden the Ko Feng and thinks that by having you under threat, you'll be more likely to tell him."

"If he had wild horses tearing me into shreds, I couldn't tell him."

"Unfortunately, there's no way of convincing a person that you're telling the truth. It's because we all tell lies at some time or other."

"Your recommendation, Sergeant?"

"I'll see what I can do about protection. Stay close to the hotel."

"Another thing . . ." I told her of the *New York Times* issues that Don Renshaw had been reviewing at the library.

"A similar theft, five years ago," she said crisply in her best sergeant's voice. "Too similar to be coincidence, you think?"

"I do. Maybe your files on the earlier theft will give some useful clues on this one."

"I'll get on it right away, sounds good. And don't forget, leave word as to your movements."

After hanging up, I called the number I had been given at the desk. A female Asian voice answered softly and put me through at once.

Dr. Li's voice was harsh and his tone guttural though the sibilants hissed in the Chinese manner. Every consonant was sounded with emphasis so that the result was conversation that was perfectly understandable yet retained a strongly foreign flavor. His telephone manner was amicable and respectful though I had a strong feeling that there was steel beneath the velvet.

"I wonder if I might crave the pleasure of an hour or so of your time?" was his question after we had exchanged pleasantries and I had been welcomed to New York and extended sympathy on the death of my friend.

He was well informed, I thought. Better than I was, for his name meant nothing to me. I cautiously asked if he could tell me what he had in mind.

"I am the director of the Methuselah Foundation. We have areas of common interest, you and I. These interface with the Celestial Spice. The Ko Feng."

"The Methuselah Foundation. I am sorry but I am not familiar with it," I said.

"That is quite understandable. Our activities are largely here in the U.S.A. though we have many contacts around the world. We are a nonprofit organization dedicated to the prolonging of the prime of life through study and research. Methuselah, as I am sure you know, lived to be 969 years old. We have chosen him to be our emblem—and our goal."

I was beginning to understand. "This is why you are interested in Ko Feng—you think it may have properties of life extension."

"Precisely. You will agree, will you not, that we have much to discuss?"

I was willing to discuss with anyone if there was any possibility at all that I might learn something that would contribute toward finding the Ko Feng and Don Renshaw's murderer.

"Of course. When and where do you suggest?"

"If you would like to come to our headquarters here in Manhattan, a limousine will collect you. As for the time, I am at your disposal."

"Is later this afternoon suitable?" That would show how interested he was in talking to me, I thought.

"Excellent," he purred. "A limousine will be at your door in an hour."

My bluff called, I said, "Fine, I'm at the—"

"The Framingham Hotel. Yes, I am looking forward most anxiously to meeting you. I am sure we will have a most rewarding discussion."

As soon as I had hung up, I called Gabriella back and told her where I was going.

"The Methuselah Foundation," she repeated, surprised. "You should be safe there."

"If I'm not out in two hours, come in with helicopter gunships."

"I'll alert the navy and the marines. Do you want the UN in on this or shall we handle it ourselves?"

"It's my life we're talking about," I protested. "Can we be serious?"

"Deadly serious," she responded and hung up.

CHAPTER NINETEEN

A smiling young Asian woman led me through a library that looked like a library should. The walls and shelves were rich, heavy mahogany and so were the tables and chairs. The floor was carpeted with thick, soft Chinese carpets that must have been centuries old. The books looked nearly as old, most of them bound in morocco leather and imprinted in gold. In sharp contrast, several computers were scattered strategically and there were a couple of large copy machines.

We went on through the building via a wood-paneled corridor and then the young woman tapped gently at a door. She opened it and smilingly ushered me in.

Dr. Li was one of the most imposing individuals I had ever met. Well over six feet tall, he had a commanding presence that radiated around him like an aura. He wore what looked at first like a conventional Western suit except for the jacket buttoned all the way up to the neck. Then at second glance, it was more like a Chinese outfit and its unusual sheen made it look even more Eastern. He wore a small round flat cap of the type we associate with mandarins.

He came out from behind his desk to shake my hand. He was distinctly yellow of skin and he had a black mustache that drooped slightly although it was probably carefully tended. His nose was large and prominent and his cheekbones high—but it was the eyes that dominated.

They were jade green and penetrating, almost hypnotic. His hand was cold and he smiled slightly as he waved me to a chair.

He sat behind a desk of Asian manufacture, on it a few books, piles of papers and two telephones. An ornate lamp of a peculiar octagonal design poured a pool of orange light onto the soft leather desktop.

The walls were papered in pastel tones and flowered patterns. Silk-shaded lanterns and ornate Chinese scrolls hung alongside bronze and ivory carvings.

"I am very pleased that you were able to accept my invitation so promptly," he said. His voice was sharper, clearer than it had been on the phone. The gutturals were still prominent and there was the same impression of words which were pronounced differently yet were perfectly understandable.

I responded suitably, aware that the English language sounds chilly and stiff when contrasted with the politeness of Asian languages.

"We all want to die young," he stated. "But we want to do it as late as possible."

He smiled thinly. "I like to open with that statement because it reveals the basic reason for the existence of the Methuselah Foundation. You see, aging is not merely the passage of time. It is a number of different processes taking place in our bodies and the sum total of these results in what we call aging. These processes include a reduction in the ability to resist disease, wrinkling and drying skin, the loss of teeth and hair, an impairment of vision and a lowering of strength, endurance and mental activity."

He steepled his hands. His fingers were exceptionally long and thin. His nails were long and clawlike.

"These are the aspects of the aging process that we wish to slow—perhaps even to stop. This is the work to which we at the Methuselah Foundation are dedicated."

If ever a man looked dedicated, Dr. Li certainly did. He thoroughly convinced me.

"Very laudable," I said. "I'm sure you're doing wonderful

work. I presume that you are connected with other organizations similarly occupied?"

"There are others," said Dr. Li. His dismissive tone implied that they weren't worth a hill of beans between them. "Institutes for the Control of Aging they call themselves. You may spend a week at one of them for $5,000 or have consultations at $500 an hour."

"Are you aware of the use of Ko Feng in ancient times?"

My abrupt question didn't bother him in the least. He responded in his urbane manner. "Many people today are aware of Ayurveda, the body of knowledge in ancient India that embraces the belief that each food has its own medical, spiritual and healing properties. The equivalent of Ayurveda occurs in all the older civilizations, and in China Ko Feng is renowned—revered even—as possessing many extraordinary capabilities."

"And one of those is longevity?"

"We have made great strides in battling the eternal enemy, great strides in medicine, in diet, in exercise and in nutrition. But these are not enough—not nearly enough. Now we need breakthroughs—quantum leaps—and the only way they will come is from chemistry and botany."

He was leaning forward, fixing his piercing eyes on me, and the glow in them was close to fanatical. I was aware of a faint aroma in the room that I hadn't noticed before. I couldn't place it but it was a little like incense, though not cloying or pungent.

"Chemistry is bringing us many new products through research. Botany cannot bring us new products"—he paused dramatically—"except in very rare instances and we may have such an instance now."

"Ko Feng."

"Exactly. If it were really new, Ko Feng would be remarkable enough. But it is not new—it is old and has been lost for centuries. We have tales in abundance of what it can do, we have old records, we have the vast experience of hundreds of generations."

The aroma was growing stronger but Dr. Li apparently didn't notice it. At least he didn't comment. It was somewhat like the smell of orchids but then it seemed not reminiscent of any flowerlike smell.

"Too many of the drugs now being used are retardants, not extenders," said Dr. Li. "There is reason to believe—hope, even—that Ko Feng has many of the characteristics we are looking for. There cannot be only one answer to true longevity. It is not unlikely that several compounds will have to be combined to achieve the results we want, but it is highly possible that Ko Feng is the most important of all—the keystone of our efforts."

"I hope it is."

"I am glad to hear that, and it is why I asked you here today. Tell me, how may we obtain some Ko Feng and realize our magnificent goal?"

It was as if I had to fight my through an invisible fog to grasp his question. Surely that aroma wasn't responsible?

"I—er, can't answer that . . . I don't know where it is."

"But you can put your hands on it."

"No, I can't—it was stolen. I don't know . . ."

Dr. Li's voice took on a steely edge. "You said you wanted to help us consummate our efforts."

"I do."

"Then tell us where we may obtain the Ko Feng!"

I wanted to help this wonderful man who was so determined to aid us all live longer, happier and more fulfilled lives. I would do anything to achieve that.

"I can't!" I groaned. "I can't. I don't know where it is!"

For a few seconds, those green eyes burned into mine and I felt him touching my very soul. My own words echoed—or maybe I said them again. Maybe more time passed. I didn't know.

Then the aroma vanished as if swept out by a giant wind. Dr. Li's eyes weren't that bright green after all, I could see that now. They were green but quite normal. When he spoke again, his voice too was quite normal. Why would I have thought otherwise?

"It must have been an incredible experience to see and touch the Ko Feng," he said.

"Incredible—yes, it really was."

"You tested it very thoroughly, I understand?"

"We did. We considered all possibilities—that it was some other plant being passed off as Ko Feng, that it was a rare plant or one not readily recognized that was mistaken for Ko Feng. We theorized that it might be some kind of hybrid, accidental or deliberate."

"And it passed every test?"

"Yes. It was impossible for us to declare with one hundred percent certainty that it was Ko Feng, of course. We have had to emphasize that point several times. No living person had seen any Ko Feng for centuries and no scientific data existed which could identify it. But we eliminated all botanical spices that could have been substituted or mistaken for Ko Feng and we established that it had a unique quality."

"And so you were completely satisfied?"

"Yes, we were."

How could I have had such unfair suspicions of this man? I was ashamed of myself. His motives were the highest—but the stakes were high too. As if he were reading my mind . . .

"This is an unprecedented opportunity," he said. His green eyes glowed again, bright in contrast to his yellow skin. His features were implacable and surely no achievement was beyond his grasp. "Such a spice as Ko Feng could be the savior of mankind, it could be the crowning glory of all the efforts and struggles of the Methuselah Foundation, it could—" His voice was rising. He became aware of it and dropped it to a normal level.

Would the director of a research foundation use hypnosis and truth gas to pry information out of me? Ridiculous—I had read too many Fu Manchu stories as a boy. I wished I hadn't thought of that. Looking at Dr. Li now, I could see a strong resemblance—no, that was absurd. He didn't look that much like him at all.

If such means of persuasion were available, would he use them? From his point of view, I might have hijacked the Ko Feng and have it hidden somewhere. After all, somebody had—and it would be exasperating to be in his position, so close to a secret he had probably pursued for years. Many a man would tell himself that the end justified the means.

He was gazing at me intently. "The prize is incalculable," he said.

"Just what I was thinking," I agreed.

We were shaking hands and he was leading me out. I was agreeing to inform him immediately if and when the Ko Feng turned up. He was repeating how much it would mean to his organization and to mankind in general. It was all very polite and businesslike.

How could I ever have got such bizarre ideas?

CHAPTER TWENTY

The desk clerk at the Framingham Hotel was getting to know me.

"You've had three phone calls," he told me when I returned. "None of them left a message."

I had barely let myself into the room when the phone rang. A muffled voice said, "There is no need to thank me for saving your life in the subway station."

"I wasn't going to thank you," I retorted indignantly. "You pushed me in the first place!"

"As I warned you, New York is dangerous place."

He wasn't very good at imitating himself. His accent was slipping again too but the muffled effect must be from the use of cloth or paper covering the mouthpiece.

"I am sure that you listen to my warning. Tell me now, where is the Ko Feng?"

"I don't know," I said irritably. "I didn't take it and I don't know who did."

"You do not tell truth!"

"I always tell truth," I said with pardonable exaggeration.

"We want the Ko Feng." The tone was one of definite menace now and I was a little scared despite the comic accent. "We will take whatever steps necessary to get it!"

"I can't give it to you if I haven't got it."

"Very well. Next time, we may not be so gentle."

"There's no point in killing me," I said, vainly attempting reason. "If you kill me, you'll never find out where the Ko Feng is." I thought that over for a couple of seconds then added, "At least that would be true if I had it. But I don't." Hopefully that would confuse him as much as it did me.

The menace was still there, maybe even a few notches heavier, as he replied, "There is pain and suffering that can be worse than death. Maybe you ask to die." He hung up.

Standard threat stuff, I told myself manfully. They can't scare me, I added. The problem was they could and they had. But I was in this situation and getting out of it might be more dangerous than staying in it. I reviewed all the options, then considered all the actions I could take. The most desirable seemed to be a further investigation of the glamorous Ayesha and her Phoenicia Restaurant.

"Of course I remember you!" she said warmly when I phoned. "I was hoping you would call. Yes, we'd love to have you visit our restaurant . . . tonight? Ordinarily, we are booked far ahead but I think we have a cancellation . . . Just a moment . . . Ah, will you be bringing a lady?"

I thought it safer not to do so. "No," I said, putting in just a tinge of regret.

"Very well, that's wonderful. We'll see you tonight, seven-thirty . . ." Her voice was warm and full of promise.

When I left to go to the Phoenicia, I tried some tricks that I recalled from Mickey Spillane novels. I walked a few blocks, staying near people, crossing at crosswalks, then returning. I could see no one following me but in case I was being watched from the other side of the street, I waited at a bus stop but didn't get on. I walked off in the opposite direction, then turned to Tenth Avenue and caught a cab at a corner as it was discharging passengers.

The Phoenicia wasn't very far and I could have walked but in my cautious mood, I directed the driver to Lincoln Center then redirected him to the restaurant. Even then I had him drop me at another restaurant on the same block. It was Chinese, and I went in and came out again and walked on to my destination.

The exterior of the Phoenicia was a warm brownstone, weathered enough to have been left over from building the Sphinx. Most of the entrance though was glass. Large glass panels led to double glass doors with massive silver door handles.

Ayesha was there to greet me as a door swung open. She looked as ravishing as before. She was dressed more formally than at the Food Fair, though in the same colors, red and green. A balloon-sleeved silk blouse with a long skirt slit to above the knee were set off to advantage by high-heeled green shoes and jade earrings.

A few items of old-world cooking equipment were in the dining area—a stone slab for grinding meal and a huge copper caldron among them. Others were the same items I had seen at the fair, though the alcove with a wood-burning fire was larger. A spit rotated slowly and chains clanked as hunks of meat sizzled and smoked. A large game bird hung from a cast-iron tripod.

She seated me at a table in a corner, Several tables were already full and Reserved signs were on the others. It looked as if she had squeezed in an extra table for me.

"I would like to bring you a number of small dishes—something like a French dégustation," she told me in her musical voice. "I think that will be better than one main dish because it will allow you to taste several of our specialties."

Waiters of both sexes were serving at the tables and a big man who looked like a retired Cossack brought a shallow wooden tray with a depression in the middle. Then he brought spoons made of bone, a silver-handled knife and sticks like single chopsticks.

The first course was chopped hard-boiled eggs with spices and what tasted like mimosa. Many dishes of ancient Rome resembled this and it was a popular way of starting a meal. The eggs were hot and served on a thin circular stone which fitted exactly into the depression in the round wooden tray. This way, the food stayed hot as the stone plate was already heated. The wooden tray insulated it so that it remained hot through the course.

The wine was one I didn't recognize. I asked the waiter and he told me it was from Carthage. He poured from a glass container with a long curving neck. For a house wine, it was very good indeed. It proved to be an excellent choice too for it went well with a range of different dishes. It was a very light rosé, fragrant and soft with just the least hint of fruit.

Next came half a dozen oysters, each one in a separate depression in another design of stone plate. They had a thick sauce of what was probably chopped mussels and mushrooms.

A basket of bread was brought and I had to exercise restraint and eat only a little of each kind. All were different shapes, some small buns, others flat cakes, others fingers and some even triangular. Different flavorings were used in each too—sesame seeds, poppy seeds, currants, celery, sunflower seeds.

Then came a fish course, tiny strips of sole marinated in garum, Ayesha told me, coming over to the table in between her ceaseless attention to all the other tables. In ancient Rome, garum had been indispensable to the chef—it was a flavoring liquid made from brine and crushed fish. It was strong enough to conceal the taste of meat that had hung too long or fish too long out of the water. Today it is made from anchovies, wine, honey, vinegar and spices, for though modern refrigeration and transport mean that the spoiling problem no longer exists, a properly blended garum gives fish a delicious flavor.

A tiny breast of pheasant came, accompanied by red currants and a sauce of chopped figs in wine. A portion of rice with it had slivered almonds and garlic. *Kosali,* a dish from ancient Persia, was next—pieces of spiced roast lamb rolled in rice and cooked over hot charcoal—an early form of barbecue. Then there arrived *mandaliya,* sausages made from entrails stuffed with marrow and spices and roasted. Next was a Roman favorite, pork with almonds and leeks, served with sautéed squash in a sauce of lovage and oregano . . .

It was at this point that I had to tell the waiter to stop. Ayesha came hurrying over to find out what was wrong and I explained that I didn't have the appetite of an Oriental potentate.

Her eyes flashed. "But there is wild boar, there is venison, there is goose, there is"—she looked indignant—"there is sheep's head . . ."

We both laughed.

"Next time," I promised.

She looked disappointed but not ready to give up on me altogether.

"A little smoked cheese from the Caucasus, then some dates from Palmyra. Just to finish—these at least you can eat!"

I did, and drank a glass of a superb Muscat from Cyprus and two cups of thick sweet black coffee from Turkey.

I congratulated her on a magnificent meal and she beamed with pleasure.

"I can't imagine how you can reproduce the ancient dishes so faithfully," I told her. "And it's even more remarkable that you can do it using the ancient cooking methods and equipment."

"I could serve meals so magnificent that your mind would reel," she said, pulling a chair over and sitting opposite me.

"You could?"

"Yes. If I had some Ko Feng."

She raised her chin and stared at me boldly.

"When it is recovered, I hope you get some of it," I said weakly. I was on the point of making a rash promise but I didn't know if I could keep it and managed to substitute this watered-down statement just in time.

"Where do you think it is?"

She was leaning closer. Her knees were almost touching mine.

"I don't know."

"Who has it?"

"I don't know that either."

"Then who do you think has it?"

"I have no idea—I can't even guess."

She leaned back, eyeing me with near contempt.

"You were there the whole time! You must have some idea!"

"I don't. I wish I did."

I didn't want to abuse her hospitality, especially after such a magnificent meal, but it was time to go on the counterattack.

"When we talked at the Food Fair, I asked you if you had contracted to buy any Ko Feng. You said no."

"I don't believe I said that," she replied with a toss of that gorgeous hair.

"You did. You said—"

"I said that I didn't know that any contracts had been issued."

"That's the same thing."

"It is not."

Our wonderful relationship was going sour faster than a bowl of goat's milk in the noonday sun.

"Ayesha—tell me—were you offered any Ko Feng?"

Her strong bold features relaxed slightly. She waved imperiously to a waiter and pointed to my glass, then to herself. He returned at once with another glass and poured more wine for us both.

"There was no mention of a contract. Alexander Marvell contacted me two weeks ago and asked me if I would be interested in buying some Ko Feng if he brought some into the country. I was astonished, naturally. He told me that he expected to have some here and said I could have some of it. I was still astonished. He told me how he had come to find the crop and said that he had FDA approval. We discussed quantities and prices. He said that the amount coming in was limited and he didn't know when there would be any more—if ever."

She was not a sipper of wine. She threw it down with a regal gesture as if it were vodka and she was Catherine the Great.

"Did you talk to Selim?"

"Yes," I said.

"What did you learn from him?"

"Nothing."

"And Abe Kefalik?"

"Nothing from him either. I didn't know New Yorkers were so reticent."

"If they do tell you anything, it will probably be the same as I have told you. Marvell offered to sell them some Ko Feng when it arrived. No contracts, no sales agreements, no purchase orders."

"Have you been contacted since the Ko Feng was stolen?"

She looked at me suddenly. "No. Why, have any of the others?"

"They don't admit it."

Voices raised in argument could be heard at the back of the restaurant. Ayesha looked, brows furrowed. Lennie Rifkin came bustling forward, anxiously staring round the room. He caught sight of Ayesha and pushed between the tables. She was about to get up and go to him but a whim of obstinacy crossed her face and she settled back in her chair. She was giving me an adoring look and a wide smile by the time he arrived.

"I was looking for you," he said in a petulant voice. "They need you in the kitchen. Ephraim isn't happy with the *passum*—Vlad says it's the same as always. Where have you been?"

"Right here," she said carelessly. "Talking with my friend—you met him at the Food Fair, remember? He—"

"Yes, yes," he said crossly, not even looking at me.

Ayesha smiled again. Addressing me, she said, "*Passum* is another of the sauces of the old world. It is made from dried grapes pounded in wine. It is one of the sauces we can reproduce with great accuracy. Vlad is our sauce chef—he has his off days like all of us but he is very good. Ephraim is our head chef and not easy to please. When something is not right, Ephraim likes to blame whoever is nearest."

She laughed gaily. "I remember once when John Lindsay was dining with us. The chapatis were very salty and Ephraim grabbed our baker by the throat and—"

"Ayesha!" Rifkin was reaching a soprano level. "Will you stop gossiping and get into the kitchen! This is serious! Go in and talk to Ephraim and—"

"You talk to him. I am busy." She leaned back in the chair again and sighed a big sigh.

"What!" Rifkin glared at her and his face turned a darker shade of olive.

"I'm busy." She sprawled even farther back, tossed her head.

Rifkin struggled to control himself. When he spoke again, he was spitting out words like bullets. He had evidently given up talking to Ayesha and addressed himself to me.

"You may not know Clive Benson. He was food critic on the *Evening Reporter.*"

"Haven't had the pleasure."

"He is an embittered man. If you meet him, don't try to shake his hand. He has two broken fingers—makes typing on a keyboard very difficult. Why"—Rifkin opened his mouth as if he had just remembered something—"he was sitting in that very chair." He pointed a finger at me. Without looking at Ayesha, he said to her, "Another of your friends, wasn't he, my dear? Your very good"—he paused meaningfully—"friends."

She ignored him and signaled to the waiter to bring more wine.

"Perhaps I leave early tonight," she said to me. "We go to a nightclub, eh? You know the Copacabana is open again? A little tame for us, though—I think the Alley Cat is best. It is very . . ." She rolled her eyes suggestively.

This was probably not an unusual scene for Lennie Rifkin. He made a gesture of anger and said a word in Lebanese that I was sure was nasty, turned and stalked back into the kitchen.

Ayesha continued as if nothing had happened. "You are investigating this terrible crime, are you not?" she asked.

"Yes—well, I mean, I'm not a real detective but I'm helping the police investigate—"

"You are making progress?"

"We're following up a number of promising leads," I said. I had heard Sergeant Fletcher at Scotland Yard say that.

"So you expect to find the Ko Feng very soon?"

"Within ten days the case will be closed." Well, that had been more or less what Gabriella had said.

Ayesha's lovely eyes widened. She clasped her hands in a little-girl gesture. "That's wonderful! Then we can have some!"

I maintained a discreet silence.

Ayesha was still enraptured, planning menus.

"It's difficult to decide which dishes to use it with first. They have to be foods that are worthy of it—I mean, we don't want to be putting it into bulgur wheat or moussaka or parsnips. But then on the other hand, although it might go well with goose, not that many people order it—no, I think we . . ."

I let her muse on, nodding here and there to show that I was listening. And I was. She was a storehouse of information on the meals of Rome, Greece, Persia, India and China, and I couldn't decide which role she excelled in—the food historian, the chef or the beautiful woman.

"But I'll decide," she concluded firmly. "As soon as you get me some Ko Feng, I'll decide. And now, I must get back to the kitchen. Your dinner tonight is, of course, with my compliments."

I started to object but she cut me off with one of her imperious gestures.

"No, no, it is the least I can do for the man who is going to get me some Ko Feng."

I had to admire her technique. I thanked her profoundly and congratulated her again on the food and the presentation.

"If I were a food critic, I'd give you five stars," I told her, "even if I had to dictate the review."

She looked puzzled.

"Clive Benson," I explained. "The broken fingers . . ."

"Poof!" She shrugged carelessly. "It was only his left hand."

I was about to say "Good" but instead I asked, "What time are we leaving for that nightclub—the Alley Cat?"

"I have much to do in the kitchen. Perhaps another time . . ." She flashed a dazzling smile as she rose to escort me to the door, no doubt considering it more than adequate substitution.

A diner at a table near the entrance caught her eye. "Why, Basil! Darling! I haven't seen you for—"

I left but she was too engrossed to notice.

CHAPTER TWENTY-ONE

It was cool and breezy but not unpleasant. Cabs were passing by and it didn't look as if it would be long before I caught one. Several restaurants were in this area and customers were entering and leaving.

Sure enough, a cab came along within a few minutes and dropped me off in front of the Framingham Hotel. It was not late and people were on the street, some in pairs, some in groups. I was going in to the hotel when I heard a faint cry.

Tales of muggings sprang to my mind immediately but I could see no sign of anything like that. A couple walked by, heedless of any disturbance. I was about to go on when I heard it again. Then I saw the source.

A very old man at the curb was tapping around him with a white stick. No one was paying him any attention and I went to ask him if I could help.

"The crosswalk," he mumbled. "Where is it?"

He had a white beard and was enveloped in an old dark cloak. He tottered uncertainly as he flailed with his stick.

"Just along here a little way," I told him. "Come on, I'll take you."

I walked him in the direction of Amsterdam Avenue where the crosswalk was about thirty yards away. He wasn't very steady on his feet and I took his arm. When we reached the corner, the nearest people were on the other side of the street. He took a step off the sidewalk and I grabbed him to stop him falling. His cloak opened and my breath froze in my throat as he pulled out a wicked-looking knife. He was a mugger, after all.

He swung the knife so that the point was only an inch from my stomach.

"You haven't heeded the warnings, have you?"

His voice was no longer feeble. It was the voice of a younger man and what's more, it was vaguely familiar. My mind still on muggers, I was trying to think who had warned me about them when he moved the knife in a terrifying manner.

"You'll have one more chance. When you're asked where the stuff is, you'd better be ready to tell."

"Stuff?" I asked stupidly but I was stalling for time because it was becoming clear what he meant.

"The spice" he said venomously. "The spice!"

I tried to see his face but the white beard was thick and bushy and I couldn't make out any features. Some people have distinctive hands and others can recognize people by their hands but his didn't look familiar. Furthermore, one of them had a dangerous-looking knife in it and that was enough to drive all other thoughts out of my mind.

"You'll be paid. Just hand it over when and how you're told—you'll be paid for it. But no tricks." The knife moved again. "Remember what happened to your partner."

There was a shout from across the street, and from a handful of pedestrians coming toward us a girl emerged, breaking into a run. The man turned to look and that was my chance to grab his arm and take the knife away from him. I didn't do it, though. I don't like violence and I don't like knives. I don't know any unarmed combat and anyway, I'm a coward.

The girl was close now and she had obviously seen the knife. She pointed as she ran and shouted again. The man gave me a push and I fell into the road. He turned and ran off, long legs pounding. The girl had a horrified look on her face as she reached me.

"Are you hurt?" Clearly she thought that when the man had pushed me, he had stabbed me with the knife.

I was winded but I dragged myself to the curb and sat there, trying to get more breath. The girl wore tight blue jeans and a form-fitting black sweater with metallic letters proclaiming SYRACUSE UNIVERSITY across the breasts. She had a black beret and strands of dark hair straggled out of it.

She sat down beside me, looking at me solicitously.

"No, I'm all right," I said weakly. There was something about her . . .

"Gabriella!" I couldn't believe it.

She was looking down the street. "Too late to go after him," she was saying. "I thought he had—anyway, let's get you mobile again." She helped me to my feet. The remainder of the pedestrians had reached us by now. One or two looked at us curiously but most went about their business as if it were no concern of theirs.

"Tell me," I said, "do you moonlight as a guardian angel or did you just happen to be passing my hotel?"

She was examining me and nodded, satisfied.

"Since you told me about that incident on the subway platform, we've had you watched. Hal said if there was going to be another attempt, it would be within twenty-four hours. Ralph, another one of our team, was following you today until you went into the Phoenicia Restaurant, then I picked you up when you left it."

"You had no trouble?" I asked weakly.

"None. You left a very clear trail for us."

"How about a cup of coffee? We could both use one."

We strolled back to the Framingham Hotel. I tossed a few nervous glances in all directions and almost had palpitations when an ambulance started up its siren but once settled in a corner booth in the coffee shop, I felt better.

Gabriella took off her beret and shook out her luxuriant dark hair.

"Do you have any idea how different you look in that beret?" I asked her.

"Sure," she said. "That's why I wore it."

"The sweater and the jeans make you look different too but they don't conceal you as much."

She smiled that delicious smile. "You're back to normal, I can tell."

She regarded me for a moment. "You know, if I hadn't thought that man had stabbed you, I would have caught him."

"Sorry I couldn't oblige."

"It's okay," she said offhandedly. "It would have been a lot of paperwork—and I hate paperwork."

We both laughed and drank coffee.

"Anything about him seem familiar?" she asked.

"Yes. It was certainly the same man as the one who pushed me on the subway platform."

"But you didn't recognize him at first?"

"Not when I first saw him, no."

"It was the voice?"

"Yes, and then something else, maybe the way he moved once he'd abandoned the old man guise."

"What did he say?"

I told her.

"Hm—so he thinks you and Renshaw stole the Ko Feng?"

"Apparently. But then Gaines hasn't given up that notion altogether either."

Gabriella pursed her lips. "He's coming around."

"Speaking of coming around," I said, "would you do something for me?" I handed her the package of King's Balm that I had bought at the Spice Warehouse. "See that he takes two spoonfuls of this in hot water, twice a day."

She looked at me, surprised. "Are you a medicine man too? Where's your wagon?"

"I know something about herbal remedies and this one gives spectacular results."

"Why should you be concerned?" she asked.

"I don't like to see a man who can't enjoy his food. This'll help his dyspepsia."

"Why don't you give it to him?"

"He probably wouldn't take it. From you, he might."

She gave a wry smile. "Okay."

"So back to what we were saying—I'm not off his list yet?"

"You're slipping down it."

"What do I have to do to get off it? Get killed?"

"Don't worry. You're near the bottom."

"I seem to be on lots of people's lists," I said.

Her dark eyes examined me thoughtfully.

"Who else?"

"Alexander Marvell."

"Anybody else?"

"Most of the restaurateurs I've talked to probably think so too."

She smiled again. "You're a really suspicious kind of person, aren't you?"

"Not really. You should see me on a good day."

She finished her coffee. "Maybe I will."

"What do you mean?

"Maybe that good day is coming up."

"Tell me more," I invited.

"We've had a tipoff."

"About the Ko Feng?" I was excited.

"Yes."

"Who was it?"

"We get lots of tipoffs, of course. The NYPD recently

loosened its pursestrings and made more money available for paying for 'information received,' as we put it on the books."

"And this is from somebody who's tipped you off before? That means you know how reliable he is."

She nodded gently. "Worth following up anyway. What we need is a person who can identify the Ko Feng." She gave me the full eye treatment. "Know anyone like that?"

"I can think of one fellow—mind you, he's kind of hard to get."

"I can handle that," she murmured.

"He's English, too."

She shrugged. "Nobody's perfect."

"Some Italians come close. Especially Italian girls."

She became all businesslike and it was back to Sergeant Rossini. "I'll call you as soon as it's set up."

"Will it be—well, dangerous?" I asked. "Not that it bothers me at all if it is," I added hastily. "I just like to be prepared, that's all."

"You're carrying, aren't you?"

"Carrying? You mean a gun! Of course not."

A hint of a smile played around her lips.

"You're kidding, of course," I said, relieved. "Anyway, how could I have brought one into the country? Metal detectors, X rays, all that stuff."

"As a detective, you could have got a pass that would let you—"

"I'm not really a detective" I insisted. "I'm—"

"I know." She was smiling fully now. "You told me."

"I never carry a gun," I said firmly.

"I know the London police don't normally carry but I would have thought that when you're on a special case, you might make an exception."

"A special case to me is deciding if the green veins in gorgonzola cheese have been put there by corroding copper wire."

"They don't!" She was astonished. "They don't do that!"

"They certainly do."

"Not Italians, surely! I can't believe it!"

I had the feeling that she was humoring me but as I looked at her pretty, animated face, I decided to let her continue . . .

CHAPTER TWENTY-TWO

$\mathbf{W}$ouldn't touch anything in there if I was starving to death!"
said Professor Walter Willenbroek.

He had left a message stating that he planned on visiting me
at my hotel at nine thirty the next morning. I was asked to let
him know only if it was not convenient and his name was too
well known for me to do that.

His comment referred to the Framingham's coffee shop so
we sat in the lobby by a palm tree of dubious authenticity and
in leather chairs of equally dubious origin.

I knew of him, of course. He was as well known to anyone interested in food as Colonel Sanders, Milton S. Hershey or
Betty Crocker. He was dapper in a lightweight linen suit that
was as white as some of the bread that had made him a rich man.
His tie was the light brown of one of his breakfast cereals and his
shoes were the darker brown of another. His eyes were bright
and lively as a squirrel's and they never stopped darting everywhere. I found this a little disconcerting at first but I quickly
learned that it didn't mean he wasn't paying attention. His carefully groomed white goatee jutted out at a pugnacious angle. He
must have been well into his late eighties but his skin was firm
and smooth and his whole demeanor that of a man thirty years
younger.

His fascinating life story was partly common knowledge and
the rest I had filled in from a visit to the library in the Hearst
Magazine Building just off Columbus Circle. As a young man
in Wisconsin, he had started work as assistant to the janitor at

the Bayfield Sanitarium. He was fourteen years old and by the time he was twenty-one, he was a manager there.

The sanitarium philosophy consisted of sunshine, fresh air and a nutritious diet. Bayfield in northern Wisconsin had a little of the first, plenty of the second and a dedicated employee in Walter Willenbroek who was determined to see that the patients got all they needed of the third. He was not hampered by restrictions which, half a century later, might have driven him into another career. As a result of the freedom given him by the sanitarium director, Walter spent his spare time (after a fourteen-hour day) experimenting with ways to make grains more healthy and more tasty.

Hard work, determination and a normal amount of luck had produced a breakfast cereal that the patients loved so much that they asked for it after they were discharged and told their friends and relations about it while they were still there. This led to the starting of a cereal company which expanded so quickly that it inspired dozens of imitators.

Walter Willenbroek then showed that he was just as astute a businessman as he was an innovator. He not only encouraged competition but he helped it prosper. Then he stepped in, bought out the best and watched the others fade from the scene.

From this base, he opened bakeries, supplying rolls for hot dogs and buns for subs and hamburgers. When the pizza craze hit the U.S., he was first on the scene to provide the dough. He knew how to turn adversity to advantage too and after he almost died from peritonitis, he set about creating a health food empire that provided everything from vitamins to energy-generating drinks for Olympic athletes.

I hadn't gleaned all of this from previous knowledge and a quick visit to a library. Walter Willenbroek was not at all reticent in telling me of his life and I was soaking up every word and using them to fill in the gaps. He had told me of his crusade to insist on the use of unbolted—that is, unsifted—whole wheat flour in the making of bread.

"It took a brave man to square up to white bread," he told me, sitting up ramrod straight with his white hair and snappy broad-brimmed hat catching stares from all who passed through the lobby. There could be few in New York City who hadn't seen this man scores of times on television, wearing the same trademark outfit, tirelessly promoting his products.

"Why, white bread was the symbol of Western civilization. Criticizing it was like criticizing motherhood or accusing George Washington of being a traitor." He went on to tell me how he had made the first rye crackers and then built up a multimillion-dollar industry out of crackers of a variety of grains.

"Not that I did all I did just to make money," he told me. Passersby in the lobby were pausing to listen and whispers confirmed their identification of a man as well known as the president of the nation. "I always had the welfare of the public at heart. Spent time and money—yes, and a lot of effort too—in getting people to eat right." He chuckled at the images that were running through his mind. "Like chewing every mouthful thirty-two times. That was important and I kept telling people so. Thought it was nonsense, some of them. I told them 'One chew for every tooth in man's natural complement of masticators'—that's how I put it. 'Stop digging your grave with your teeth,' I used to say." He chuckled again.

The assistant manager of the hotel was having to move people on now, as they were blocking the entrance. He gave me a smile which I presumed was acknowledgment that he was enjoying the publicity even if residents couldn't get in or out. There was no doubt that he recognized the famous professor.

I recalled a phrase in one of the biographies in the Hearst library. It described Walter Willenbroek as being responsible, more than any other man, for making Americans "the most health-conscious nation in the world." Like many a great man, he had not always been right. He was often accused of being a crank, expressing intolerance at one time or another of milk, eggs, pork, shellfish, and salt. But then he had been ahead of his time in most cases and right far more often than wrong. It had happened more than once that within a decade after one of his campaigns against some food or other, scientific evidence emerged supporting his prophetic views.

His stream of recollections and anecdotes concerning persecutors, supporters, friends and enemies, famous and infamous, could probably have continued unabated all day as he was far from forgetful. He certainly wasn't boring even if the flow was remorseless, but he knew exactly why he had come here.

He rapped his cane on the floor twice as if to remind himself.

"Now—this here Ko Feng thing."

I didn't want to go public on the topic. When I waved to the manager and made a rueful face while regarding the avid listeners, he knew what I meant. A bellboy dragged over a large folding screen and the small crowd was dispersed.

Restored to relative seclusion, I said, "Yes, Professor Willenbroek. I presumed that was what you wanted to talk to me about."

"You tested it, tasted it, all that sort of thing, didn't you?"

"I did."

"Said it was genuine."

"That's right."

"Then it disappeared." He looked at me accusingly.

"I know. I was as appalled as you are. I couldn't believe it. I couldn't understand it—I still can't."

"Know the history of Ko Feng, do you?"

"Some of it."

"Amazing spice."

"Several of the spices of the ancient world were."

"We don't have them anymore. We have Ko Feng. Or did have."

He could have added, "Until you lost it, you jerk." He didn't, though, and I mentally thanked him for that. I wondered if he did think I had "lost" it—or was he here because he thought I had done more than lose it?

Like steal it?

I was getting tired of protesting my innocence but he had no way of knowing that. I was about to go into my James Stewart impersonation of a man falsely accused of a crime when he stared at me keenly and said, "You look like an honest man to me. Wouldn't have got where I am if I wasn't a good judge of men. Renshaw must have thought so too—he was the one who brought you here, wasn't he?"

"Yes, he did. That's why I'm staying here in New York as long as I have to—to help the police find out the truth."

"Hmph." He appeared to be debating with himself. It was the first moment of silence since we had shaken hands. Finally, he said, "I was offered the Ko Feng, you know."

I was dumbfounded. Eventually, I found some words.

"You were?"

They weren't the greatest of words but they were the best I could manage upon hearing this startling revelation.

I asked the big question. "Who offered it to you?"

"That's the funny thing. I don't know. Well, maybe that's not so funny—he wouldn't want to identify himself, would he?"

"When did this happen?"

"About two weeks ago. I thought he was some kind of crank. I didn't know that Marvell was bringing the stuff in—he didn't announce it till the last minute. I expected Marvell to call me and ask if I wanted to buy any. He didn't, though, so naturally I started to wonder what was going on after I heard about the stuff being stolen."

"This means that the person offering it to you planned on

stealing the Ko Feng," I said slowly. "To approach potential buyers after the theft wouldn't carry any conviction—all kinds of weirdos claim to have committed major crimes. But by offering it before the theft . . ."

"That's what I thought." Professor Willenbroek nodded briskly.

"If you're offered it again, will you buy?"

"Don't believe I will." He rapped his cane sharply on the floor. "Don't hold with encouraging wrongdoers—especially murderers to boot." He eyed me. "I suppose there's no doubt that the man who stole the Ko Feng also killed your friend Renshaw?"

"It looks that way."

"Can't say it isn't a temptation, though," he said ruminatively.

"Ko Feng would be a valuable ingredient in some of your health foods, wouldn't it?"

"Certainly would. Maybe you know this but a couple of thousand years ago, spices weren't used that much for cooking. Their main uses were in ointments, curatives for whatever ailed you, pick-me-ups and drugs and medicines of all kinds. They were the ingredients that cured people and helped them live happier lives."

"Just as you're doing today with your health foods."

"Precisely," he snapped. "I'm not one of those old fogies who doesn't believe in trying things. When I heard about this Ko Feng, I thought to myself, Here's something I've got to have. And if it's only ten percent as good as its reputation, then it's something I want."

I didn't like his implication when he said that Ko Feng was something he had "got to have" but I took it to be a figure of speech.

"They used Ko Feng in Babylon—did you know that?" he asked.

"Yes, I did."

"And China, and Egypt, and naturally in Rome."

"Yes. All of the pre-Christian civilizations made extensive use of it. Alexander the Great is said to have taken it regularly and made it a part of the diet of his officers. The Emperor Charlemagne was a firm believer in it too and so was King Roger when he led the Normans in that amazing invasion of Sicily around 1000 A.D."

"You've done your homework, I see." He nodded approvingly.

"Which products do you plan adding it to?"

"Don't know that there's any of them wouldn't benefit from it. Take breakfast cereals for instance." He snorted indignantly. "These lists that some outfits show on the box—all those vitamins and minerals! Why, they're a joke! Wouldn't be surprised if one part per million of Ko Feng didn't do far more good!"

I smiled.

"You're certainly a believer in Ko Feng."

"Belief," he said. "Belief—it's a wonderful thing, belief. I've always believed in it!"

"Because," I reminded him, "we don't have any knowledge of Ko Feng that is the result of scientific research."

"No. But don't think that those ancients didn't know a thing or two about nutrition. They had to—did you know that every work battalion that built the pyramids had its own nutritional expert?

"I didn't know that," I admitted, "but I'm not surprised."

"The ancients had a lot of extremely valuable herbs—ginseng, yohimbe, gingko biloba—now there's a good example for you! Five thousand years gingko biloba's been around and people have sworn by it all that time. Scientific research has only just proved that it contains heterosites, the most powerful energizers known to man."

"I don't doubt that Ko Feng is going to prove one of the greatest nutritional benefits to mankind. First things first, though—and top of that list is to get the Ko Feng back from whoever stole it."

"You're the detective," he said, though I could have wished that he'd put more conviction into the statement.

"Actually, I'm not." And I launched into my explanation of what I was.

He was looking more and more disappointed as I went on. I tried to reverse that trend. "I'm working actively with the police on the case. They feel that a knowledge of food may prove to be very important in solving this crime—well, both crimes. Two of the finest detectives in the Unusual Crimes Unit have been assigned and between us, we're confident of success."

"Hmph." It wasn't an overwhelming vote of support and I hurried on to catch him before he cooled any further.

"Can I ask you to tell me immediately if you're offered the Ko Feng again?"

"I'll do that."

"Or if there are any other developments that you think I ought to know about?"

"Right. And I'll expect you to tell me as soon as you've found it."

"Deal," I said.

We shook hands and I walked outside with him. A sleek gray Rolls-Royce materialized and pulled to a smooth stop. I watched him go.

CHAPTER TWENTY-THREE

Back in the hotel room, I phoned JFK airport and after being advised to try various numbers, I got Karl Eberhard. He didn't ask about the Ko Feng case and I supposed that was because his position gave him access to any information on it. He offered his condolences on Don Renshaw's death.

"Were you in security at the airport five years ago?" I asked him.

"I was, yes."

"There was a robbery in May five years ago. Do you recall it?"

"No, I don't believe I do."

"A shipment of birds' nests from China disappeared after being cleared through customs."

There was a pause. "Ah, yes, I think I recall it," he finally said.

"You said you were there then."

"Yes."

"Did it strike you—the similarity between that theft and the theft of the Ko Feng?" I asked.

There was another pause. "Now that you mention it—yes, they are similar," he admitted.

I waited for him to elaborate.

"You see, I was just a security patrolman then. I wasn't involved in that case at all. I remember hearing about it, seeing it in the files, but I had nothing to do with it. I have had many promotions since that time," he went on proudly.

It sounded feasible. I wondered if he was going to ask me how I had heard about the earlier case but he didn't so I didn't volunteer anything.

"Perhaps you can look through the files on it again," I suggested. "Any similarities between the two cases might be helpful in this one."

"I will do that," he promised.

I thought of asking him to transfer my call but decided it might be a problem and furthermore there was no need for Eberhard to know who I was going to talk to next. So I hung up and redialed. This time it was easier and I was promptly connected with Michael Simpson.

"Still with us?" he asked in surprise. "Oh, I guess the police want you to stick around . . . That Ko Feng didn't show up yet, eh? Nasty business about that fellow Renshaw. I didn't know him that well, only met him a couple of times. Is there something I can do for you?"

I picked my words carefully. "Someone was telling me about a theft there at JFK about five years ago—you were there then, weren't you?"

"Yes, I've been here twelve years now." He hesitated. "What theft was it? I don't recall."

Eberhard hadn't recalled either. Must be all that engine noise affecting people's memories.

"A shipment of birds' nests."

"Birds' nests?" He sounded astonished.

"From China. Hijacked—either at the airport or on the way to their destination. As a matter of fact," I added as if I had just thought of it, "the shipment disappeared in a very similar manner to the Ko Feng."

There was a long pause.

"Yes," he said slowly. "Yes, now it comes back . . . birds' nests. I wasn't involved in the clearance of it myself," he hastened to add, "but I recall seeing it in the files and I know that the police were here investigating." There was another pause. "It was similar, you say?"

"There were a number of similarities," I said. "Did you ever hear any more about the case? Did they recover the shipment?"

"Not that I ever heard."

I hardened my tone. "I'd appreciate it if you could check the files on it for me."

"Well, I don't know . . ."

"There may be more similarities to the Ko Feng case than we realize," I said, introducing a ring of authority. "Which, as you know, is now a murder case."

"I—er, well, I'll be glad to cooperate any way I can, of course. I'll call you back."

I didn't place much hope in Eberhard calling me back as it was unlikely that he would run across anything even if he made the effort. With Simpson, I needed some facts.

"I'll wait," I said firmly.

"It may take some time."

"I won't be near a phone for some time. I'll wait."

He didn't sound too happy about it but he agreed. It was some minutes before he returned. "I have the file right here."

"Can you give me the classification number it came in under when customs cleared it?"

He did so.

"And it was described as what?"

He read off the Chinese names, letter by letter.

"Translated into English as . . ."

"White birds' nests."

"Good," I said. That was what I had been hoping for.

The phone rang again, almost immediately after I hung up. I noticed that the hotel operator's manner was more deferential than before. A visit from the famous professor, veteran of a thousand TV commercials, had boosted me up the ratings chart.

A deep male voice confirmed my identity, then said, "Please

hold the line. This is Paramount Pharmaceuticals. Our Vice-President, New Products, Research and Development Division, wishes to speak with you."

I waited. A woman's voice came on the line, rich and melodious, just husky enough to be exciting.

"This is Gloria Branson speaking, Vice-President, New Products, Research and Development Division, Paramount Pharmaceuticals."

"What can I do for you?" I asked.

A rough idea of what I might do was already in my mind. After the conversation with Professor Willenbroek, a call from a woman who was in a new products division for a pharmaceutical company wasn't likely to have too many bombshell surprises.

"I'm calling because I'm sure we have a great deal in common."

It was a sensually attractive voice, full of promise and allure. Many women are able to project such a vocal image but few are able to sound completely natural and sincere. This one did. I wanted to meet her and drink in more of that marvelous voice.

I reminded myself sternly that I was a professional and did not intend to be influenced by anything as inconsequential as a woman's voice, no matter how fascinating.

"I was hoping we could get together over lunch—perhaps today?"

"That would be great," I said promptly.

"Do you like intrigue?"

It was a question that caught me without an immediate answer.

"Vienna Intrigue. It's on Fifty-second Street near Second Avenue," she explained, a touch of exasperation in her voice. Then she turned on the full power of her oral intimacy. "Oh, I'm sorry. Of course, you're a stranger to New York. It's one of the better of our new restaurants. I know you'll love it. Ernst-

Erich Vogeler from the Goldener Pferd in Salzburg took over the kitchen only a couple of months ago and already he's doing wonders."

"What time?" I was trying not to sound too anxious.

"Noon. I'll reserve a table. It's not much notice but they know me."

We had hung up before I realized that she hadn't even said what we were going to talk about. Nor had she elaborated on what it was we had in common. Not that I had much doubt on that score . . .

I went up to my room. It wasn't very large and I wondered if my raised status in the eyes of the manager would get me a larger one. It would be worth a try. In the meantime, I phoned Gabriella.

"Do you know Paramount Pharmaceuticals?" I asked her.

"I know the name. Nothing specific. Why?"

"Are they big?"

"Huge. Are they involved?"

"They may be. I just had an invitation from their vice-president in charge of new products. Lunch."

"Did he say what he wanted to talk about?"

I saw no reason to correct her. After all, it was only results that counted.

"No but it can't be anything except Ko Feng, can it?"

"I suppose not. Where's the lunch at?"

"Vienna Intrigue."

There was a low whistle.

"Know it?"

"Not on my salary," she said promptly. "From what I've heard, it's pretty ritzy. Well, it should be safe anyway. Just to be sure, stay away from dangerous people."

"Absolutely," I assured her. "I just had an interesting chat . . ." I told her about Professor Willenbroek. "You might want to talk to him, perhaps he'll recall something he forgot when talking to me although there's absolutely nothing wrong with his memory."

She agreed and I asked, "Anything new?"

"A lot of work and not much to show for it. We've checked out the New York and Asian Bank—clean. We've checked the route that you took, all the way from the bank back to JFK. We've talked to a dozen police officers who were on that route—not one of them saw anything unusual. We've covered the airport itself. We've run a thorough check on Arthur Appleton and Michael Simpson—no prior convictions. We even checked Karl Eberhard, the security man—squeaky clean."

"Eberhard's clean, is he?" I asked, interested

"Yes. The only one we don't have a handle on is Sam Rong."

"Why's that?" I asked.

"We're waiting for an answer from Bangkok. The time difference may be the holdup there, not necessarily any other reason. We've talked to staff in the entire cargo area—nothing."

"It's baffling," I said. "It's too ridiculous for words. How could the Ko Feng disappear like that? Even Houdini couldn't have done that."

"Houdini?"

"Yes, you know, the magician—"

"I know who he is. I was just musing . . . That's a thought."

"What is?"

"An idea," said Gabriella, "just an idea . . . I'll tell you about it later."

"All right. Meanwhile, when are you calling me into action?"

"Just waiting for a couple of things to fall into place. It may be tomorrow. Keep in touch."

"One other thing . . ."

"Yes?"

"It is possible, I suppose, that the thief has sent—or taken—the Ko Feng overseas."

"Hal thought of that. He's ordered a special watch at ports

and airports and asked the post office to be on the alert."

"It could easily slip through."

"I know. But Hal doesn't think it's likely. He feels that the U.S. is the big marketplace and that the spice is still here."

"All right," I said. "One other thing . . . You remember I mentioned that Don Renshaw had wanted to see copies of the *New York Times* from five years ago?"

"Yes. I told Hal about it. He ran it through the system. There are similarities in the MO but nothing else came out."

"Well, I'd like to follow it up. I know who the importers were."

"What do you expect to learn?"

"Maybe the two cases have more in common than just the MO. Whatever we learn about the first theft might help with the second."

"Hm, and it might take a food expert like you to spot it."

"It's the birds' nest angle that intrigues me."

"I don't see how you can learn much that way," she said. "No restaurant owner is going to admit stealing it."

"No, but they might know or suspect who did."

"The Chinese are a tightly knit community," she said.

"Like the Italians?"

"Comparisons are not appropriate," she said in a school-marmish voice. "Anyway, do you know how many Chinese restaurants there are in New York?"

"No. How many?"

"I don't know either, but I do know there are seventeen thousand of all kinds and a fair proportion must be Chinese. An investigation like that could take weeks."

"Gabriella, let me tell you about birds' nests. In the first place, many Chinese restaurants use substitute materials."

"You mean, not birds' nests at all?" She sounded horrified.

"Right. Second, a lot of them use the black birds' nests."

"From blackbirds?" Now she was puzzled.

"No, no, the nests are black, not the birds. It's because they're different birds. That's the inferior grade, the cheaper one. That leaves a relatively small number of top restaurants which use the expensive and much rarer white birds' nests. Well, not just top ones—there are some that pride themselves on using genuine ingredients."

"I see." She was beginning to sound interested.

"Now we can whittle that down even more," I said, getting more enthusiastic by the minute myself. "Birds' nest soup is not that popular a dish in the West. It still is in the Far East but not here. It's an acquired taste—many Westerners find it bitter. There are lots of Chinese and Indo-Chinese here, of course, and they will go to a place which serves a good soup, expensive as it is."

"It might be worth following up, after all," she conceded. "But remember that the Chinese are clannish. They won't let much out to a Westerner—especially one as foreign as you."

I let that one go by. "I know—but let's suppose there were several Chinese restaurants that wanted those birds' nests. What if only one got them? Wouldn't the others feel irritated?"

"We say PO'd."

"That abbreviation has now crossed the Atlantic," I told her. "So, might one of the others still be nursing a grudge and therefore love the opportunity to spill the beans?"

"It's an idea," she admitted.

"After all, it sells for somewhere around $150 an ounce."

"What! That's outrageous!"

"It's more than caviar. Quite a lot for bird spit, don't you think?"

She gurgled. At least, that's what it sounded like. "What did you call it?"

"The birds are called salanganes—they're found only on a few small islands just off the coast of Java. They're small—smaller than hummingbirds. They make their nests on the walls of grottoes overlooking the sea and always on the tops of high, almost inaccessible cliffs. Their sticky saliva forms a crust that is the tiny nest. The natives have to make dangerous climbs to get the nests and the birds are rare—"

"That's what pushes the price so high?" Gabriella asked.

"Right—and it's pushed even higher by the long, tedious manual work needed to remove the soil, feathers, dirt and other—"

"You don't need to spell it out" Gabriella said. "I get the message. Remind me never to order birds' nest soup. Thank goodness Italian cuisine is pure and clean."

"You think so? How about—"

"No. Not now. Anyway, thanks for narrowing the field. Go for it."

"I have your backing?"

"Give it a try," she said. "Oh—and take care."

I appreciated her solicitous concern for me but it gave me a slight shiver. I consoled myself with the thought that the person who had threatened me on the subway platform and at that street corner hadn't wanted to kill me, just scare me. Besides, that person couldn't be the thief because the thief knew I didn't have the Ko Feng.

So I couldn't really be in danger because if the person threatening me wanted me to tell where the Ko Feng was, I had to be alive to do it. I didn't like the corollary to that—namely that once I told, I was no longer of value. But then that didn't apply because I didn't know so I couldn't tell.

Worst of all was the thought that the thief—or someone else connected with this whole mess—had already killed Don Renshaw. The most likely reason was that Don had learned something which might identify the thief. And here I was, contemplating a solo expedition into Chinatown to learn something . . .

CHAPTER TWENTY-FOUR

Like several New York restaurants, Vienna Intrigue was underground. There was no clue to this from the outside. A black awning trimmed in silver and double doors of a black hardwood seemed normal, but then the doors swung open as the customer intercepted an invisible beam and an empty lobby with mirrors led to an automatic elevator. This came to a stop that was so gentle it was undetectable. The door slid open and the maître d' was there, smiling, dressed impeccably.

The ambiance was dark but not gloomy, with black and purple the dominating colors. The restaurant was divided into several areas, each with four booths, separated so as to provide complete privacy. Black wood paneling and hidden strips of silvery light maintained the atmosphere suggested by the restaurant name.

The mention of Ms. Branson's name brought a murmured invitation to follow the maître d' to a table. She had not yet arrived but the wine waiter arrived promptly and I accepted his proposal of the house cocktail.

The menu contained a description of the restaurant. It was a replica of one in Vienna which had been a meeting place for men and women of the aristocracy who wished their affairs to be conducted in privacy bordering on secrecy. There were several Viennese specialties on the menu but also a few other dishes from various European cuisines.

My companion was twenty minutes late, though she saw no need to apologize for it. In any case, her appearance drove all other thoughts right out of my mind. Her smooth blond hair glowed with a golden sheen. It fell straight and was cut medium short. Her face was classically sculptured and made even more striking as she was maturely beautiful. She had a serenity that suggested an inner peace, though I wondered how that was possible in the highly competitive pharmaceutical industry and in the supercharged arena of New York City. She was slightly above medium height but her slim figure and gliding carriage made her appear taller. She wore a severely tailored business suit in dark forest green that molded the curves of her body precisely.

"I like this place," she said. Her voice was as enticing as it had been over the phone though a tone lighter.

"Vienna is a good model to use for a decor of intrigue. All that's needed are curtains that can be drawn."

She smiled, a placid smile—or so it seemed at first. Then, and without changing, there was a hint of delicious wickedness in it.

"Look behind you," she said.

I had thought that the walls were covered with drapes, mostly black and some purple, but now I saw that the purple ones were in fact curtains and that they had cords.

"Not only attention to detail but realism," I commented.

She ordered the same house cocktail. It was champagne with some fruit juice in it—I thought a blend of guava and mango.

We sipped. I waited for her to open the conversation.

She said nothing. Her composure was extraordinary.

To break the silence I said, "I'm glad they haven't thought to add more atmosphere by playing *The Third Man* theme on a zither."

"Ernst-Erich is half Swiss, half Austrian. He's too subtle for that."

Another short silence followed. It must be her technique, I thought, her way of throwing me off balance. Then she started to speak and I decided I had been wrong. She spoke when she had something to say and didn't feel the need to bridge gaps of silence.

"Let me tell you about Paramount Pharmaceuticals first of all. We are the seventh largest pharmaceutical company in the Western world. Our total sales last year were twenty-three billion dollars. Our operating profit was a record high at eight hundred percent and our net income was five hundred million dollars . . ." She broke off to smile apologetically. "Numbers get so boring, don't they? Especially when millions and billions get thrown around so readily. We have one hundred and four subsidiary companies all over the globe and our long-term earnings are growing at nineteen percent per share. Last year was a record year in every respect—for the fifth year in a row."

She paused to assess what effect she was having on me.

"A remarkable achievement," I said. "Especially in these tough times."

"My responsibility is new products. Developing new products isn't easy. Few chemical products are really new. Most are simply improvements on the old. Occasionally, we succeed in synthesizing one of nature's original products but that is expensive to do and manufacturing them is even more expensive. So you can see why we become excited when we hear of a genuinely new natural product."

We were getting there at last. I nodded encouragement and waited for her to continue.

"I decided to establish a new group a few months ago. A new group to develop and market a new category of pharmaceutical products. Products that have never been marketed before."

I frowned.

She smiled, her red lips perfectly shaped with a tantalizing crinkle at the corners. "Does that surprise you?"

"It certainly does. It must be very rare for a product group that new to be developed."

"Rare indeed," she agreed. "The group I'm talking about are aphrodisiacs."

That got my full and undivided attention.

It also brought a silence down on the table that must have been noticed by the waiter for he deemed the moment appropriate for bringing menus and he was promptly followed by the maître d', who appeared to be accustomed to giving Ms. Branson the personal treatment.

She introduced me as a visitor from London.

"He has a reputation as a gourmet," she told the maître d', "so you had better give him your finest recommendations."

"I'm looking forward to hearing them," I told him. "Viennese cooking has a unique pedigree—drawn from a dozen cultures."

He gave a slight bow of agreement.

"In the days of the Emperor Franz Josef, sixteen languages were spoken freely in Vienna and there were even more national cuisines," he said. His slight accent was smoothly and definitely Austrian. "Many contributions were made—from herdsmen of the Hungarian plains, Czech peasants, Serbian mountaineers, Alpine guides, Turkish pashas, Polish noblemen, Italian seamen, Levantine traders. The best was taken from each, for the Viennese were choosy. They also blended a little of this cooking with a little of that and evolved new dishes."

"Didn't you tell me that everyone in Vienna ate well except the emperor?" asked Gloria.

The maître d' smiled. "Yes, indeed. He wanted only boiled beef every day."

"Tafelspitz," I commented. "I enjoy it when I can find it, but once or twice a year is enough."

"So what do you recommend for twentieth-century capitalists?" Gloria asked.

"Hapsburg Soup would be very suitable . . ."

We both smiled.

"It's very good," conceded Gloria, "but too creamy."

"Dumplings are, of course, very much a Viennese specialty . . ."

"I've had them several times," she said. "I'm beginning to look like a dumpling."

The maître d' and I responded simultaneously with protests that nothing could be further from the truth. Gloria smiled, having achieved her desired result.

She decided on the Russian Eggs and I ordered the Barley Soup. Discussion continued on the next course. Gloria favored the Hot Oysters and I chose the Eel in Dill Sauce. For the main course, she went for the (a true Viennese specialty, the maître d' assured us) and I eventually selected the Fricasseed Goose, as goose is unfortunately becoming increasingly harder to find.

The wine waiter came and confided that he had a few bottles of Austrian wines in the cellar.

"They are drier and more alcoholic than the German wine varieties drunk most often in this country," he added. We accepted his recommendation of a Klosterkeller Steigendorf, a full-bodied but dry Riesling.

When he had gone, Gloria returned to her theme.

"Apicius, the Roman cookbook writer, had recipes for increasing sexual desire. Homer, Ovid and Pliny all described sexual stimulants in their writings," she said.

"Both garlic and onions were considered as such stimulants, weren't they?" I asked.

"And still are. In fact, there was a period in India when they were banned because they were considered to be too stimulative. And in Europe for centuries, both of them were forbidden food in nunneries and monasteries. Nero ate huge quantities of leeks—which, of course, are the same family."

"I remember reading that the workers on the pyramids in Egypt went on strike when their garlic ration was cut."

She nodded. "But the Middle Ages were the times when

the search for love potions was at a peak—every wizard, every sorcerer and every alchemist was brewing up a newer and better one. Repressive governments and ignorant populations made an ideal environment for even the most outlandish concoctions. Yet some of these contained ingredients which we have since come to find very useful."

"Presumably they hit on them by sheer chance," I suggested.

"Trial and error too. Even without any scientific method, centuries and centuries of trial and error produced a small body of knowledge."

The first course arrived. My barley soup tasted authentic and had asparagus tips in it.

"Another heavily favored aphrodisiac," commented Gloria when I remarked on them.

She was studying her Russian Eggs but evidently didn't miss a trick. She continued to expand on the theme.

"Many vegetables with what was considered to be a phallic shape had that reputation—even carrots and parsnips."

I asked about the eggs when she had tasted them. The layer of black caviar was generous and she indicated approval.

"Yet another stimulant," I pointed out.

"An inaccurate belief," she said. I was quickly learning that she was a lady of strong opinions. "Based on cost and scarcity—false bases, both of them."

"And then there was Casanova, who believed in oysters. They too have been scarce and expensive at certain periods in history."

I said it fully aware that she had ordered oysters for her second course.

"Casanova ate fifty a day," she agreed. "When it was later found that oysters are very rich in zinc, a search began for other zinc-rich foods."

"And now it's a search for any product which will act as a sexual stimulant."

She nodded. "Flowers have always been very popular for the purpose. Henry VIII ate primroses and violets at meals while jasmine, lotus, saw palmetto, fuchsia and verbena are just some of the others that many people swear by."

"Isn't it surprising that flowers are not used more in modern cooking?" I asked.

"Very surprising. I think we are due for a resurgence of interest in them. At PP"—I looked askance and she explained— "Paramount Pharmaceuticals, we are analyzing and testing numerous flower groups to determine what chemical compounds of value may be in them."

The second course had arrived by now. Gloria's oysters were in a milk-and-butter mixture only, the chef presumably not wanting any other flavors to obtrude. I considered asking Gloria if she preferred that no spices interfered with their stimulating purpose but did not, concentrating on my eel. There was a fraction too much vinegar in the dill sauce, which prevented the full flavor from coming through, but it was acceptable. I knew from personal experience that no chef can please all tastes.

The wall drapes had a sound-deadening effect which made the restaurant very quiet. It lived up to its name as even the most secretive intriguer couldn't be heard in the next booth. This was just as well as our conversation would have proved fascinating to the average eavesdropper.

Gloria continued. "The discovery of hormones brought a new approach. The male hormone was identified as testosterone and the female as estrogen. Products which contain these or initiate their production by the body are the target of investigations on which millions of dollars are being spent."

The wine waiter poured us the last of the Riesling. It is always a problem when a dish contains vinegar as mine did, because vinegar affects the taste of the wine. Salads are equally difficult from the wine drinker's point of view, as most dressings are acidic. We asked the wine waiter for his suggestion on a wine to go with the main course and, after lamenting that he had no suitable Austrian wines in the cellar, he proposed a German Spätburgunder, adding that they had a case in the cellar from Assmannshausen, universally considered to be the best. We ordered a half bottle.

One thing I liked about Gloria—well, there were a number of things but one of them was that she paid full attention to her food and when the main course arrived, I was still admiring her for that reason as well.

Her sweetbreads looked appetizing and she nodded approval upon tasting them. It had been a long time since I had eaten goose but the chef had lived up to the reputation that Gloria told me had accompanied him from Salzburg.

We were almost through when she resumed our conversation.

"As it was my idea that we should form a new group to produce and market aphrodisiacs, my job is on the line. If the group isn't profitable, I'll be looking for another job."

"I'm sure you would have no trouble getting one."

"That's not the point." She put down her fork to concentrate on her words. "This was my suggestion, my idea. If it doesn't succeed, I've failed. That is important to me."

"I can understand that. Still, you can't have much to worry about—it seems like an infallible notion from a marketing viewpoint. Aphrodisiacs will surely sell like—well, I don't suppose 'hot cakes' is exactly the right metaphor . . ."

She smiled and took a hearty swallow of wine. "The concept is right, that's true. Even if our marketing forecasts are off by fifty percent, we should still do very well."

"Isn't it odd that no one has thought of this before?" I asked.

"A number of products are on the market but the FDA

doesn't permit describing them as aphrodisiacs, and we can't advertise them as such. Yohimbine, avena sativa, and gotu kola are all herbs which have some effect as sexual stimulants. Some claims are made for ginseng while others swear by gingko biloba. Then among the chemical stimulants are bromocriptine and acetylcholine."

She stopped eating and drinking temporarily and I knew she must have something important to say. "With Ko Feng, it's different. Ko Feng offers us our first clear chance of marketing a substance that can be accurately described as an aphrodisiac."

"How do you know?"

"Robert Barker's book *The History of Spices,* published in 1911, John Arthur Evans's earlier work, *Sexual Stimulants* and Erika Farber's *The Venus Factor* deal with the subject in general and make numerous references to Ko Feng. Rabd-Al-Manah's books in Arabic contain extensive mentions of natural products effective as aphrodisiacs and Ko Feng is described as the most powerful of all. A lot of other titles have accumulated in our library since I began this project and Ko Feng is mentioned frequently."

We finished our meal. We drank another glass of wine.

"The FDA will hardly accept the authority of deceased writers, will they?"

"We will, of course, have to do a considerable amount of research," Gloria said carefully. Her lovely eyes were on me, calm and yet inviting.

"Rats, guinea pigs, fruit flies, you mean?"

"No matter how much laboratory work of that type is done, it will still be essential to make tests with humans."

"Do you have a staff for this or—?"

"We sometimes use volunteers."

"I suppose with any work this vital, you have to participate yourself?"

"Of course," she murmured demurely. She sipped more

Spätburgunder and the dark red wine left drops on her lips. She dabbed them at them delicately. "I could hardly ask my staff to undertake any research work that I am not prepared to risk myself."

"Management has its responsibilities," I agreed.

"Tell me who else is interested in recovering the Ko Feng," she said softly.

It took me a few seconds to switch subjects. I had been immersed in her plans for testing the Ko Feng and was still at the stage where I was speculating on exactly how results would be judged . . .

"Other potential buyers are on the scene, of course," I said, being as noncommittal as I knew how.

"Competitors?"

"No, not competitors of yours. Different areas of business. I don't know that there are any others working in your, er— more sensitive area."

I wasn't absolutely certain that was true. There might be a shading of overlap, although putting aphrodisiacs into breakfast cereals did strike me as being too innovative to be likely.

"Are you making any progress in recovering the Ko Feng?" she asked me anxiously.

"Several promising leads have shown up," I said. "They are all being pursued."

"Do you have any idea of when you expect to get it back?"

"We operate on the basis that we have to succeed in ten days," I said, quoting Lieutenant Gaines but not crediting him for it.

"That means only about another week left." She looked concerned and I looked noncommittal. It was easy to do.

"I could use your help on this," I said.

She looked at me, inquiring but cautious.

"Let me know immediately if you're approached by anyone offering to sell."

"Do you think I will be?"

"It's possible."

When we left, she simply gave a nod to the maître d. It was an impressive way to pay the bill but out of a twenty-three-billion-dollar turnover, I suppose she had a generous expense account.

After such a delightful lunch, I had a lot to contemplate. An investigator's life is tough and a food investigator is no exception. But I was prepared to do what an investigator has to do and when I got back to the Framingham Hotel, I decided to walk over to nearby Central Park and get some fresh air to stimulate my thinking processes. It was a pleasant afternoon with a light breeze and if I stayed with the crowds, I should be safe.

The nuts and the kooks were out in strength. A young man with a propeller on his hat was being pulled along on a skateboard, the power being provided by eight cats, all on strings like huskies pulling a sled. A group of monks in yellow robes were ringing bells and chanting. All had begging cups and a poster carried by one stated that the proceeds would go to building a temple on Staten Island. Bicycle messengers were using the park as a shortcut across town, and life and limb were being threatened in order to deliver office memos ten minutes sooner.

Two women went by, talking. "Know why the animals in the zoo are behind bars?" one asked her companion. "It's for their safety." The other sniffed as they passed an overflowing garbage can with a particularly offensive odor. "I wish this city would collect its garbage as often as it does taxes."

On the way back to the hotel, I stopped and bought a fifth of Jack Daniel's, some limes and a bottle of ginger ale. Some bourbon purists throw up their hands in horror at such a mixture but I find it a delicious combination—so delicious it deserves a name. At the Fairway Market near Seventy-fourth Street, the day's specials were chalked up and I made a few purchases.

While enjoying the first drink, I watched television, still with an air of disbelief. On one channel, an uptight, egotistical, bombastic white male was the anchorman on a fictitious television news station while a gruff producer with a heart of gold was avoiding complimenting a competent white female assistant. On another channel, a gruff talk-show producer was avoiding complimenting his assistant, an unappreciated white female and trying not to fire his bombastic, fatuous, uptight white male sidekick. A third channel seemed to have the same characters but now they were in a newspaper office. A fourth channel had the same characters only now they were all black.

The lunch had been satisfying but by eight o'clock, all the food commercials on television had made me hungry again. I peeled and sliced a large potato and put the slices in an oven-proof dish. I added salt and pepper and put the dish in the oven. Ten minutes later, I took out the tenderloin steak I had bought and pounded it thin. I heated a skillet really hot, added a little butter and as soon as it melted, added the steak. I swirled in some sherry, added an ounce or so of brandy and ignited it. I turned up the temperature on the oven to brown the potatoes, then put another piece of butter and some chives in the skillet.

This quick and easy version of Steak Diane is one of my favorites when I don't feel like really cooking. A second bourbon came and went during the cooking process. I should have been stimulated into brilliant hypotheses of the case but I wasn't. Watching Columbo, Jessica Fletcher, Perry Mason and Jim Rockford didn't help either—they made it look so easy. I had a third bourbon and made it an early night, not looking forward at all to tomorrow.

CHAPTER TWENTY-FIVE

The inquest was a somber affair. It was held in a grim, high-ceilinged room somewhere in the rear of the County Court complex. Voices echoed eerily and the dark green walls were oppressive. The court recorder's machine clicked away remorselessly and from outside came the frequent howl of a police siren.

I gave my evidence and so did Peggy. Lieutenant Gaines gave the police report and the medical examiner said death had been instantaneous and the result of a single gunshot. It was over as quickly as if it had been carefully planned.

The verdict of murder by person or persons unknown was not a surprise to anyone. Peggy was pale but controlled and her sister-in-law was brisk and energetic with a very matter-of-fact view. Her husband, Don's brother, was a pragmatic north of England type, already thinking of early retirement from the brokerage business. We talked for a while and I was as optimistic as I could be about our chances of finding the killer. Peggy told me that the funeral was to be in Connecticut and apologized that it would be for the family only. I told her that I understood, not adding that I was confined to New York anyway.

I said, "There's a question I want to ask you. I'm sorry to do it now but it might have some bearing on the investigation."

"Go ahead," she said, "you know I want to help all I can."

It was a point that had slipped to the back of my mind. It didn't seem relevant and yet . . .

I described the woman I had talked to at the Spice Warehouse just before Don had been killed. We had talked about ginger, she had told me that she had an appointment with Don, then she had headed toward his office shortly before we had heard the shot.

Peggy looked alarmed. "You don't think she killed him!"

"No, I don't. I talked to her for a few minutes and got an impression of her that doesn't fit with her being a murderess. But it was only a few minutes and impressions can be wrong. I thought you might know something about her."

"I don't think so. Describe her again."

"Early thirties, light brown hair, brown eyes, blue suit with a white blouse."

"Did she say she was a regular customer?"

"No. Perhaps she had only been in a few times. I don't know."

"She doesn't sound familiar to me," Peggy said, "but I'll tell you what I'll do—I'll talk to Maisie when I get back. Maisie works on checkout mostly but she's a real chatterbox and she helps out in the shop too. She loves to talk to people and if this woman is known to anybody, it'll be Maisie."

Minutes after arriving back at the Framingham Hotel, the phone rang.

"I'm here with Maisie," Peggy said. "She's seen the woman you were asking about."

"That's great! Does she know her name?"

"I asked her. She doesn't."

"Has she bought anything there?"

There was a brief discussion, then Peggy came back on. "Yes. She bought some tarragon not too long ago."

"Does Maisie remember how she paid for it?"

Another discussion took place.

"No, she doesn't," said Peggy when she picked up the phone again.

"Tarragon doesn't cost much," I said, disappointed. "She probably paid cash."

"Why does that matter? Oh, I see, if she used a credit card there'd be a receipt in the file."

"Right."

"We don't seem to have any way of finding her, then," Peggy said glumly.

"If you think of any way, call me."

"I will." She hesitated.

"Is there something?" I asked her.

"Well, it may be silly—I mean, it's so trivial . . ."

"What is it?" I urged.

"Well, when Don and I came in to the warehouse that morning, as I left him he snapped his fingers and said, 'The most obvious . . .' "

"Go on," I urged.

"That's all. I thought he was going to say more but he didn't."

"Thanks for telling me," I said.

"Doesn't help, does it?" Her voice was bleak.

"You never know. Give me a call if you think of anything else—no matter what."

She promised she would and we hung up.

I called Gabriella.

"Special Spice Operator checking in."

"All in one piece?"

"Yes. Why?" I asked, alarmed.

"You've been the subject of a lot of attention lately," she said reassuringly. "Just a routine query."

I was relieved. "I thought maybe you'd heard something."

"As a matter of fact, I have."

"What is it?"

"Tell you in a minute. What happened with your vice-president?"

"Ah," I said, "yes, the vice-president . . . Well, Paramount is striking out in some novel areas of research. They are extremely anxious to get hold of some Ko Feng."

"How anxious?"

"I can't say. But the vice-president's job is on the line. This new research has to produce some startling results or this VP is out of a job."

"What impression did he have on you?"

"I—er, pretty impressive, I'd say."

"Ruthless?"

"Well—if it came right down to a ruthless decision, yes, I'd say the decision would be made."

"Is it risky for you to keep in touch with him?"

"There might be some risks," I admitted. "Paramount is thinking of some tests. They hinted I might be asked to take part—if the Ko Feng is recovered."

"Would you want to do that?"

"I'm willing to do whatever I can," I said bravely.

"Well," said Gabriella, "first we've got to recover it. And as to that—we've had a tipoff. It's from one of our regular informants. Often, these turn out to be useless but once in a while, there's one that can be helpful."

"What's the tipoff?"

"Some Ko Feng may be offered for sale."

"What!" I shouted.

"For now, that's all we've got."

"You'll let me know?"

"Of course. I want you there when it's offered."

"To authenticate."

"Yes. I'll call you—be ready."

"I'm ready," I told her. "Any hour of the day or night."

"All right. Keep in touch—and be careful."

I wished she wouldn't say that but it was nice that she did.

She was well-balanced—she kept telling me to be careful but she kept taking me or sending me into risky situations. I consoled myself that she wouldn't take a chance on losing a valuable authenticator if they were that risky . . .

CHAPTER TWENTY-SIX

New York is a friendly city, as everyone will tell you. There's no problem meeting people, they will add. Well, I certainly wasn't having a problem. If I had any more visitors, the Framingham Hotel was going to add a charge to my bill to cover the service.

Now here was another one. I didn't even know his name for he had called the hotel and left a message for me saying that he would be here at this time and a number to call in case it wasn't convenient. Of course, I wasn't going to turn him down, I wasn't going to turn anyone down. There was always a chance that the next visitor might have some scrap of information that would lead to the capture of Don's killer and the recovery of the Ko Feng.

He was right on time. We went into the coffee shop, which was almost empty—presumably Professor Willenbroek was not alone in his assessment of it. When we had sat at a corner table and ordered coffee, we took stock of each other.

He was about six feet tall and had a powerful, muscular frame. He looked as if he worked out in a gym a few times a week. He also had the look of an amateur polo player, that barely definable air of superiority which stops short of supercil-iousness but only just. His steely gray hair was cropped an inch short all over his head and he had a tan which suggested Florida rather than New York, but there were machines that could do that too. He had a square broad face, a strong chin and very light gray eyes. If a submarine movie were being cast, he would be perfect as the commander—no, better than that, the chief executive officer who takes over when the commander turns neurotic and wants to fire all weapons.

He handed me a card. It read BOSENDORFF, ZACKAROV, LIEBOWITZ AND SCHELLENBURG and the address was Pine Street, which as near as I could recall was close to Wall Street.

"You're Mr. Bosendorff?" I hazarded.

When he answered, his voice was clipped and carefully modulated. I would have bet he was president of his local toastmasters.

"Mr. Bosendorff was killed on the Somme in 1917."

"Oh, then you're Zackarov?"

"Mr. Zackarov died in 1927. He had been retired for some years."

"Liebowitz?" I was shooting in the dark now.

"He died of pneumonia in 1930 and, to save you the trouble, the late lamented Mr. Schellenburg died in a nursing home three years later."

"It's an old firm," I commented. It was too long after the events to offer condolences.

His light gray eyes were steady. His face might have been carved out of granite. Only his mouth moved.

"Very old. I like to open an acquaintanceship this way, though. It establishes us as a reliable establishment of tradition and integrity."

He handed me another card. This one said *New York Fidelity Bank.*

"My name's Eck," he said. He was right, it was. Tom Eck, right there in the corner and perhaps it should have been in larger letters—especially if it had been on the other card where it would have been outnumbered and outlettered.

"The earlier name was well known and widely respected," he went on, "but in today's more harsh business environment, unfortunately those virtues are no longer as meaningful."

"So now you're a bank."

"We were always a bank. Many establishments of a century ago didn't use the word, but we have always been in that business."

A century ago, Bosendorff and his team were probably money-lenders, which was why they didn't call themselves a bank, but I wouldn't judge until I'd done some checking. In the meantime, if he wanted me to open an account or offer me a gold credit card, he was wasting his time.

"Let me tell you why I am here," he said in his clear, crisp tones. "Our principal activity is providing capital for new and expanding businesses"—my guess had been right, I thought, and they were still in the same line—"and these businesses are mostly in the food trade. There are several of us loan officers, each with our own area of specialty. It so happens that commodities such as spices fall into my bailiwick."

My attention quickened. I should have been expecting it. He was hardly likely to be here asking about the health of the queen but even so when he said the word *spices,* my mind focused sharply.

I gave him my half smile, which is supposed to encourage a talker to go on talking. It must have worked or maybe he intended to tell me anyway.

"When Alexander Marvell arranged for the Ko Feng to be shipped here, he contacted several potential buyers. He had no difficulty finding them, of course. Any restaurant owner would want some of it. Well, a couple of them came to me—independently—to ask for financing."

He paused. I waited for him to go on. It was getting interesting. Maybe I was going to learn something.

"You can see my predicament," he said. I couldn't so I scratched my chin and said, "Hm."

"I am responsible for approving loans of significant amounts of money but the commodity that the money was intended to buy has disappeared."

Now I did see his predicament.

I suppose we have all become cynical about banks. After the debacles at BICC and S&L, the scandal at the Vatican bank whose director hanged himself on London Embankment, the multibillion-dollar blunder that put Barings out of business and other headline-making disintegrations in the financial world, we are apt to dismiss their problems and casually assume that insurance will cover their losses. Sadly, the insurance business has become tarred with the same brush and even Lloyds of London has not escaped. Consequently, tears are not shed readily and while I was sorry about the bank image that had been tarnished, I still wasn't sure what it all had to do with me. But then he had come here—I hadn't gone to him—so I was going to listen.

"A difficult situation," I admitted.

"I'm glad to find you sympathetic," he said heartily. "Not everyone feels that way about banks anymore."

"I suppose not," I said cautiously, hoping he would come to the point.

He sat back and regarded me much as the chief exec on the submarine *Starfish* might regard his trusted second-in-command.

"I'll be honest with you," he said, and I hoped I was looking worthy of it. "When I came to see you, I wasn't certain how I was going to approach you. The fact is, there was the chance that you were involved in the theft of the Ko Feng yourself."

"I can understand that," I said. "I'm a foreigner, I was brought in to do a job of refereeing that some might think could have been done as well—perhaps better—by an American, I was on the scene at the time of both crimes so on the basis of means, motive and opportunity, I'm a prime suspect."

"That's a fair assessment," he agreed. "However, on the gut feeling I have after talking to you, I don't think you were involved in either crime."

"Thanks. You're right, as it happens. I wasn't, though there are people who don't agree."

"You mean Alexander Marvell for one . . . yes, I know." I wondered who the others were but didn't want to hear a list.

"The point now is, if you don't have the Ko Feng, who does?"

"I wish I knew," I said earnestly. "And I'm doing all I can to help the police find the answer."

He looked off into the distance, pensive.

Finally he asked, "How many of the restaurant people here have you talked to?"

"Only a few. Ayesha and Lennie Rifkin, Abraham Kefalik, Selim Osman—that's about all so far."

"There are, of course, many more."

"I'm sure. I'd like to talk to as many as I can—plus others in the food business besides restaurant owners."

He didn't seem too interested in any others but he asked in an offhand manner, "Who, for instance?"

About to mention a few names, I drew back. Instead I said, "Oh, people in the bakery trade, candy makers, vitamin producers . . . not that this is significant. Any food or medicine that's put into human stomachs is a candidate. If Ko Feng has even some of the properties we think it has, it could be added to any foodstuff with beneficial results."

He nodded slowly. "Yes, I suppose so."

He moved around in his chair, probably trying to decide how to phrase his next question.

"Can you tell me what progress the investigation has made?"

I was getting adept at answering this one. There was no reason, though, for me to pussyfoot with Eck. "We do have a few leads but nothing concrete so far."

"Tell me something else." He leaned forward. "Has the Ko Feng been offered—actually offered—to anyone?"

"No, it hasn't, as far as we know." I was interpreting his question to mean an offer since the theft.

"Won't the person who has it be taking a risk when they do offer it?"

"I hope so," I said fervently.

"Ah, then you'll be able to grab him?"

I nodded. I wasn't convinced that it was going to be that simple but that was as far as I was prepared to go with Tom Eck.

"You've talked to the police, I take it?" I asked.

"Yes. I was directed to a Lieutenant Gaines at the Unusual Crimes Unit. He wasn't very forthcoming. In fact, he was on the verge of being rude. Felt I was wasting his time—at least, that's the impression I got."

"Don't be fooled," I said sagaciously. "Hal Gaines is one of the best detectives in the NYPD."

Tom Eck grunted. "Didn't seem that way to me. He needs to remember he's a public servant. People might cooperate with him better."

"He's a man you need to get to know."

"I'd rather not," Eck said with a rare flash of emotion. This one was contempt.

He was shuffling a little. He had asked all his questions and he wanted to go. I stood up.

"Glad you stopped by. And I hope you resolve your financial problem. It must be a worry."

"Financing business is a worry. Financing the food business even more so, and the complications involved in this affair are just not worth it. I wish we'd never gotten into it. Still . . ." He stood too.

We shook hands and I walked with him to the lobby. We parted with mutual expressions of keeping each other informed. I wondered which one of us had held back the most.

CHAPTER TWENTY-SEVEN

From the phone in my room, I called the *New York Times* and asked to speak to their food editor.

"If I wanted the best birds' nest soup in New York, which restaurant would you recommend?" I asked.

The busiest people are seldom too busy to talk on their specialty. This man chatted in friendly style, making distinctions like "best," "best for the money," "most authentic" and others, but he had no hesitation in giving me one name that stood out above all the others. It was the Shanghai Palace.

Outside, gusty winds were blowing rain showers in unexpected directions and people on the street were struggling to raise umbrellas, cover their heads with newspapers or wave frantically for a cab.

I waited in the doorway. It was not likely that I would be pursued or observed here but I wasn't taking any chances. The rain stopped as quickly as it had started and I caught a cab in a few minutes.

The Shanghai Palace was at the south end of Mulberry Street and just inside New York's Chinatown. Winding alleys and narrow streets were packed with people—"nearly ten thousand" said the cab driver, "and more coming in from Hong Kong every day." The exotic atmosphere of the East was dulled only by the Western clothing that most residents wore but the shop and store windows were no different from those in the rest of New York although I caught a glimpse of one shop offering thousand-year-old eggs.

Restaurants abounded. Every third or fourth establishment was a restaurant and I saw more dragon motifs than a jeroboam of champagne has bubbles. They came in every color and I was wondering how the Shanghai Palace could compete with all of them when the cab stopped.

The front of the place was spare but imposing. Long black windows in trim green woodwork and the name in block letters along the top with no attempt at a cute Chinese effect. Inside, a warren of handsome rooms went on and on into a limitless interior. The entrance and bar area were finished in high-gloss black lacquer and tile. The bar stools were black velveteen and the decor was accented with white monkey sculptures that were eerily effective. In the eating areas, tall booths encircled large central sections and high banquettes provided privacy. Bamboo furniture, hemp walls and red and green carpeted floors were cleverly combined with leafy green plants as dividers. Tables were set with pink table linen and black tableware.

"The large numbers of new residents from Hong Kong and Taiwan are accustomed to Cantonese cooking," explained T. R. Koo, the owner. "As a result of this, most Chinese restaurants in New York serve food Cantonese style. It is pleasant and healthful but it is not spicy.

"We serve Cantonese dishes too," he continued, "but I like to present the cuisines of Szechwan and Hunan with their lush and fiery sauces—resplendent with ginger, garlic and chiles."

I had been passed along to him through a chain consisting of a waiter, the headwaiter and the maître d'. He received me courteously and we sat at a table where he ordered tea and I apologized for the hour of my visit. It was between mealtimes so it was more convenient for him, I pointed out, but it robbed me of the enjoyment that I had no doubt I was missing by not being able to partake of his food. I noticed how I had slipped into an Asian mode in saying that, although I meant it.

I had studied the menu while waiting for Mr. Koo to come from the kitchen and the food looked tempting. The cold appetizers included chopped chicken in a thick sesame sauce—a Szechwan specialty—and there was another, shrimp with mint and fresh coriander with crushed chiles. The julienne of jellyfish was not often seen on Western tables and the hot rice cake soup was uncommon too.

Several sea scallop dishes were among the main courses. Hunan, being an island, is a major seafood producer and scallops are prominent. Some dishes were served with tofu cubes, others with a sauce of ginger, garlic and scallions. The chicken steamed in lotus leaves and the dry shredded crispy beef offered interesting variants from seafood and, naturally, several delicious-sounding duck dishes were present.

Mr. Koo nodded his appreciation of my comments. He was of that indeterminate age that is a prerogative of Chinese men, who remain in an aging limbo between forty and seventy. He was slight and stooped, possibly from many years over cooking pots. His voice was wispy but his words demanded attention. He listened respectfully while I told him why I was there.

During the taxi ride, I had prepared a thoroughly convincing story of being with a travel agency which wanted to put on a banquet for a large group. Birds' nests soup of the finest quality had to be the first course . . . and I intended to wing it from there. When I talked to Mr. Koo, I abandoned the subterfuge. His manner was courtly but beneath it was a perceptiveness that would quickly see through me. I followed the sage advice I had been given early in my career: when in doubt, try the truth.

"Yes, I remember the occasion well," he said in his gentle voice. "The Pacific storms had been extremely severe and white birds' nests were hard to find. The price was climbing rapidly. I had to agree to a very high price. It was a devastating blow when the shipment was stolen."

"Did you ever have any clues as to who had stolen it?"

"Not I. Nor, I understand, did the police."

"What do you suppose happened to it?"

Did I imagine it or did he glance away for a fraction of a second?

"Other restaurants in New York serve birds' nest soup. I suppose that one of them bought it."

"At a time of shortage, wasn't it obvious which restaurants were still meeting the demand?"

Mr. Koo shook his head slowly. "Oh, no. Unscrupulous chefs sometimes use the black birds' nests—much cheaper—in place of the superior kind. Some even use other ingredients—not birds' nests at all." He smiled sadly at the idea of such perfidy on the part of his compatriot chefs.

"How many customers do you have who can tell the difference?"

He smiled. "You are thinking of tourists, perhaps not sophisticated in the appreciation of Chinese cuisine?"

It was nicely put. That had been what I was thinking. I nodded.

"We have many of those, of course. They are an important part of our clientele. But we have another very important part—the diplomats from Asian countries. Many of these eat here regularly and we also arrange banquets for embassy receptions and parties."

He waved a hand toward the interior. "We have facilities for several hundred people in there."

It was an extraordinary claim but I didn't doubt it. Several New York restaurants seem to go on and on, level after level, down into the—well, bowels wasn't appropriate but certainly into the earth.

"So you have no idea who got the stolen shipment."

He shook his head gravely. "I do not know," he said and I realized that it was not a precise answer to my question.

"It would be a shame if visitors came to New York expecting the finest birds' nest soup and were unable to get it here," I said. "In such circumstances, where do you imagine they would have gone?"

There wasn't a crack in his imperturbable facade and he answered smoothly. "The Forbidden City would be the restaurant answering to that description."

"Presumably you were insured for your loss?" I asked.

"Yes, but that is poor recompense for the damage to reputation. Imagine a restaurant like the Shanghai Palace unable to offer its customers birds' nest soup!"

I sympathized with his embarrassing position.

"Can you tell me who you are insured with?"

"There is nothing confidential about such information. The company is New England Assurance."

I thanked him. I had learned more than I had expected. Perhaps the truth was underrated, after all.

"I sincerely hope that you recover the Ko Feng," he said, pouring the last of the tea.

"I was wondering if you'd ask me about that. Doesn't the idea of using it appeal to you?"

"It is a fascinating concept, employing a spice lost for centuries," he admitted. "Perhaps age has drained me of ambition, however. The thought is seductive but the will to innovate has declined."

Midmeal diners were drifting in. New York is a nonstop city and time doesn't govern all stomachs. I went out into the squally rain that had started again. Taxis were in great demand but I got one eventually.

The Forbidden City was not far away. The exterior was modest in design but ornate with gilt, and inside, huge gilded pots stood everywhere, spraying out fronds of palm leaves. The ceiling was high and gilded, adorned with heads of mythical animals. Gilded chandeliers cast discreet pools of golden light in which the tables were crisp and white. Quite a few of these were occupied, so Mr. Singyang took me into the small office of his accountant.

He was rotund and almost jovial in comparison with the slight and reserved T. R. Koo. I used the same truthful approach that had been so effective before but in a scant few minutes it became obvious that the truth was like lightning—it didn't strike twice on the same topic.

Mr. Singyang was polite but, though he never seemed to be evasive, he never answered the question.

"Suitable birds' nests have always been rare and expensive," he agreed.

"They must be even more expensive than they were five years ago."

"Five years ago . . ." he mused.

"Yes. That was when a shipment of birds' nests was hijacked at JFK. I'm sure you remember it."

"Very well."

"And I am sure you have heard of the theft of the Ko Feng?"

"Very sad," he murmured. "Most regrettable."

"The similarities in the two thefts must have come to your attention."

"Yes, indeed."

"Mr. Singyang, I'm not concerned with the theft five years ago or what happened to the shipment. I came here to help authenticate the Ko Feng. A friend has been murdered because of that and I might be next."

He regarded me with a little more interest and when he said, with Oriental sincerity, that he hoped not, he might even have meant it. I came to the point in crude Occidental fashion.

"Whoever stole the birds' nests shipment also stole the Ko Feng. Can you tell me anything that might help me find the thief?"

He continued urbane and amiable but he wasn't helpful. He

would ask around the neighborhood, he said but of course, after five years . . . He chatted about Ko Feng but I knew I was getting nowhere. I thanked him for his time and left, aware of him watching me all the way out.

A message awaited me at the hotel. It was signed "Gabriella" and it said that she would pick me up the next morning at 9:30. It was the next sentence that really excited me. It stated simply, "We're going to a sale."

CHAPTER TWENTY-EIGHT

Variety may be the spice of life as one of the oldest of old clichés has it, but variety can also be the spice of food. That was why I walked about four blocks down Broadway to The Klatsch, proposed by many addicts as the perfect place for morning coffee.

All chrome and glass and with a floor that looked like black glass and a ceiling of mirrors, it brought a bright, purposeful look to the new day that must bring a beaded sweat to the brow of many a reveler of the night before. If so, there were plenty of nonrevelers for the place was packed. It was certainly no place for those with a thick head and a problem with decisions—the glaringly brilliant sign offered so many choices of coffee that a dedicated ditherer could find himself at lunchtime before he had ordered.

Regular, espresso, latte, cappuccino, decaf—small, medium, large and jumbo—those were merely the beginning. There was flake, grain, chip, filament and globule—and these could be grated, granulated, milled, ground, chopped, flocculated, pulverized or powdered. The devotees crowding the bar for their quick fix had their own serious preferences for the origin of the bean and I heard mention of Arabica, Jamaican, Colombian, Brazilian, Venezuelan, Hawaiian, Kenyan and a score of others. Some customers were even specifying roasting times and brewing times. The air was dense with fumes and shouted orders.

Nutmeg, cinnamon, cardamom and mace were among the more popular toppings—some sprinkled on, some stirred in. The blending of aromas was heady and many a customer must stagger out, his hangover cured but a new intoxication mounting.

To make judgment yet more shattering, bagels were on display in another multiplicity of choices—cracked wheat, rye, raisin, chocolate, cranberry, coconut, mango, onion, basil, garlic, tomato, poppy seed, papaya, sesame, chipped almond, pineapple, grated apple . . . I walked back to the hotel, presuming that New York had plenty of psychiatrists specializing in patients afflicted with "excess of choice" syndrome.

I had only got as far as page two in the lobby copy of the *New York Times* when I heard a toot-toot from outside. I went to look but all I could see was a tan-colored Ford that hadn't been washed since it was new and with a badly dented fender.

The toot-toot came again before I had got back to the newspaper so I went back and took another look. A head of untamed blond hair poked out of the window and a voice that sounded familiar called, "Get in!"

Even from a few feet away, I wouldn't have recognized Gabriella. Sitting next to her, I still couldn't.

"Do you always get into a car when a strange blonde invites you?" she asked. "Thought I'd warned you to be careful."

"I don't believe it!" I was dumbfounded. "What show are you auditioning for now? *West Side Story* or *Grease*?"

She released the brake and pulled away from the curb. The engine sounded rough and there were several rattles. The interior of the car was as disreputable as the outside.

"Don't mind the car," she said. "Part of the image."

"Very convincing. It certainly fooled me—and so did you. Are you sure you don't want to go back on the stage?"

"I get plenty of acting opportunities still—like today, for instance."

"Did you dye your hair?" I asked curiously.

"Of course not. This is a wig."

"But what have you done with your own hair?"

"They make a very tight-fitting latex skullcap now, and the wig fits right over it."

"Amazing," I said and meant it. "But your eyes—they look different too."

"Just different makeup," she said offhandedly.

In fact, everything about her looked different but it had all been very subtly done. None of the changes were major but the sum total was the evolution of a new person.

One aspect was not subtle, though . . .

She caught me staring and smiled. "Like the outfit?"

She was wearing a skintight, flesh-colored blouse that was only one short step away from see-through. Over it was a minuscule garment like a waistcoat. It was in dark blue with a lacing of black running through it. The shiny black skirt was extremely short and so tight that it rode up her thighs as she drove, exposing enticing lengths of very shapely legs.

"Four inches longer and it would be a miniskirt," I said weakly.

"Suits today's purpose," she said matter-of-factly.

"Just one question about the costume . . ."

"What's that?"

"Makes it impossible to carry a gun."

She shook her head. "Not at all. Beretta has a new model that is very flat and very small.'

I looked her over very carefully—several times in fact. I finally shook my head.

"I give up," I said. She smiled but didn't enlighten me.

"I used to think a disguise meant you needed to be inobtrusive, not readily noticeable, blend into the background sort of thing."

"You're right, that's how it used to be. The latest advice from the police psychologists is to be noticeable. Once you've been registered in a memory, the automatic assumption is that you must be okay or you wouldn't want to risk attracting attention."

"Sounds as if you do this kind of thing often," I said.

"You mean undercover work?"

I looked her over again, twice.

"I wouldn't call it exactly undercover—but yes."

"No, I don't do it often, only when the occasion demands."

"Okay. Now the next question is, what am I going to wear?"

"You're wearing it."

I glanced at my lightweight slacks and gray flannel jacket.

"This? This isn't a disguise."

"You're not going in disguise. You're going as you. The more people recognize you the better."

"Isn't that a little—well, dangerous?"

"Not very," she said with a careless toss of blond locks.

"Let me get my position straight. You mean I'm sort of a Judas goat pegged out waiting for the big bad wolf to show up?"

She smiled wickedly. "No, I see you more as a pot of honey—and we're going to wait for the flies to swarm all over you."

"And you're the girl with the fly swatter?"

"The Beretta."

"In that outfit, you're more of the honeypot. You'll have men four deep around you."

She neatly avoided a motorcyclist and speeded up through a yellow light.

"Impossible. I'm on duty."

"But you'll be too engrossed with all those men just when I need you to protect me."

"In an emergency, you'll find a way," she said confidently.

"Speaking of duty and impossible—just what is today's mission?"

She settled down to a position in a stream of traffic. We were heading north and went past the massive stone edifice of the Cathedral of St. John the Divine.

"We're going to the Bronx. This is the background. There's a group of merchants who got together some years ago to have an annual sale of all the products they hadn't been able to sell. I know that sales are not a novelty in New York—stores are having them all the time. But this was a bumper affair with tremendous bargains and it always resulted in a complete sellout."

The car sputtered a couple of times. Gabriella expertly juggled the choke and it settled down to as smooth a rhythm as its aging engine would permit.

"A few of those merchants had a further idea," she continued. "They had done so well putting on sales of goods they hadn't been able to sell that they decided to step over the line and start selling goods they shouldn't be selling."

"In what way?" I asked.

"Electrical appliances that had been declared potentially dangerous, clothing that could be inflammable, toys and games that were hazardous—that kind of thing."

"Nice people," I said. "And these are big companies, well-known merchants?"

"Oh, yes. They operate through several layers of other organizations so that we can't get to them."

"And you don't know who they are?"

"We suspect one or two but it's hard to get proof. Most of them, we don't know who's behind them."

I knew where we were now. We were cutting across Harlem and heading for one of the bridges over to the Bronx. Our whereabouts was only registering on the back of my mind. My primary attention was on Gabriella's story.

"So today we are going to one of these?"

"These people have got very specialized. A girl on Staten

Island was electrocuted recently and it came out that the VCR she had bought at ninety percent off the regular price came from one of these sales."

"Couldn't you—I mean the police—do anything about that?"

"How? The sales are not advertised, it's just word of mouth. The sale is one day only and the venue can be anywhere. A stadium, an empty theater, a church hall . . . Oh, once in a great while we manage to bust one of them but we never get to the people behind it."

"I can see it's a tough nut to crack. Which brings us to the present—"

"Yes, well, we've never heard of one of this type of sale before but whenever there's a whisper on the street, it gets circulated through the department. There's one today and"—she paused dramatically, probably her theatrical training—"this one is foodstuffs only."

"I see. And you're thinking that one of these dubious food items that will be on sale just might be Ko Feng?"

"It's a long shot but when Hal heard about it, he suggested that I go."

"And take me with you?"

"He had the idea that if any Ko Feng is offered for sale, you should be on hand to identify it."

We were crossing the Harlem River, a sullen, slow-flowing mass of dark water. The Bronx was a sharp contrast to Manhattan and we hit the bottom of a big pothole, stretching the Ford's suspension to the limit.

"It can't be too dangerous then," I said. "I mean, we're talking about people who run department stores, chains of shops—they're not gangsters, they don't kill people."

"No, no," Gabriella said, curling past a truck carrying a heavy overload of gravel and spraying a goodly amount of it through the Bronx. "It's not really dangerous." I wished she hadn't said it so quickly.

"Then why are you carrying a gun?" I asked.

"Routine."

"I don't believe you are carrying one."

She threw me a smile and honked to warn a garbage collection vehicle not to pull out of an alley.

We reached our destination a few minutes later, a run-down neighborhood with derelict shops, empty storefronts and dirty windows. A liquor store was open and a man looking like a hobo came out with a large brown paper bag. Across the street, a fruit and vegetable stand was doing a small amount of trade. Two young men lounging by a fire hydrant turned to stare at Gabriella's legs as we got out of the car.

"See what I mean about a honeypot?" I muttered.

"Ignore them. Come on."

We walked briskly along the cracked and decaying pavement. A siren shrieked in the distance. The air smelled dusty and sour.

We had parked near a corner. We turned and ahead of us, past a shop selling "adult" videos, stood an enormous building, easily one of the ugliest I had seen in a long time. An uncomfortable blend of brick and old stone that looked more like concrete blocks, it had evidently gone through several building and rebuilding stages. It had been a church as I could see when we got close but not very recently. All the windows were gone, some boarded over, others covered with crisscrosses of barbed wire. Weeds had sprung up everywhere and were climbing the walls. A pile of garbage had grown higher than a man.

"Looks deserted," I said. "Are you sure this is the place?"

"It's the place, all right. Let's find an entrance."

That was harder than it sounded. The chipped stone steps led to what had been the main doors but they were now barricaded with planks. We walked along the outside looking for another way in, but the side doors were barred just as effectively.

"Those planks have been there a long time," Gabriella said thoughtfully. "Let's walk around again."

We did but could find no other entrances. Then she pointed. "Look there!"

A large steel panel was set in the ground against one of the walls. We had missed it the first time as it had a sprinkling of soil and grass over it. Gabriella reached out with one shapely leg and rubbed the soil aside with her three-inch-spike-heel shoe. She tapped. It sounded hollow.

"There's another," she said, and sure enough another steel panel was set in the ground next to it.

"And another," I added. A whole row of them stretched out in a line and Gabriella's finger traced the line across the desolate ground to the ruin of a building about forty paces away. It had probably once been the church hall but only a corner of it was left.

We followed the line of panels. The ruin looked like a junction of two crumbling walls at first but it had a rough wooden structure about the size of a normal room. There was a door with peeling brown paint. I turned the knob and it opened. We went in.

CHAPTER TWENTY-NINE

A man sat at a desk reading a newspaper and smoking a cigarette. The walls were the same rough wood as outside and a bare
electric bulb hung from a fraying wire. A wide flight of wooden
stairs led down and out of sight.

The man had scrubby black hair and hadn't shaved recently. He glanced at us over the top of his paper but didn't put
it down.

"Something?" he asked, without moving the cigarette.

"Whistler sent us," said Gabriella.

He looked her up and down, then again more slowly. I
think he knew I was there but he said to Gabriella, "Whistler?"
as if he had never heard of him.

She nodded coolly. "Whistler."

He looked at her without speaking for a long time. Then
he nodded toward the stairs. "Go ahead."

We went down the stairs. At the bottom, a long tunnel was
ahead of us. A trench just deep enough to walk in and wide
enough to accommodate only two people at a time had been dug
and covered over with the steel panels we had seen from outside. A dim light at the far end shed just enough illumination for
us to walk on the hard-packed soil.

When we arrived at the end of the tunnel, we encountered
a heavy steel door with no handle and no lock visible from this
side. I banged on it with a fist and the booms echoed down the
tunnel.

A "boy" in his late teens opened it. He looked aged beyond

his years, with a thin face and hair pulled back in a ponytail. He opened the door only partway and looked questioningly at us.

"Whistler sent us."

He looked at Gabriella as if he had never heard of Whistler. "Who?" he asked.

"Whistler," she said, cool as ice.

He eyed her a while, gave me a hundredth of a second glance, then swung the door open. We went up another flight of stairs that curved, then led into the main body of the church.

It was a huge place, vast and cavernous as an Italian railway station. The ceiling was out of sight with the dim lighting of haphazardly strung wires and bare bulbs. The walls were in fairly good shape and columns soared up to be lost in the darkness. The concrete floor was patterned with cracks but serviceable.

And there were a lot of people.

That was the most striking thing of all. After the barren approach and the gloomy tunnel, it was a shock to find so many people but after the initial surprise had worn off, it was like being in Macy's at Christmastime.

Well, almost . . . Counters and tables had been set up and bare wood shelving erected against the wall in several places. These gave the place more the air of a hastily conceived charity sale in a village, raising money to send boys and girls to summer camp. Boxes and crates were piled high everywhere, cans and packets were in untidy heaps, confusion was prevalent, but the people were intent on getting bargains and trade was brisk.

Gabriella and I stood for a few minutes, absorbing the scene. Then she said to me, "See any supervisors, bosses, that kind of person?"

I didn't. The hard-working sales staff were a mixed crew. Mostly young, some even teenagers, but a fair number of older people, probably retirees making a few extra—if illegal—dollars. About half and half male and female, and a mix of races and ethnic backgrounds. As they called out the quality of their wares and the irresistible bargains to be had, a bewildering array of accents could be heard. But nobody was in sight who looked to be in any position of responsibility.

A young Hispanic with slick black hair and a trim mustache stood behind a pile of cans. We moved closer. They were five-pound cans of ham. A couple had been opened and it looked fine. Cut pieces with toothpicks in them were spread on a dish as samples and they were going fast. The young man was taking orders as fast as he could scribble. Each time, he handed the buyer a slip of paper and money changed hands. Gabriella picked up one of the cans and studied it critically. I did the same.

"Can't see anything wrong with it," I murmured.

"Looks all right to me," Gabriella said.

"Then how can they make any money?" I asked her. "Even at a good wholesale price, they can't make enough to cover expenses."

"He isn't selling these cans individually. The orders he's taking are for crates."

"Even so, there isn't enough markup, surely . . ."

Gabriella made a motion with her head and we edged out of the crowd around the table. When we were out of earshot, she said, "He has a terrific markup. Everything he gets is profit."

"How can he—oh, I think I see . . . This stuff is hot?"

"Sure. When the big stores have sales, they take the opportunity to bring out merchandise they couldn't sell before. When the people behind these ventures put on one of these illicit sales, they bring out stolen goods too."

We moved on. People were still coming in and the noise level was rising. There weren't any low-value items on sale—no soap powder or cereal, no sugar or flour, and of course no perishable goods like eggs, bread, butter or fruit.

We came to a stand with jars of jams, jellies, chutneys and marmalades and another with cans which all appeared to be the same. We stopped to examine them. The first was lobster and the only thing wrong with it was a red stain on the label. I looked at another can and it was the same. Gabriella was looking at a can and it had the same red stain on the label.

She looked at her can, then mine. "Funny," she said. "The stains are similar."

"All the cans are like this. Notice where the stain is?"

"No."

"Exactly where the 'sell-by' date is."

We came to a stand with a few large trays of what looked like fat dry herrings. The little wizened man attending the stand was short on teeth but made up for it with a booming voice. He was arguing with a prosperous-looking man with gray hair.

"What is it?" asked Gabriella.

We watched and listened.

"We're getting warmer," I murmured.

"But what is it?" she persisted.

"Japanese fugu fish."

After a moment, she asked, "Isn't that the poisonous one? Didn't some people die last year in San Francisco?"

"There are twenty species of fugu and all are deadly poisonous except one. That one is only edible from October to March and even then only certain parts are safe to eat. The fish contains a poison called tetrodotoxin, which is found in the ovaries, liver, entrails and in the skin. The Japanese describe the fish as 'touch and go'—one touch they say, and you go."

Gabriella shuddered. "Is it that good? That people will take that kind of risk?"

"A lot think so. Or it may be that it appeals to eaters who also enjoy Russian roulette. Before it can be cooked in Japan, the poison must be removed by a qualified cook, and those qualifications are issued only by a government department. Only one cook in five passes the tests. It's admitted that at least five hundred people die in Japan every year from eating fugu and the true figure may be very much higher."

The next stand was selling an even stranger-looking edible, though Gabriella didn't want to believe that it was. Two or three inches long, they were pinkish brown strips of puffy flesh and I told Gabriella that they were duck's tongues.

"They eat those?" She wrinkled her nose.

"Italians eat spider crabs, don't they?"

She shrugged. "Well, in Venice, yes."

"Goat meat and turnip tops?"

"But they're good—"

"And what about squid, carp and cuttlefish?"

"Delicious. They're different, they're real foods."

"Everyone doesn't think so," I told her. "Anyway, duck's tongues are a highly valued item in zen cooking. Hong Kong imports them from all over the world."

"I think they look revolting."

"Cooked with broad beans, onions, ginger and white wine, you'd love them."

"Not if I knew what they were," she said firmly.

I knew better than to press the point any further so instead I said, "In any case, you might be wrong with these. Duck's tongues are easy to duplicate and the ones here could very well be phonies."

Our onward progress led us to a bar where an elderly woman with orange hair and far too much makeup beckoned us. She held out a balloon glass with the tiniest amount of pale emerald green liquid in the bottom.

"Only five dollars," she urged as her face cracked into a persuasive smile.

"What is it?" I asked.

She waved a hand almost hidden under a weight of rings and bangles. The wave indicated a double row of bottles behind her on the bar. They carried a label which had a curving crimson band against a background of yellow and brown flowers intertwined. Along the crimson band was a word in large white letters: ABSINTHE.

"Too early in the day for me," murmured Gabriella. To the woman, she said in a chatty tone, "I didn't know anyone still drank it."

"They do if they can get it," said the woman meaningfully.

"What's in it?" Gabriella wanted to know.

"Try it and see," enticed the woman.

Gabriella was still playing hard to get. "I heard it was dangerous."

"It's dangerous, all right," she leered. "He knows, don't you?" she said, looking at me.

"It was banned because it was believed to encourage moral laxity," I said. "Ernest Hemingway drank a lot of it for that or, well, a parallel reason."

"Tell her they used to give it to the French Army," the woman insisted. "Wouldn't have done that if there was anything wrong with it, would they?"

"What's in it?" Gabriella asked me.

"Wormwood was in the original recipe. It affected the nervous system and destroyed the brain."

"Van Gogh drank it all the time—him and those other French painters," said the woman, not willing to give up.

"The word *absinthe* to me conjures up a picture of Toulouse-Lautrec wandering through Montmartre with a glass of it in his hand," said Gabriella thoughtfully.

"There! See!" said the woman triumphantly. "And look at all the wonderful paintings he did! And just with those little legs of his! Not only him either—what about all those others? That one who looked like Anthony Quinn and went to Hawaii!"

"It used to be 140 proof," I contributed. "That's almost twice the strength of bourbon or scotch."

"Right," said the woman. "It's good and strong. Don't want to taste it? Take a bottle home."

"How much?" I asked.

"Hundred dollars—special price."

"Think I'll stick to Chianti," said Gabriella as we shook our heads sadly and walked away, the woman's voice still calling after us with progressively reducing prices.

"It'd be a great price for the genuine stuff," I said to Gabriella.

"Surely there isn't any of the original still around?"

"Oh, yes," I assured her. "Bottles keep showing up at auctions quite often. One sold at five thousand dollars recently. At a state banquet in Switzerland, President Mitterrand of France was the guest of honor and they served soufflés made from authentic absinthe."

"I suppose there's an awful lot of the fake stuff on the market, then?"

"Lots. The herbs that were in the original were fennel, aniseed and hyssop and those are still used. Industrial alcohol made from sugar beet is sometimes used as it's cheap."

We were looking for the next stand to examine. Gabriella said, "Well, we seem to be running across items that are a bit nearer to what we're looking for. Somehow, though, I can't see us finding any Ko Feng here."

"No, you're right," I agreed. "There isn't—"

A tap on the shoulder stopped me.

A deep voice asked, "Looking for Ko Feng?"

I turned to find myself facing the biggest and the blackest man I had ever seen in my life.

CHAPTER THIRTY

He wore a light gray suit, a waistcoat that had a thin red-thread pattern running through it and a cream shirt with a flowing red and white tie.

I was able to see these details clearly because my eyes were on a level with the middle of his waistcoat. He was so large that the suit had to have been specially made, but even so it was extremely tight and the pearl buttons looked as if they might pop off under the strain at any moment.

He was a huge man, huge in every direction. He might have been described as fat but he looked to be bubbling with energy so maybe it was muscle. There was a tremendous amount of it, whatever it was. His legs were like tree trunks and he had arms which appeared long enough and powerful enough to strangle a water buffalo.

His head was like a big globe on top of his immense shoulders and it was a startling black—an intense coal black. I know it has always been said that the Ceylonese have the blackest of all black complexions and now that they are known as Sri Lankans, their color is just as dark. I didn't know if this man was a Sri Lankan but none of that island race could be any darker.

He was probably used to people staring at him. He must encounter that everywhere he went. The whites of his eyes were quite clear and there was a gleam of intelligence in them which hinted that he might be a dangerous customer with such a combination. He didn't look unfriendly but with that bulk and build, he didn't need to.

Gabriella was as dumbstruck as I. He repeated his question. "You folks looking for Ko Feng?"

I found my voice. "We're very interested in it. Are you selling?"

He laughed, a deep laugh that seemed to boom up from the depths of a barrel. It went spiraling upward to disappear into the unseen void above the lights.

"What do you want to do with it?" he asked, looking at us from one to the other.

Gabriella looked at him calmly. "Are you in charge here?"

His features were not Negroid and his mouth, though big, was not full-lipped. It became even bigger as he grinned, showing a large number of dazzling white teeth.

"In charge? Of this?" He waved a hand of black fingers the size of bananas. "No, ma'am, I'm not in charge of this. I'm just here like you, looking around, looking for bargains."

There was a shrewd glitter in his eyes and he was evidently sizing us up. He came to a decision. He stuck out his hand. "My name's Yaruba Da. I'm from the Congo."

Gabriella shook the proffered hand cautiously and I did the same, both of us concerned that we might come out of the encounter with the nickname of "Lefty." But he was aware of the danger too and his grip was firm yet gentle.

We gave our names and he nodded. I was trying to place his accent and it wasn't easy. It had a decided British undertone so perhaps he had been to school there. He spoke like an educated man but without affectation.

Gabriella leapt in, taking the initiative.

"So you're looking for Ko Feng? What do *you* want to do with it?"

He chuckled. It was like a warning sign that a volcano was about to erupt. I hoped it wasn't symbolic.

"I want to cook with it—like everybody else," he said.

"Where do you want to do this cooking?" demanded Gabriella. She was not one to be intimidated.

He dived into his waistcoat pocket and came out with some cards. He handed one to each of us.

African Dreams it read and had a Manhattan address.

"Oh, you have a restaurant . . ." Gabriella said, a little mollified.

Authentic African Cuisine, the card announced.

"That's an original idea" I told him. "The cuisines of Africa get very little attention in the Western world and they have so many great dishes to offer."

He eyed me, assessing. "You know Africa?"

"Not very well. I know something about cooking, though."

Gabriella wasn't going to let him off the hook that easily. "So you came here to look for Ko Feng?" she challenged.

"I didn't truly expect to find any here today but this is the kind of occasion and place where one might pick up some rumors, talk to folks who might know where to find it." He studied us thoughtfully. "Folks like you two."

"We don't know where to find any," Gabriella said, truthfully. "We came here today for the same reason as you."

He nodded. "You two got a restaurant?"

"No," Gabriella said, looking him right in the eye. He waited for her to expand on that brief answer but she just looked back and said nothing.

"You sound like you're English," he said to me and I nodded.

"That's right."

"Went to school there—Cambridge. Went to the Sorbonne in Paris before that because I spoke French first, the language of the Congo. Then went to Harvard later."

"What did you study?" Gabriella asked and I was glad she didn't add, Was it cooking?

"History," he told her. "Then philosophy. But I never felt like either one was something I wanted to pursue the rest of my life. Neither one was practical enough for me. I got interested in cooking and did some research on the history of food and cooking. I went to Cairo and opened a restaurant, then came here to New York and just opened African Dreams."

Gabriella was easing up a little now. His statements could be checked so he no longer looked as threatening, though he didn't look any smaller.

"How did you hear about this event?" she asked, ever the policewoman.

"Same way you did, probably," he said with the same wide grin.

Gabriella and I both knew he hadn't leaned on a police informer but he obviously wasn't going to tell us any more.

"You see a way to use Ko Feng in African cooking?" I asked him curiously.

"Sounds to me like it's a spice that can be used in any cooking," he said seriously. "If it's what they say it is, it's wonderful stuff." He studied us, then said abruptly to me.

"You say you're English?"

I nodded.

"The fellow who was killed after the Ko Feng was brought into the country was English."

"I know."

"You can't be him . . ." He was thinking as he spoke. ". . . So you must be the other one."

I wasn't sure how much of my undercover role should be blown so I said nothing, hoping that Gabriella would pick up on the answer.

"He *is* the other one," she said firmly.

Yaruba Da was still studying her. "And you're in the food business too?" he persisted.

She didn't answer right away and he spread two big hands.

"Hey, in a place like this, you like to know who you're talking to," he said.

"That's true," she said.

He grinned in resignation. Turning back to me, he asked, "Having any luck finding that stuff?"

"Getting close," I said confidently.

He moved a half step closer. "Between you two and me, I really need something new like this Ko Feng. The restaurant business is tough anywhere. I don't have to tell you how tough it is here in New York. A genuinely novel flavor like Ko Feng could make sure I stay in business."

I nodded in understanding. Gabriella looked sympathetic.

"Listen," he said, "come and eat with us sometime. Get to know African food."

I nodded again.

"Good." He looked pleased. "Just give me a call."

We shook hands and left him. He was heading for the absinthe counter.

"Biggest man I ever saw," she said. "I'm glad he didn't turn out to be in charge of this operation."

"We still haven't found out who is. Or anybody who knows anything about Ko Feng. Let's move on."

The next stand was easy to find. It was spaced well away from its neighboring stands and the reason became very obvious when we got closer.

"Whew!" Gabriella said. "Are they ever high!"

Venison carcasses dangled from hooks and a man with the skin coloring and prominent cheekbones of an American Indian was extolling their qualities. I thought they had been hanging too long.

"Will he able to sell those?" asked Gabriella.

"Probably. I know they don't smell that good but well

cooked and with a red currant sauce or one equally tangy, they'll be edible."

"For how much longer?"

"If he's smart, he'll sell them today."

A knot of people was untangling from a nearby stand and for a second, I thought I saw a face I recognized. I was telling myself it couldn't be as I didn't know anybody here when I saw her again. She was visible only for two or three seconds but I knew her—it was the mysterious woman I had seen in the Spice Warehouse just before Don Renshaw's murder.

CHAPTER THIRTY-ONE

What's wrong?" asked Gabriella.

The woman had disappeared in the crowd of people and try as I might, I couldn't see her.

"I thought it was someone I knew," I said, "I must have been mistaken."

But I knew I wasn't. I kept looking but there was no sign of her. I watched the crowd flow past us and break up as small groups went on to other stands.

Gabriella looked at me strangely but said nothing.

At one end of the massive building, an entire area was devoted to wine. Here were some incredible bargains.

"Look at those!" I said to Gabriella in astonishment.

Cases of red Bordeaux were being offered at $150 a case.

"Doesn't look like such a knock-down price."

"That's the Pomerol 1990, the Certain de May, anything under a thousand dollars is a great price."

Another Pomerol, the Petrus, a year older at 1989, was being offered at $1,100 a case. "Worth nearly ten times that on the normal market," I told Gabriella in amazement.

There was a rare Sauternes, the Chateau de Suduiraut, one with a rich creamy texture. Cases offered at $250 were worth at least $2,000 and even a Santa Maria Chardonnay from California, a 1993 and market priced at about $250 a case, was selling fast at $50.

I relayed these figures to Gabriella.

She shook her head in dismay. "Hot, every one of them."

"Hm," I said, "not this one, though."

"Austrian wine?" Gabriella looked at the label. "Nineteen eighty-four? How do you know it's not hot?"

"Maybe it didn't get as much publicity here as it did in Europe. The story began a year later when a sharp-eyed inspector in Austria's tax office noticed that a wine producer was claiming high added-value refunds on diethylene glycol. That's antifreeze and it's also used as a disinfectant. But when the inspector did some calculating, he found that the quantities consumed by this vineyard were excessive and he began investigating.

He went so far as having some of the wine analyzed, and to his horror the wine contained three times the lethal dose of antifreeze, which is a deadly poison."

"Smart investigating," commented Gabriella.

"It really was. Further testing showed that more than five million liters of adulterated wine were known to be out on the market. Two hundred different brands were affected and fifty companies were blacklisted by the Health Ministry."

Gabriella looked at the wine bottles on the stand with a new respect.

"And you think this is some of it?"

"Most of it had already gone to Germany, Austria's biggest customer. Most of it was never traced."

"The importers held on to it, waiting for the furor to die down," guessed Gabriella.

"Without a doubt. Every once in a while, a few bottles are reported. And one dealer, intent on preserving his image, poured several hundred bottles into the local river." I paused and Gabriella looked at me, waiting.

"Go on," she urged, "I have a suspicion there's a punch line coming."

"All the fish in the river died and the water treatment plant broke down."

"But what about all those experts who taste wines when

they first come on to the market? Didn't they notice anything?"

"They said it had a rounded smooth sweetness and they praised its body."

"So much for experts," she said. "Is a ten-year-old Austrian wine valuable?"

"It sure is," I told her. "Not only that but there are those who speculate that as adulteration of wine in Austria had been going on for years, the amount of wine spiked with diethylene glycol might be nearer to ten million liters."

"All lethal!"

"All dangerous. As the spiking was done in vats before bottling, the amounts probably vary. Some may be very lethal, some less so—some of it may even be harmless. Want to try some?"

Gabriella shuddered. "Not me. You say that this isn't the first time the Austrians have been known to do this kind of thing?"

"Sweet wines can be very, very expensive. Adding diglycol, as it's called, is a cheap and easy way of turning an ordinary white wine into an expensive sweet wine. Then too, lots of artificial wine has been produced there."

"Artificial how?"

"Made in the laboratory from all-chemical products. And here's a story you'll love—in 1985, an Austrian was arrested and charged with adding gunpowder to his wine."

"Gunpowder? What on earth for?"

"To make it sparkle."

"And sell it as champagne?" asked Gabriella in astonishment.

"Right."

"The wine industry in Europe is a fertile field for criminal investigation, isn't it?"

"With good reason. The president of the German Wine Association was brought to trial for illegally adding liquid sugar to wine. Politics comes into the picture sometimes."

"That happens here too," Gabriella said, straight-faced.

"So I've heard."

We successfully resisted the blandishments of a doll-faced Japanese girl selling cases of sake and a brown-skinned young man with gold earrings who was promoting several unusual liqueurs in strangely shaped bottles. According to the attractive labels, they were made from various Asian fruits with bizarre names. Gabriella was trying to make out the ingredients on one label when a face at a distant stand caused me to do a double take.

I looked again, hard. There was no mistaking the close-cropped gray hair, the tan, the lithe athletic carriage. It was Tom Eck.

What was he doing here? I wondered. Well, this place seemed to attract a wide clientele and if I knew more people in New York, I'd probably see a lot more faces that surprised me.

He was talking now to someone I couldn't see, someone hidden from my sight by the crowd at that particular stand. All of them were moving, some coming, some pushing their way out in search of another bargain and as positions shifted, the person talking to Tom Eck came into view.

It was the mysterious woman I had seen at the Spice Warehouse again.

Gabriella was still marveling at the weird names of the fruits on the liqueur bottles. I grabbed her arm.

"Let's go over there."

"Where?"

She put the bottle down and came willingly enough.

"What's over there?" she asked.

"I don't know," I said, "but it must be terrific. Look at the crowds."

The place was nearly packed now. Even the spaces between stands and stalls, previously ample, were filled and it was difficult to follow a desired course. Elbowing, jostling, people of both sexes, a dozen nationalities and even more ethnic backgrounds crammed the church in quest of food and wine bargains.

Muttering complaints about being pushed and shoved by others, we pushed and shoved our way through but when we got close to the stand, neither Eck nor the girl could be seen.

"What is it now that we're here?" grumbled Gabriella. "Hope it was worth all these bruises."

"If it was Italy, you'd have more bruises from pinches."

The attraction was of historical interest rather than practical. Still encased in ice and kept frozen by slabs of solid carbon dioxide, were what looked like slabs of meat. We listened to the spiel of the seller, a hoarse-voiced elderly man whose smoker's cough caused him to break into hacking fits. The tale he was telling was an extraordinary one and described the terrible ordeal of an Arctic expedition which ran out of food and, unable to find any game, was fortunate enough to find the corpse of a mammoth, frozen into the ice.

The way he told the story, they had hacked enough ice away to be able to reach the corpse, which they had promptly torn into pieces and eaten. Their hunger temporarily assuaged, they had built a fire and eaten more of the mammoth flesh the next day, proclaiming it quite tasty.

"Liven up your next dinner party," the man wheezed. "No need to serve the same old filly mignons—give your guests something they'll talk about for years—serve them mammoth meat."

"What do you think?" I asked Gabriella.

She eyed the hunks of meat in their shell of ice. She looked doubtful.

"I don't think I'd like it."

"I don't mean that. I mean, is it genuine?"

"In a place like this—who knows?" she said.

"Something wrong with this place?" asked a hard voice.

His face was as hard as his voice. Thin-lipped, cold-eyed, he studied us suspiciously. He wore a dark suit with a black shirt.

With so many people in there, I didn't know how he had heard us. Gabriella might have spoken slightly above a normal tone so as to be heard over the hubbub of voices but he must have had very sharp hearing.

Gabriella was cool as the ice that had allegedly come from the North Pole.

"Kinda crowded," she said disparagingly. "Hard to get around."

He nodded, assessing us both.

"Regulars here?"

"No," said Gabriella. "Our first time. You the guy who runs this show?"

"Who sent you?" he asked, ignoring her question.

"Whistler."

"Who?"

"Whistler," she repeated.

Whistler seemed to be a character who was recognized by no one the first time around.

"He couldn't have sent you," the man said and I felt a slight chill.

Gabriella shrugged a take-it-or leave-it shrug.

"He's still inside," the man said.

Gabriella stared insolently back at him. "So? He hasn't been struck dumb, has he?"

The man said nothing at first then he asked, "See anything here you like?"

"Lotsa things," Gabriella said, "but the prices are too high."

"Best in town," the man said.

"What we were hoping to find," said Gabriella, "was some Ko Feng."

I hadn't been expecting her to be that forthright. The man hadn't either. He gave her a quick glance and his expression changed.

"That's that spice that went missing?"

She nodded.

"You call these prices high and you're looking to buy some of that?" he asked.

She looked uninterested. "Have any?" she asked casually.

He shook his head. She wasn't going to give up.

"Know where we can get any?"

He gave a noncommittal grunt.

"We can raise the cash," she said.

He shook his head again. "The word is that that English guy snatched it."

"He was shot," said Gabriella.

"Then the other English guy's got it."

"Is that a fact?" Gabriella drawled. "Know where we can find him?"

The man's eyes were on me but I didn't think there was any significance in it. I hoped I was right.

"Shouldn't be hard," the man said.

He eyed me a moment longer, then gave us a nod and walked away.

This time I waited until he was out of earshot—and everyone else in the place too.

"Don't believe a word he said," I advised Gabriella.

"Maybe he knows something," she said.

"He's wrong."

She half smiled.

"Is Whistler still inside?" I asked her.

"Who?"

"Now, don't you start with that!"

"I don't know."

"You don't know!" I said, appalled. "You don't know and you risked our lives!"

"Police work occasionally entails risks," she said carelessly. "What's on that stand over there?"

It was more hot merchandise, large restaurant-size cans of

oysters. We listened to the presentation being repeated by a heavy, overdressed woman who Gabriella thought was moonlighting from her regular job in a brothel.

The numbers of cans she was offering brought a further comment from Gabriella. "Just about a twenty-ton trailer load."

It was then that I saw another face I recognized. Gabriella saw me looking. "Know him?"

"His name is Lennie Rifkin. He has a restaurant called Phoenicia. It prepares and cooks dishes of the ancient world—Greece, Rome, Egypt and so on. He's hoping for some Ko Feng."

His course brought him directly into our path. He stopped when he saw me. He stared at Gabriella, then looked her over again, more slowly. Tearing himself away from that pleasurable action, he gave me a curt nod.

"Might have expected to find you here," he said.

"You too," I said. "Come here often?"

"Just like to look," he retorted.

He looked Gabriella over again appreciatively, waiting for me to introduce him. When I didn't do so, he said in a surly voice, "Haven't seen any Ko Feng here, have you?"

"Not yet."

"Expect to?"

"Going to keep looking until I find it."

He sniffed, either unconvinced or disbelieving, and went on by.

"Not one of your admirers," commented Gabriella.

"Not even a supporter," I admitted. "Yet another of the legion who doubt me."

"Speaking of doubters," said Gabriella, her voice changing, "look who we have here."

It was the cold-faced man from before.

"And this time, he's brought help," she added.

The two of them approached us directly. The second man

was bigger and looked even tougher. The man we had talked to previously raised a hand to detain us.

"This is a buddy of Whistler's," he declared.

Gabriella gave him a nod.

"Pleased to meet you," I said. "Any friend of Whistler's is a friend of ours."

Gabriella gave me a glance of warning not to get too flippant. The fact was, I was annoyed. The man's face darkened. "Tell us when you talked to him," he invited and I didn't like his tone.

The resourceful Gabriella was about to say something when we were joined by another. This one was the biggest of all. He dwarfed the big man confronting us and easily outweighed the two of them. It was Yaruba Da from the Congo.

He came up from behind them and clapped a hand the size of a shovel onto the shoulder of each.

"You met my friends already!" he said jovially. "That's good. I like to see folks getting along. It's a pity they have to leave but you gentlemen and I can have a chat—as a matter of fact, I wanted to ask you about this olive oil over here. It seems very reasonably priced and I was wondering about its origin. I shouldn't sound so suspicious, I know but at this price, well . . ."

His formidable grip turned the two of them away from us.

"Our cue to leave," muttered Gabriella. We slipped through some bunches of eager customers and the teenage boy with the ponytail standing by the steel door gave us only the briefest of glances—and that was at Gabriella—before letting us out.

We hurried along the tunnel, gave the man at the other end a nod and emerged thankfully into the daylight. I didn't let out my breath until Gabriella had pulled away from the curb and the Ford engine was hammering out a farewell.

CHAPTER THIRTY-TWO

It was about two o'clock as we reentered Manhattan.

"How about some lunch?" I suggested.

"I really should get back to my desk . . ." Gabriella said but I have always been a firm believer that when people say they "really should" do something, it means that they can be persuaded to do something else.

"Even hard-working cops get time off for lunch," I told her. "Anyway, this will be police business—I want to tell you about my inquiries yesterday. So where do you recommend?"

"To a gourmet? I wouldn't be so bold."

"I don't eat gourmet all the time."

"You don't? What about the Bull Moose—can't get any more gourmet than that."

"That was a culinary experience not to be forgotten," I said carefully. "Can we ever match it?"

She laughed. "Okay, I can't stop too long but there's a place near here—we go right past it on our way back. By the way, do gourmets eat chili?"

"I do. Love it. I often cook it at home. I'm always trying different ways—there can be few dishes that have so many variations on one theme."

"Good," she said. "When you cook at home . . . does your wife like chili too?"

"I'm not married," I told her. "I live alone."

She made no reply and in about ten minutes, she stopped to put the Ford in an outdoor parking lot. It had barbed wire around the top of a rusting steel fence, the ground was sand and gravel, which must be a mess in rainy weather. A black man came out of a battered, tiny wooden shack to collect money, and even he looked at the Ford with disdain.

"I thought he was going to give us half price when he saw the car," I said to Gabriella as we walked into the restaurant.

"I'll get a Cadillac next time."

"No, no," I said. "This one is certainly good camouflage."

The name of the restaurant was Chili Today. It was a big, barnlike building that Gabriella told me had been converted from a dance hall that had been put out of business by police order. The wooden benches with plank seating and wooden floors gave it an air rather like a German beer hall. Flags hung on the walls and I asked Gabriella about the name.

"Why only today?"

"It's a line from a Peggy Lee song," she said. " 'It may be chili today but it'll be hot tamale.' "

As we read the descriptive and informative menu, the significance of the flags became apparent—they were the flags of all the places that claim they serve the best chili—Texas, Arizona, New Mexico, California, Colorado, the Mexican Republic and a number of other states including, of course, New York.

We ordered Mexican beer, Carta Blanca, then Gabriella said, "Well, we didn't find any Ko Feng but it was an interesting day and we got an invitation to an African barbecue."

I nodded. "I doubt if the people running that sale have any Ko Feng but they might hear who does—they may travel in the same circles."

"I'll do some checking when I get back. What about that Rifkin character? He looked shady."

"Check on him by all means," I said. "He would love to get his hands on some Ko Feng and he might not be too choosy about how he did it."

The beer arrived. "Like Mexican beer?" Gabriella asked.

"Oh, we can get it in London. It's not uncommon. Not as full bodied as English beer but more flavor than the run-of-the-mill American beers."

We examined the menu and exchanged comments on the numerous chilis offered and on the flamboyant text that accompanied them.

There were all the regional variants and many adventurous deviations. For instance, there was turkey chili and even a venison chili. The menu explained that real chili purists insist that chili is never made with minced beef but only with beef cubes and furthermore, it never contains beans. In Texas, it went on, they break both rules. The New Mexico variant is called chili con carne verde and the "verde" refers to the small green chiles that it contains.

"Good heavens!" I exclaimed and Gabriella looked up. "What?"

"Did you know there was an Italian chili?"

"I don't believe it."

"Right here on page four. It uses tomato sauce of the kind used for pasta, lots of tomatoes, mushrooms and sliced pepperoni."

"I'll tell my mother about it," said Gabriella, "but doubt if her regular patrons will ever forgive her if she serves it."

There were recipes originated by, or beloved by, many famous people—Harrison Ford, Bob Dole, Mick Jagger, Jim Florio (the former governor of New Jersey), Linda Ronstadt, Reggie Miller, an astronaut, a neurosurgeon who had won the Nobel Prize, Jacques Cousteau, Ernest Hemingway, Zubin Mehta . . . the list went on and on.

There was a paragraph on Cincinnati Chili and I pointed out to Gabriella that it is served over spaghetti there, which might appeal to her mother. All of the familiar chili names were present such as Three Alarm Chili, Rockbottom Chili and Texas Red, and an inset warned that the longer chile peppers are cooked the hotter they get. "For a real taste thrill," it said, "ask for chili from last August."

The establishment's own recipes were graded in order of hotness. First, there was Aunt Susie's Saturday Night Special. "Mild but still tangy, assertive without being aggressive," said the poet in the kitchen. Next came My Way, the chef's own statement of how chili should taste. "Moderately inflammatory" was the comment.

Tame with Flame was moving fast up the heat scale and the accompanying advice was to eat it slowly so as to give the paramedics plenty of time to arrive. Mrs O'Leary's Revenge was ripe with roasted hot jalapeño peppers and was said to have a smoky taste which endured—"Probably to the end of the century," remarked Gabriella.

Anyone who thought that dish was hot should try the Doomsday Express, said the menu writer, adding that it had initially been developed for testing tank armor.

"Better bring us two glasses of water," Gabriella said to the waiter, a skinny fellow with spiky hair.

"I thought water came with everything," I said.

"It used to but not anymore. Now you have to ask for it. Shows how long it is since you were last in New York."

"You folks from out of town?" the waiter asked.

"No," Gabriella said.

"Yes," I said.

"In that case, can I suggest that you try our combination platter? It has some of each, and you can write your own comments on the asbestos paper we supply."

We agreed and it arrived quickly, I still marveled at the speed of the service in American restaurants, no matter what their status. We had a choice too of corn bread, coleslaw, potato salad, rice—all foods to counteract the hotter chilis, as Gabriella observed. Simultaneously, she asked for more ice water.

The waiter grinned. "No problem. We have a couple of glaciers anchored outside—we get daily delivery."

"What do you think of that Doomsday Special?" I asked Gabriella.

"Towering Inferno would have been a better name" she said with a shudder. "I can handle everything up to that level, though."

We were entering the last lap and had cleaned up everything except that really hot one when Gabriella said, "That was fun." She looked at me anxiously. "Did you enjoy it?"

"Terrific. Now I know how the West was won."

"I think you'd rather have had a French meal."

"No, no," I insisted.

"It's all right for food to be fun once in a while, isn't it?"

"Absolutely. Food and cooking have been put on a pedestal that has led to their getting too stuffy an opinion of themselves."

"You mean they need bringing down to earth—the way Gene does, for instance."

"Right. And anyway, there's room for all kinds of food and the great thing about a dish like chili is that the food itself is more important than the presentation. Too many chefs have let themselves be carried away by presentation—it became not so much cooking as interior decoration."

"I blame the French for that," said Gabriella.

"Any true Italian girl would. No, no—" I waved off her protest. "I'm not saying it's just an ancient rivalry. Nouvelle cuisine was largely responsible for the shift in emphasis from taste to appearance."

"Luckily, it didn't last long."

"It was food as an art form," I said, trying not to sound too opinionated. "It was a boon to food magazine photographers and gave them all kinds of new challenges. But to be fair, nouvelle cuisine did play a part in changing cooking styles. It brought about a lighter, healthier approach. It cut down on excessive amounts of butter and cream."

"It must have focused on the hazards of deep-frying, too," Gabriella said.

"It did—and in doing so, refocused on techniques like stir-frying, which we knew about but didn't make enough use of in Western cooking."

"So once again, we drew knowledge from the East."

"Michel Guerard certainly did—he was probably the most famous French chef at the time that nouvelle cuisine was taking a hold. He ransacked the Chinese and Japanese cookbooks of the seventeenth and eighteenth centuries and applied both their food and their methods."

We had been obliged to order more beer by this time. Water was not enough to hold back the fiery onslaught of the chilis. As the beer arrived, Gabriella said, "Speaking of the Chinese, tell me about your adventures in Chinatown. You seem to have emerged without any scars from the hatchet men."

"It was a terrifying experience," I said. "I never expected to come out alive. If it hadn't been for this exotic Chinese girl—Lotus Petal, her name was—"

"Just the facts, man."

I outlined my talk with the affable Mr. Koo at the Shanghai Palace and my abortive efforts to pry any information out of Mr. Singyang.

"You did well," Gabriella said. "The Chinese are not known for being talkative and there are people who would label them secretive."

"I thought of turning it over to you after I had been to the Forbidden City," I told her, "I suppose you could have sent in a Chinese cop."

"They don't give away any more to them than they do to any other kind of cop."

"Well, Mr. Koo was friendly enough and he tried to be helpful."

"And how much did you actually learn?" she asked.

"Well, having had the birds' nests stolen from him at a time when he really needed them, he was willing to finger Mr. Singyang but there I hit the Great Wall."

"You think he got the shipment?"

"Yes, I do."

"So he knows who stole it."

"Maybe he did and didn't want to tell an outsider."

"Or it could have been arranged so that he didn't know," she mused. "By the way, did you happen to ask who handled the insurance on the birds' nest shipment?"

"Yes. They're called New England Assurance."

Her expression changed. "Are they now? That's interesting."

"Why?"

"That's the same insurance company that covered the Ko Feng."

"Could be coincidence—"

"Could be. They're big, do a lot of insuring. We'll do some checking—it's good to be able to rule out coincidence."

"One other thing . . . . . . whenever I have the chance, I'm spreading the word that parcels of phony Ko Feng are being offered."

Her brown eyes regarded me thoughtfully. "The result being . . . ?"

"Hopefully, it will cause potential buyers to focus on me. With Don Renshaw dead, I'm the only person who can identify the Ko Feng."

"Is that a good idea?"

"It should also make it difficult for the thief to dispose of it before we catch up to him. Nobody will want to take the risk of paying a lot of money for a sack of worthless flower stamens."

"I may have to arrange extra police protection for you," she said, finishing her beer.

"I'll just get an order of the Doomsday Special—better than a flame thrower."

She didn't debate the idea any further, conceding that it was worth a try and warning me to be careful.

"This case would be getting out of hand if we lost another Englishman," she concluded.

Another beer would have been necessary in order to fully assuage the ravages of the chili but we agreed to call it a day. I asked Gabriella if she was sure she didn't want some chocolate cheesecake for dessert but she rolled her eyes in horror. She insisted on going Dutch on the bill, which was surprisingly reasonable.

The attendant at the parking lot seemed glad to get rid of the Ford. No doubt it lowered the tone of his place. Gabriella dropped me at my hotel and gave me a cheery wave as she drove off.

CHAPTER THIRTY-THREE

If I stayed in the Framingham Hotel much longer, they would be wanting to charge me for secretarial services. There was a call from Professor Willenbroek and I punched his number.

"Yes, I called you," he said in his brisk voice. "Wanted to ask you a question."

"Go ahead, Professor." I knew it was an honorary title, possibly self-bestowed, but I felt he liked to be addressed that way.

"Might want to get you to do a little job for me."

"What kind of a job?" I asked.

"It's a job you've done before," he said and I felt a tightening in my throat as I replied.

"What job is that?"

"Authenticate some Ko Feng."

It wasn't a complete shock. He had put no particular emphasis on his words "a little job," but they had foreshadowed what was to come.

"You have some?" I asked in a flat tone.

"No, no. I will be getting some, though."

"I'm surprised." I picked my words carefully. "It's still regarded by the police as stolen property."

"Oh, I wouldn't buy it under those conditions," he said quickly. "But it's sure to be recovered sooner or later, isn't it? And when it is, I want to be ready."

"When it's found, of course I'd be glad to authenticate it for you," I said.

"I mean—you did it before, didn't you? You're the only

one who knows all its characteristics. You could do it again."

"It's a wise precaution on your part," I told him. "Phony Ko Feng is already being offered around the city."

"Is it?" he said in a thoughtful tone. It was clear that I had given him something to think about.

"Excellent then," he said heartily. "Good man. Need to have you coordinate with our laboratory people, naturally. Just a formality . . . Right, then. I'll call you."

After we had hung up, I pondered—not for the first time—on what could only be my misjudgment of human character. The wily old bird had been offered some Ko Feng. It had shown up on the market. He must want it very badly, for he was evidently prepared to buy it knowing that it was stolen property. Well, it had been the most valuable spice in the world two or three millennia ago and it was up there again.

Why just the professor, though? Well, it didn't have to be . . .

I looked up the number of the Methuselah Foundation and asked for Dr. Li.

His hissing sibilants came on the line almost at once. I introduced myself and he told me how delighted he was to hear from me and hoped that I was in excellent health. I affirmed the fact and took the initiative.

"Dr. Li, I understand that you have been offered some Ko Feng."

There should have been an astonished pause but I reminded myself that I was dealing with a very wily man who would never show astonishment. Indeed, he was prompt with his reply and bland in his manner.

"You are indeed well informed. Your understanding is only partial, however. I have not been offered any Ko Feng as yet but it has been suggested to me that some will soon be available. I was asked if I would wish to buy some when it comes on the market. The legitimate market, of course."

Horsefeathers, I thought.

"As a matter of fact, I was about to call you," he continued.

I'll bet you were, I thought. Then I had the uneasy notion that he might think me well informed not because he considered me a brilliant detective but because he believed I had been involved in the crime. After all, he had tried to brainwash me into telling him where the Ko Feng was. He might be as convinced of my guilt as was Alexander Marvell, just a little more devious about showing it.

"I wanted to ask you . . . When the Ko Feng does come on the market, would you be willing to authenticate it?"

"Well," I said, in an uncertain 'You've caught me unawares' tone, "possibly, yes, I would."

"Your expertise would be very much appreciated and you would be well compensated for it."

"Very well, Doctor." It was my best 'I know how to make up my mind quickly' tone. "You are wise to beware of imitations," I added breezily. "It seems that people are being offered imitation Ko Feng. It looks like it, has its aroma and is superficially convincing."

"I suppose that is only to be expected," said Dr. Li smoothly.

He told me that he would be in touch very shortly. I wondered what approach he and Professor Willenbroek would use to smooth over that small gap between legal and illegal Ko Feng. Probably something along the lines of "This is too wonderful an opportunity to miss. Here is a remarkable plant which will benefit all mankind . . ." and so on.

I thanked him for taking me into his confidence and if the sarcasm was noted, it was not commented on.

I called Gloria Branson at Paramount Pharmaceuticals and came straight to the point.

"Gloria, what was your response to the offer of Ko Feng that you have just had?"

She didn't have the suavity of Dr. Li in dealing with the

abrupt question but she was pretty good. I might not have noticed the split second of hesitation if I hadn't been listening for it so intently.

"Well, as a matter of fact, I have had such an offer. I was going to call you about it. How did you know?"

There seemed no hint of suspicion in her voice that might suggest she thought me guilty too. Or was she just good at concealing it?

"The word is out that fake Ko Feng is being put up for sale."

"What!" There was a breathy alarm in her voice that was good to hear.

"I thought you should know," I said blandly.

She thanked me pleasantly enough but I could almost hear her mind working as the line clicked.

A pattern was beginning to develop in my mind and I made another call, this time to Abe Kefalik.

No, he said. He hadn't been offered any Ko Feng. Then he turned cagy. Did I know where he could get some? I gave him the warning of the day—just in case he was contacted, I told him.

I called Ayesha. She was in the middle of a slanging match with her husband and I caught some of the side spray. No, she hadn't been offered any Ko Feng, she said curtly. I suggested she be very careful before buying any without making absolutely sure it was genuine and hung up quickly.

Selim Osman was in the kitchen of the Topkapi Castle but he took my call and must have been successfully inventing some spectacular new dish because he was almost friendly. He hadn't heard of any Ko Feng being available, adding quickly that when it was, he would be in the market.

"Phony Ko Feng is being offered," I cautioned him. "I thought you should know." Imperturbable as ever, he thanked me amiably.

I called Gabriella. She was still in the office and I was put through at once. I told her of the Ko Feng offers and of my efforts to muddy the waters and delay any transactions.

"Presumably all the people the Ko Feng has been offered to are aware of the penalties attendant upon the receipt of stolen goods." Gabriella was firm and officious.

"All due respect to the authority of the New York Police Department," I replied, "but I'd say that not one of these people gives a hoot about that."

"I suppose so," said Gabriella. "Keep me informed."

I turned on the great brainwasher and watched a few minutes of television. The time wasn't a total loss—I learned about Elizabeth Taylor's new husband's chicken pot pie recipe; heard that a woman accused of smothering her two children had been acquitted because she was suffering from premenstrual depression; and saw three commercials in rapid succession, one for hemorrhoid cream, one for a diarrhea remedy and one for a foot deodorant. A governor of one of the Southern states announced his plans for running for president as soon as he was released from jail.

I called London and made sure that the data I had faxed to explain my inability to be present at the salmon hearing was adequate. I called Mrs. Shearer at the answering service/reception/general secretarial operation on the floor above my office. She was still awestruck at the thought of my being in New York and I thought it better not to tell her that I was here because the police had my passport. As for being involved in a murder . . . There are some things that it is better for people not to know.

Other trivial details of surviving in a foreign city took up some time too and when it came to early evening, there arose the vital question of where to eat. There is no greater array of ethnic cuisines in the world than in New York but I reminded myself that I was still on duty. I called African Dreams and asked Yaruba Da if he had a table. He said he was delighted to hear from me and was most anxious to extend his hospitality for dinner.

CHAPTER THIRTY-FOUR

Irregularly shaped rooms led from one to another in a carefully planned pattern of geometric eccentricity. All the rooms had the same basic design—pyramidal ceilings of narrow glass panels which climbed up to an apex of dizzying height. Plants, bushes, indoor trees and flowers grew in profusion and maintained the jungle theme of African Dreams. A waterfall became a gurgling stream that threaded its way through the rooms. Small wooden bridges crossed it in places and a native hut with a thatched roof doubled as a serving station for the waiters.

All the staff was black, though none achieved the ultimate blackness of my host, Yaruba Da. His teeth gleamed an impossible white against the smooth coal-black skin and his huge size made him an imposing figure.

He led me to a table by a stream. A banyan tree was behind me and a banana tree, loaded with its yellow fruit. Occasional jungle noises could be heard, the distant trumpeting of an elephant, the cackling of a tribe of monkeys and the roar of a lion but they were never obtrusive. A rhythmic drumbeat replaced them periodically and became a soothing tune.

"You've done a wonderful job with the decor," I congratulated Yaruba Da. "It's not easy to achieve the jungle effect and still remain sophisticated."

He spread his huge hands in an appreciative gesture.

"Thank you. We are still struggling for recognition, though—as you see."

He waved toward the half-filled room. As it was the peak

time of the evening, that wasn't good. I consoled him with stories of acquaintances in London who had battled for a year or more to become established.

A beautiful brown-skinned waitress in a white robe with a lacy gold belt and high-heeled sandals brought me a Mozambique cocktail.

"Drinks brewed from fresh ginger can be found all across sub-Saharan Africa," said Yaruba Da. "They are mainly soft drinks as alcohol and the African sun are not a good combination. Then too, many Africans are Mohammedan and therefore forbidden to partake of alcohol. So we have used one of these, a blend with lime and pineapple juices, and added a little alcohol to it."

"The Dark Continent's version of a Moscow Mule," I commented.

He nodded. "With much less of a kick."

The girl returned and with a shy smile put on the table an ornate silver-inlaid tray of appetizers. Yaruba Da identified them for me, one by one.

"Hot plantain crisps, samosas—you have seen them in many countries—these are filled with a spicy mixture of potato and beans. Those are roasted melon seeds, these are *kulikuli*—crispy peanut balls, a Nigerian specialty—and over here, this dip is *meshwiya* from Tunisia. Vine-ripened tomatoes are chopped with garlic, cumin, green peppers, black olives and hard-boiled eggs. These are prawns *piripiri*—you may know this from other parts of the world."

"It's popular in the Philippines, I know."

"Yes. And just as popular in Mozambique—in fact, *piripiri* is to the cuisine of Mozambique what curry is to Indian cooking. Crushed red peppers and garlic are the essential spices."

I was enjoying the appetizers, all of them delicious.

"These samosas are excellent," I told him. "Too often they ooze cooking oil but these are extraordinarily crispy without being dry."

He accepted the compliment with a bow of his head.

"I must leave you for a few moments. Please study the menu and tell me if there are dishes you would especially like to taste. Venandra will bring you another Mozambique cocktail whenever you wish it."

"The cocktail is very good but rather than another, I'd prefer wine if you have it."

"Of course. We have many European and Californian wines and we also have a few specialties—which are actually variants on rice wine. You will find them quite palatable."

I agreed to have a glass of rice wine and when he left, carefully easing his bulk through the table-strewn jungle, I looked at the menu.

It was a very eclectic array of African dishes and from the descriptions of the ingredients and the cooking methods, an ingenious adaptation of genuine originals, making as few modifications to Western taste as possible.

I recognized a few. Djedj b'l-qasbour is a coriander chicken dish from Algeria and very popular throughout North Africa. Chicken Tagine, with chickpeas and beans, is Moroccan. Bamia is a lamb and okra stew found in many countries. I had once eaten Egusi Soup, a Nigerian classic which contains crayfish, the African type sometimes called rock lobster.

The waitress returned with a glass of rice wine, which tasted remarkably like a Riesling, then Yaruba Da came back and we discussed the menu. I congratulated him on offering such a range of dishes.

"Perhaps it is too wide a range."

"It's the way to start," I told him. "You will quickly learn which dishes don't appeal to customers and you can drop them from the menu. You have several very unusual dishes which will attract the more adventurous."

His large face cracked into a wide smile.

"Wildebeest, for example."

"Yes. And Bstila, the Moroccan pigeon pie. But I doubt if you get many calls for camel."

He chuckled. "I added that just for sensationalism. It is eaten in all the Saharan countries, though, served in couscous as an alternate to goat meat."

"You don't have many fish dishes," I remarked.

"I can see that you find that surprising. With twenty thousand miles of coastline, you might expect a lot of fish to be eaten but the problem is the climate and the lack of refrigeration in much of the continent. Fish has to be eaten soon after it is caught. The fish dishes that we do serve are pickled fish, which is very popular and avoids the spoilage difficulty."

At Yaruba Da's recommendation, I eventually settled for some pickled fish to start. I followed it with a bowl of Doro Wat, the famous chicken stew of Ethiopia. It was served with an *injeera,* the Ethiopian pancake which is a little like a tortilla. Next came Skudahkharis, one of the staple dishes of Somalia, consisting of lamb and rice and superbly spiced. It was accompanied by *maharagwe,* spiced red beans in coconut milk, and *fufu,* boiled yams from Ghana.

It was a delicious and unique meal and when Yaruba Da rejoined me, I told him so.

"I am very pleased that you enjoyed it," he murmured. "And now, if I may ask—what is the situation with the Ko Feng?"

"First, I must thank you for coming to our rescue at the sale," I said.

"It was nothing."

"It was very timely."

"My size is often an embarrassment," he said with a smile. "But there are times when it is very helpful. That was one of those times."

He eyed me for a moment. "I heard of that sale and was intrigued," he said. "It was an interesting experience. I don't know who the organizers were but they have an unscrupulous approach. I am sure that many of the goods on sale were stolen property."

"Yes, I'm sure they were."

"It was logical, therefore, that you should think it possible that Ko Feng might be there too."

"After seeing the place, I doubted it," I said. "Ko Feng can demand a very high price and it would have no place alongside cans of stolen ham. Still, it was worth a try."

"And it was feasible that the same people running the sale might also be the people who had stolen the Ko Feng," he said thoughtfully.

"Possible," I agreed. Then I added, "Have you been offered any Ko Feng?"

"Just before it was stolen, I had a talk with a man who hinted he might be able to get me some. But then I saw him at the sale and asked him again. He told me he was no longer in a position to do so."

"You saw him at the sale?"

"Yes."

It was a long shot but I had little to lose. "Was it Tom Eck?"

He inclined his head. "You know him?"

"A little." I was thinking it might not mean a thing. As a broker, Eck might have been hopeful of marketing some Ko Feng before but now, since the theft, he was no longer able to do so.

"If you do recover it, I would very much like to obtain some," he told me earnestly. "It could be instrumental in improving my business here, which, as you see, is in need of it."

"If I'm in a position to help you, I will," I told him. "A word of advice however . . ."

He leaned forward expectantly. "Yes?"

"You may hear of Ko Feng being offered, or it may be offered to you directly. Be very careful. Substitute material—not

Ko Feng—is out on the market. I wouldn't want you to be deceived."

"How could I be sure it was genuine?" he asked seriously. "Perhaps you could assist me in deciding?"

"I'd be glad to."

He insisted I try some Liberian gingerbread, made from plantains, and it was excellent. He watched me eat it, seemingly deep in thought. He raised his head as if he had made a decision and his large black face confronted me.

"I appreciate your offer to help," he said in his deep, resonant voice. "And as a token of my goodwill, allow me to tell you that you need not be concerned about any more attacks."

I wasn't expecting that at all. I stared at him, astonished.

"You were responsible for those?"

"No, of course not," he said with an emphatic shake of his head. "But I was aware of them."

"And who was responsible?" I asked angrily.

"You need not worry. There will be no more of them— and you were never in any danger," he added hastily. "There was never any intention of harming you—only frightening you. A small group thought you had been implicated in the theft of the Ko Feng and wanted to scare you into selling it to them."

"You have nice friends," I said bitterly.

"Not friends, merely business acquaintances." He seemed relieved that he had got his confession off his chest. I pushed for one more admission.

"Other restaurant owners, you mean."

He shrugged. It was agreement enough and it cleared the air a lot. A few of the hotheads, probably inflamed by Lennie Rifkin, had decided to put a scare into me. They'd hired someone—or had they? Rifkin . . . The more I thought of that phony accent and the bizarre get-up with the black clothes and the beard, the more it sounded like his style. He didn't like me anyway and probably enjoyed playing the part.

Yaruba Da ordered mint tea.

"No African meal can end without it," he told me.

"Why do you say there will be no more attempts?" I asked. "How do you know that?"

"One or two others and I objected to such terrorist tactics. Not all Africans are barbarians."

The tea came and we sipped it amicably. The drumbeat melody faded away and after a moment of jungle silence, there was the hideous howling of jackals. I was reminded of Lennie Rifkin again . . .

CHAPTER THIRTY-FIVE

Gabriella had phoned me while I was still at breakfast to say that she was picking me up. She was driving a dark blue Isuzu four-door sedan this time—a definite step up from the battered jalopy of our earlier adventure. She looked delightful in a crisp light brown suit with cream-colored buttons. I congratulated her on her new disguise and she gave me a shriveling look.

"The girl of a thousand—well, not faces exactly . . ." I said.

"It's not hazardous duty today."

"That means you're not packing?"

"We say 'carrying' these days. Oh yes, I have my protection with me."

"It's as well hidden as it was when we went to church."

"It's here this time." She tapped a raffia bag that lay on the seat between us.

"You didn't carry one at all the other day. A bag, I mean."

"In that area there's a risk of bag-snatching. Didn't want to chance that."

"So today's a no-risk day? Good. Where are we going?"

"We're going to see an old friend of my father's."

"A *paesano?*"

"Yes."

"He knows something?"

"He knows a lot—a lot of very surprising information."

"You're not going to tell me, are you?"

She laughed that delightfully intimate laugh. "You'll see. We'll be there in a few minutes."

Even though it was past the morning commuter hours, it was still rush hour as far as the traffic was concerned. It seemed like it was always rush hour in Manhattan. We went south down Columbus Avenue, which turned into Ninth, past all sorts of restaurants, bars and shops, then we turned west on Forty-third Street. There was a fire station, a used-car dealer, and Gabriella pulled into a metered parking place almost in front of a theater.

"Too early for a matinee, isn't it?" I asked but she gave me an enigmatic smile.

Large free-standing letters proclaimed THE MAGIC MUSIC HALL and there were posters on both sides of the entrance. One showed a man, resplendent in a scarlet Chinese robe and a long black pigtail. A globe behind him was crowned with frothy clouds and silvery flashes of lightning darted past him. Another showed a girl in tights inside a glass cage which was suspended above an audience. They were all staring up in amazement as a man in an elegant tuxedo and top hat fired a pistol at the cage. THE WONDER SHOW OF THE UNIVERSE said the poster in an utter abandonment of modesty.

"You're sure we're in the right place?"

"I'm sure," Gabriella said and led the way to a side door beyond the main entrance. She pressed a bell and a wizened old man opened the door.

"Monty's expecting us."

The old man nodded and opened the door. We went in.

The narrow passage had been recently repainted, though the floor still had some ancient linoleum and boards that creaked as we walked. The old man was sprightly despite his years and led us at a brisk pace down to the end and through a lounge, also recently decorated. We went through double swinging doors and a heavy curtain and into the theater.

It's a shame that television and the cinema have dimmed the appeal of the live theater. There is no greater thrill in entertainment than seeing live actors on the stage. This building had obviously been popular as a theater fifty and more years ago and I wondered what great names had paraded across that now dark and curtained stage.

"Vivien Leigh was in *A Streetcar Named Desire* here," said a croaky voice. "Olsen and Johnson ran nearly a year with *Hellzapoppin*. Helen Hayes was in *Mary of Scotland* on that stage. Orson Welles, Katherine Cornell, Paul Robeson, Lunt and Fontanne—they all played here."

While he was speaking, we had turned to find a dumpy little man behind us. Gabriella gave him a big hug and he laughed with delight and lifted her off the ground. He had a round pudding face, crinkled and seamed, and his faded gray eyes had clearly seen a lot of tragedy. It was a happy face, though, and its owner obviously enjoyed life even while it buffeted him.

"This is Monty" said Gabriella as she introduced us. "Christened Bernardo Montefalcone but no one except his mother has ever called him anything but Monty."

"You like the theater, eh? I can tell from the way you look at the stage." He had a very definite Italian accent.

"Love it," I told him. "I live in London where I have plenty of opportunities to see good theater."

"London!" His face lit up. "Hey, I spent five years there. We had this show that . . ."

He was an irrepressible raconteur and had known theater people all over the world. Loud noises from backstage interrupted him after Gabriella had made one unsuccessful attempt.

"Listen!" he said to us. "I just gotta check through this one act, then we can talk. Come and siddown and watch." He led us down the center aisle and installed us in the second row, then slipped out though a nearby exit. The footlights came on and then that most emotional of moments in the theater when the curtains parted.

Music filled the auditorium. It had an insistent drumbeat that had a familiar ring. There was a clattering of hoofbeats and a horse and rider came prancing onto the front of the stage. The rider was an Indian chief in full regalia, a splendid war bonnet on his head, a quiver of arrows on his back and a bow in his hand. They made a spectacular tableau against the black velvet drapery. The familiarity of the music was now clear—it was the music heard in a hundred Western movies.

The horse was a magnificent palomino with a mane of flowing silvery hair. The saddle was studded with silver and the horse had silver bands around its ankles. It stepped high, throwing up its head. We were so close that we could plainly see the whites of its glittering eyes.

Center stage was an inclined ramp, climbing six feet to a large horizontal platform supported by two trestles. The rider urged his mount up the ramp and onto the platform where the horse stopped, quite composed. Stagehands ran on and carried away the ramp.

Horse and rider stood there and the music switched tempo, more mysterious now but still with that throbbing beat.

From above, a curtain pole descended, supported by a chain at either end. It stopped above and in front of the Indian chief and his horse. He reached up and pulled down a bright blue shade from the roller on the curtain pole. Both horse and rider were now hidden from view.

Indian war whoops sounded. The music faded, then a slow drumroll started. The curtain pole rose taking the blue shade with it. Gabriella gave a gasp of astonishment. Horse and rider had disappeared. The platform was empty.

The stage curtains closed. Gabriella and I clapped as enthusiastically as school kids.

"That's impossible!" Gabriella gasped.

"They couldn't have gone down," I said. "Only those trestles support the platform. They couldn't have got off the platform in any direction—it's too high. How on earth did he do it?"

"Absolutely impossible," came Monty's voice from behind us. He chuckled.

"Monty," Gabriella demanded. "Tell us how you did it."

"Illusion." He was still grinning with satisfaction. "It went real well. We've been practicing all week. I'd like to knock two more seconds off, though; then it's okay."

"No, come on, Monty, we have to know," Gabriella coaxed.

He settled into a seat behind us. "No. Let's talk about your problem. The way you outlined it over the phone—"

"Monty, I'll never speak to you again if you don't tell us." Gabriella was firm.

"Suddenly, I realize why we're here," I said to her.

"You didn't know?" Monty laughed. "Hey, Gaby, you didn't tell him why you brought him here but you want me to tell you the secret of the Vanishing Indian!" He laughed again.

"And don't call me Gaby! You know I hate it." She turned to me. "It was that remark you made about Houdini. Well, it started me thinking. Monty knows as much about magic as Houdini did—"

"Except he was a better showman," Monty said.

"Monty has devised tricks for all the greats," Gabriella continued. "Maskelyne, Blackstone, Flip Hallema, David Copperfield—all of them."

"Blackstone," Monty said. "We might start with him when we look at your problem. He did the Vanishing Automobile, the Vanishing Horse—that's the one you just saw"—he broke into a reminiscent laugh—"and the Vanishing Camel—now that was a show and a half. That camel never did want to work as part of the team. It hated show business. It gave us the hardest time every performance. Then it died—on stage already!"

"So I thought, Why don't we get Monty to tell us how *he* would do it? Maybe the thief used the same technique—or something like it."

"Sure," said Monty.

"But first," Gabriella said sternly. "The trick we just saw. How did you do it?"

"Promise not to tell?" His pudgy face was jovial. He was a man who got a lot of enjoyment out of life and people.

"Yes," Gabriella said promptly.

"Lighting. The stage seems brightly lit but all the illumination comes from the front and the footlights. All the overhead lights are turned off and you'll notice that the entire stage is curtained with black velvet. Between the two chains that hold up the pole and the blue shade is another black velvet curtain. It's invisible to the audience and they can't distinguish it from the curtains behind. As soon as the shade comes down, hiding the horse and rider, a harness drops down and the two of them are hoisted up."

Gabriella gave a hiss of annoyance. "It's so simple."

"All stage illusions are," Monty said. "The simpler the better. You know Siegfried and Roy?" Gabriella did but I didn't. "Well, they're German but they've made their name over here—Las Vegas mainly, where they've made seven-hundred-pound Bengal tigers disappear right there in the MGM Grand Hotel."

"They've done tricks with lions and black panthers too, haven't they?" Gabriella asked.

"They sure have. They did it with a cheetah too once—it was a benefit performance before Princess Grace and Prince Rainier. They made it disappear. Then, when it reappeared, it got away and strolled through the audience."

"Well, we don't have animals in the illusion we're facing," Gabriella said. "Just people."

"Let's go talk about this," Monty said, and led the way backstage where we went into an empty dressing room. He pulled up chairs.

"Now," he said, "tell me about it."

I ran through the story from our arrival at JFK. I included

as much detail as I could recall. He asked an occasional question, then when I had finished, Gabriella gave him a brief rundown on the activities of the police.

Monty leaned back in his chair. "A nice trick—if you can do it. And somebody did."

He asked more questions. Finally, he looked at Gabriella. "Need to look at the scene of the crime, kiddo."

CHAPTER THIRTY-SIX

Gabriella's expert driving got us to JFK airport in barely an hour. The journey was lightened by Monty's reminiscences of his life creating magic and mystery. He told us some of the secrets of Kreskin, the mentalist—"not a hypnotist," Monty said firmly; of Doug Henning and his Magic Boxes, which contain four different parts of his female assistant; of Johnny Thompson, "the Great Tomsoni" and his tricks with doves and bowling balls; and of the great Channing Pollock and Jimmy Grippo, "the magician's magician."

It was Karl Eberhard's day off but Gabriella said it didn't matter, we only wanted to spend some time in the hangar where the Ko Feng was brought in. Eberhard's deputy handed over keys and directed us. Gabriella drove the Isuzu through the maze of buildings until we came to hangar BLS 12.

The smell of burning jet fuel, typical of modern airports, hung heavy in the air. Aircraft were taking off and landing but there was no activity in the area around our hangar. Gabriella unlocked the side door and we walked in.

The hangar was empty and it looked bleak and cheerless. Monty studied the interior carefully, saying nothing. Finally, he turned to me.

"Okay, from the beginning. From the time you came in here, tell me exactly what happened."

I went through it, step by step. At the end, Monty pointed to the bays.

"Which one were you in?"

"This one." I led him into it. Monty was looking everywhere, his eyes never still. Gabriella followed, silent.

"So you were in the second one from the left. And the others?"

"Sushimoto Electronics were in the first one, on that side of us. The next one—the one on the other side—was empty except for a big black limo."

"What about the other shipment that came in?"

Gabriella was flipping through her notebook. "That was the Chicago Museum of Oriental Art, right?"

"That's right. They took the fourth bay."

"So you parked your truck just outside the bay?" asked Monty.

"Right."

"Where exactly?"

I showed him.

"Oh . . . a few feet."

"There was never anyone in that third bay?"

"No."

"Okay," shrugged Monty. "Now, the tables in here all had this lab equipment on them right?"

"Yes, all of them."

"And where were you all standing?" I thought carefully then showed him.

"The equipment—where did it come from?"

"Rented for the day," said Gabriella.

"By—"

"Renshaw listed what he needed, Cartwright ordered it."

"Now, what was the timing?" Monty asked, and as near as I could remember I ran through the sequence of the testing.

"Where was the sack all this time?"

"Sitting here." I pointed.

"And when you'd finished?"

"Cartwright tied up the sack and took it out to the truck, put it in the chest, locked everything up."

Monty looked at Gabriella. "You checked the chest, of course."

"I know what you're thinking," she said. "But no, it was the same one. There was no switch."

"Okay," said Monty, turning back to me. "All the time you were here, did anyone come over from the next bay?"

"Their customs man came over to ask our man a question. He answered him right away and he went back."

"The Chicago Museum people . . . Have any contact with them?"

"None at all."

Monty nodded again. He walked in circles, looking, musing and asking a few more questions. Gabriella and I answered them and finally Monty snapped his fingers.

"Got it?" asked Gabriella in surprise.

"Nearly got it," said Monty. "I've gotta get back and rehearse an escape from a tank full of water. I can give you what I've got right now. Purely an opinion, of course, you can take it or leave it—and I wanna make one thing plain. I'm telling you what I think from an illusionist's point of view. Beyond that is up to you."

"Go ahead," said Gabriella.

"The most likely scenario is that one of these three guys did it," he told Gabriella but he looked directly at me. "Either you—or this Renshaw—or that Cartwright guy."

"Now, wait a minute—" I began hotly.

"Hold on," said Gabriella. She could be very authoritative when she chose. "Let Monty finish."

"Finish nothing!" I said furiously. "He's named three suspects and one of them is dead! I'm the third one—what does that suggest?"

"Let. Him. Finish!" rapped Gabriella. "Go on, Monty."

"From what you've told me, it must be Cartwright," Monty said, giving me a placatory grin, "and he had an accomplice."

"Cartwright!" I echoed, astonished. "Why would he steal his own merchandise?"

"Hey, come on," Monty said with a grin. "Didn't I say anything beyond the illusion is the problem of Miss Gaby here?"

She gave him a withering look but all she said was, "Keep going, Monty."

"Okay, here's the way I see it. This guy Cartwright wraps up the sack after he's done with all that testing stuff. He puts it on the barrow and takes it back out to the truck. He locks it up. Then—unseen by you other guys—he hides the keys outside in an agreed place. The accomplice is hiding in the vehicle which is only a few feet away from the truck. He gets the keys, removes the sack and puts the keys back. He gets back into the other vehicle."

He paused, watching us.

"Wasn't he taking a chance on being seen?" Gabriella asked.

"Sure," said Monty, "so he needed a diversion."

"The timer bell that went off . . ." I said.

"Right—it was also a signal to the accomplice to go into action."

Gabriella turned to me. "And then there were some wrong numbers on a form, you said. Did everybody get involved in that?"

"They did, you're right," I said. "When Simpson said, 'This is wrong,' we all crowded around. That would have given a person in the vehicle time to get the sack of Ko Feng, transfer it, return the keys and get back."

"I checked on the vehicle in the next bay," Gabriella said slowly. "The limo—it had been there for some time. Nobody knew if it still ran."

"It just looked like a big black car to me," I said. "I didn't pay it that much attention."

"Bet you a dollar to a doughnut that vehicle was out of here as soon as you guys left in the truck," said Monty.

Gabriella picked up a phone from one of the benches.

"Security?" She identified herself. "A vehicle was here in hangar BLS 12 the day the Ko Feng arrived. Would you check your traffic log? I want to know what time it went out." She waited a couple of minutes. "Okay, thanks."

When she hung up, she read off the time. "Twenty minutes difference. The limo left just twenty minutes after you left."

She picked up the phone again. "DMV? I want to trace a vehicle . . ." She gave her identification and listened. She hung up with an irritated sigh. "The license is a phony."

"I wonder who made all the arrangements for this," I said speculatively, waving a hand to the contents of the bay. She picked up the phone again and when she put it down, she said, "Cartwright. He was out here twice, making sure everything was arranged and picking a place to leave the keys."

"And probably putting chalk marks on the floor so he could put the truck just where the space between the limo and the truck couldn't be seen from where you guys were standing," said Monty. "Another thing—who prepared the documents that had had the wrong numbers on them?"

"They were the receiving documents," I said. "Must have been Cartwright. And," I added, "he had had goods come in through Simpson before. He would have known what a stickler for details he was. He could have been sure that Simpson would spot the errors right away."

"You done good," said Gabriella. "Thanks, Monty."

"Any time," he grinned. "Well, that's to say any time after I make sure that I can get this guy out of the sealed tank of water every performance. I keep telling him four out of five is pretty good for an act this tricky but he won't go along with that. Wants to keep practicing."

We went back into the maelstrom of New York traffic and dropped Monty at his theater. It was just past noon.

"I can see that lunch look in your eye," said Gabriella.

"Something simple?" I suggested.

"And quick."

"Any ideas?"

We went to a tapas bar, which Gabriella told me had become a recent craze in New York. The deliciously tempting little appetizer dishes that are such a tradition in Spain had now caught on here and were ideally suited to the fast food market. We had marinated mushrooms, stuffed mussels and vegetable croquettes. One small dish of each between us was satisfying without being too filling, though we had to pass on the huge triple-decker sandwiches that any tapas bar in Bilbao serves as well as the batter-fried shrimp of Gijón and the savory chorizo pies of Galicia. The Vina Sol from Penedés was the only white wine from Spain on the list, the remainder being Californian but its dry, lemony character went well and a glass each was marginally enough for a quick meal.

"Sorry I blew up back there," I said.

Gabriella smiled. "It would have been suspicious if you hadn't. Now, if Monty is right, that's the way the theft was pulled off."

"Which means that only Cartwright could have done it. I must admit that I have been thinking of him as owner of the Ko Feng and therefore not likely to be stealing it. But, of course, he isn't the owner—Marvell is."

"This fits in with what we heard from Selim Osman."

"Right. It means that Marvell was planning on selling the Ko Feng to the restaurant people. Cartwright realized that there was a far wealthier market out there which would pay much more—the research people who want it for life extension, better health and fitness and"—I was thinking of Gloria Branson—"other advantages."

"That's why the Ko Feng hasn't shown up for sale yet. The research people are naturally reluctant to buy a stolen property—not for reasons of scruples but because they are suspicious of who has it and they want to be sure it can be assured of being genuine."

"And the accomplice?" I asked Gabriella.

"Well, we're a step closer to that person—whoever it is."

"In the meantime, you can interrogate Cartwright, knowing that he is almost certainly guilty." I stopped myself just in time—I was about to add that I was sure now that Cartwright had been the one who had tried to eliminate me in the Marvell laboratories but I remembered I had not shared that incident with Gabriella. I went on quickly. "Gives you an advantage, doesn't it?"

"It certainly does."

"And as for Don Renshaw's murder, evidently Don remembered the earlier theft of the birds' nests and in some way tied it to Cartwright."

Gabriella nodded. "We'll be able to confirm that too. Well, that's eliminated a number of blind alleys."

"Coming back to the people who want to buy the Ko Feng," I said. "As I told you on the phone, I've spread the story that phony Ko Feng is being offered and hopefully given the impression that the only way any buyer can be sure of getting the real thing is to have me authenticate it for them."

"Hm," she said, spearing a remaining solitary mussel, "I've been thinking about that. You're making quite a target out of yourself, aren't you?'

"Just doing my best to contribute," I said modestly.

"Just don't contribute a third corpse," she said, looking in vain over the table for something else to eat.

I told myself it was New York humor and that she really was concerned about me.

CHAPTER THIRTY-SEVEN

Gabriella dropped me off at the hotel, but this time no one was clamoring for me. I was pondering my next move when the phone rang. It was Peggy. She spoke fast and her voice was high pitched and excited.

"That woman—the one you saw here—you know, the one you described to us? Well, she just came in! Maisie saw her too and she agrees it's the same one. What should I do?"

"Keep her talking, don't let her get away," I said urgently. "I'll be there as fast as I can."

"What if she wants to leave?" wailed Peggy. "How can I stop her?"

"Lock the doors, say you've lost the key, tell her it's an emergency—do anything you have to do but keep her there!"

One of the desk clerks had told me that on the corner of the block was a suite of doctors' offices which had a steady flow of taxis. It was the best place to catch one, he said, and he was right. I got one almost immediately and I was lucky enough to have a driver who was incredibly not only American but a New Yorker. After congratulating him on being the only one of his kind, I offered him an extra twenty dollars if he got me to the Spice Warehouse fast.

He narrowly avoided losing paint at least three times and left a trail of curses, shaken fists, screeching brakes and terrified pedestrians but he earned his twenty and I dashed into the Spice Warehouse. The door wasn't locked, several customers were there and I couldn't see any signs of struggle or commotion.

Maisie came hurrying toward me.

"She's in the office with Peggy."

"Well done," I congratulated her. "Did you have to tie her to a chair?"

"Oh no, she's quite nice, really."

"Nice! We'll see how nice she is."

I stormed across to the office. Peggy and the woman were drinking from cups that wafted an aroma of chamomile. They sat in the small office that held such unpleasant memories but I was pleased to see that Peggy was adjusting so well.

"Like a cup of herb tea?" she asked.

"In a minute. First, I want to ask this woman a few questions."

I glared at her. She was wearing a neat business suit in dark blue and looked cool and attractive.

"Remember our last conversation?" I asked. "It was here, a few days ago. We talked about ginger."

She nodded, bright and friendly. "Yes, of course."

"You have some explaining to do," I said hotly.

"It's all right," Peggy said. "She's been telling me about herself."

I looked at her. The brown eyes, the firm chin and the straight nose made her face just as pretty as I remembered it. Ignore her looks, I told myself—interrogate her.

"You were with me . . . that day," I said, not wanting to refer to it in front of Peggy as "the day of the murder."

"Yes, but I left if you remember."

"You left *me* but I don't know where—"

"She's told me all about it," Peggy said.

"Please, Peggy, let me do this."

Peggy drank some tea and nodded. She really was being very placid about it all; perhaps it was the tea. The woman turned to me.

"I left here immediately after I left you. I told you I had another appointment that I couldn't break. I had to go. I didn't know anything about Mr. Renshaw's"—she looked apologetically at Peggy—"well, death, until later."

"But you were there just before!" I told her. "Why didn't you come forward and tell the police that?"

She stared in astonishment. "I did."

I returned her astonishment. "You did?"

"Of course. I went to my other appointment and finished the day in the office. It wasn't till evening when I turned on the news. I could hardly believe it but I called the police and told them all I knew."

"Didn't you know you were my alibi?"

"I wasn't," she said resolutely. "How could I be? I had already left."

"I was a prime suspect—still am to some extent."

"Ah, yes," she said. "The Ko Feng. I guessed you must be the Englishman who was brought over for the authentication."

"She knows more about this than you think," Peggy told me.

"I don't doubt it," I said, regarding her sternly.

"She can explain all that," Peggy said.

"Peggy, please! I don't mean just what's on the television news and in the papers. She also turns up in a lot of places where things are happening."

"If you'd just let me tell you," the woman said in an exasperated tone. "About the Ko Feng, about the Marvell Corporation . . ."

My suspicions returned. She might look delectable but she wasn't off my "doubtful" list yet.

"You know a lot about it."

"Yes, I believe I do," she said coolly.

"How much do you know about the Marvell laboratories in Leonia?"

"I go there from time to time."

I goggled at her. "When were you there last?"

"Oh, several days ago," she said cheerfully. She scrutinized me and some kind of memory dawned. "That surely wasn't you there that day . . . pulling those funny faces . . . pretending to be trapped in the environmental lab . . ."

She looked like she was about to laugh but my face must have resembled the proverbial thunder and she managed to control herself.

"I thought I saw you down the corridor but I told myself it couldn't be. Then there was the pandemonium when the alarms went off . . . That wasn't really you in there, was it?"

She had a sudden attack of coughing but she mastered it and had to dab away a few tears.

"You turn up in a lot of places, don't you?"

I wasn't done with her yet. She couldn't laugh at me and get away with it.

"Why were you at the sale in the church?"

She looked puzzled. "Church? I don't know what—"

"The food sale—stolen, dangerous, dubious food and drink of all kinds—absinthe, duck's tongues, mammoths . . . Isn't that enough to identify which sale? I mean, how many sales like that do you go to?"

She smiled. It was a sunny smile and she tilted her head to one side in the same charming gesture I recollected.

"I go to all sales like that," she said.

"Why?" I asked darkly.

She opened a small clasp bag with a silvery mesh material over it and handed me a card. It read KAY GRENVILLE and underneath the name was NEW ENGLAND ASSURANCE COMPANY.

"So that's how you knew about the Ko Feng," I said weakly.

"Of course. We insured it."

"So-o-o-you're not a mystery woman at all." I was voicing my thoughts.

"I'm not? What a shame!"

"Wait a minute," I said suddenly. "You insured that shipment of birds' nests five years ago, didn't you?"

She regarded me sharply. "You noticed the similarity too, did you?"

"Don Renshaw noticed it. That was probably what got him killed."

"Yes, Lieutenant Gaines asked me about that. We didn't have anything to add, unfortunately."

Another thought occurred to me. "You went to the sale with Tom Eck, didn't you?"

She shook her head firmly. "No. I ran into him there. I've known him for some time."

"I can understand why you'd want to be there—you must pick up some useful tips on stolen items. But why does Eck go to sales like that?"

"He puts up the financing for purchases of food products. I see him occasionally at various events. He likes to keep in touch with customers, actual and potential, as well as keep contact with the market."

"Even the black market?"

"Yes. It's not too surprising. You'd be staggered at some of the people I see at those sales."

I nodded. I was recalling that Eck had told me he had been approached by restaurant owners wanting financing from him to buy Ko Feng from Marvell.

"Something else you can tell me," I said. "What's the situation regarding the policy that Marvell has with you on the Ko Feng?"

"Funny you should ask . . ." Those calm brown eyes were examining me contemplatively.

Peggy poured more tea and looked at me inquiringly. I nodded. It seemed to have had a calming effect on the two of them so I might as well join in, although Kay's role now made more sense.

"Funny how?" I reminded her.

"Marvell filed his claim today."

"Did he! Now that's interesting."

"You know," she went on and her voice was speculative, "I avoided any contact with you after the murder—after all, I didn't know you and a few minutes' conversation about ginger is hardly a basis for forming any judgment about a person. Then during a recent exchange of information with Hal Gaines, he said that Scotland Yard had given you a clean bill—"

"So now you feel it's safe to talk to me," I said tartly.

It didn't upset her a bit. "You're no longer a prime suspect and Hal Gaines is giving you enough leash that you can do a little investigating. So, I see no reason why I shouldn't tell you about Marvell and his policy."

"How much is the policy worth?"

She smiled candidly.

" 'Tell you about it,' I said—that doesn't mean I'm going to tell you how much it is."

"So what can you tell me?" I asked. "For instance, are you going to pay off?"

"Our immediate reaction is no. It's too soon."

"It's reaching the police limit. Another two days and it'll be dropped from the active file. That means they'll no longer have any faith in the Ko Feng being recovered."

"True."

"And what's your policy?"

"We don't have one for shipments of this nature. We judge each one on its own merits."

"You know, you can be very irritating," I told her. "You say there's no reason why you shouldn't tell me about Marvell and his policy and then you proceed to tell me nothing."

"What else do you want to know?" she said, smiling sweetly.

"You're judging Marvell's case on its merits, you said. Okay, what are its merits?"

"We don't intend to pay off right now. We're going to give it longer than ten days. How many days? There's no decision on that yet. We'll see what comes to light in the next week or two then look at the case all over again."

"Won't Marvell be yelling for a settlement all that time?"

She shrugged. "Probably."

"Your card doesn't say what you do. Are you an investigator?"

"I do some investigating. We have other investigators too—some of them are working on this case."

"Any promising leads?"

"Nothing that the police don't know about. Naturally, some aspects might get more attention from us than the NYPD might give to them. Our interest is primarily to establish what happened to the Ko Feng—theirs is to solve a murder."

"I'm at the Framingham Hotel," I told her. "Can we keep in touch?"

"Of course." A thought occurred to her. "You're coming to the All-Charities Buffet, aren't you?"

"Haven't heard about it, but it sounds like a function I ought not to miss."

"It's run by the food and restaurant trade and they hold it at the Park Avenue Towers. It's an annual affair and it's tomorrow. Everybody comes."

"Thanks," I said. "I'll be there."

"I'll arrange for a ticket at the door for you—be there about noon."

There was a tap at the door and Maisie entered. "Sorry," she said. "I need the duplicate register for the storage rooms."

"Right there." Peggy pointed to a shelf.

"So it is," said Maisie with a sigh. "Just where it should be."

She lifted it down. "Things never are in the most obvious place, are they?"

She went out. Kay was about to say something when she caught the exchange of looks between Peggy and me.

"The most obvious place . . ." I breathed. "Do you suppose that's what Don meant—?"

"What is it?" Kay wanted to know and Peggy told her of Don's last words.

"Where is the most obvious place to hide the Ko Feng?" I asked, excited. "In a spice warehouse! Anything that valuable should be in a controlled atmosphere, carefully monitored temperature, protected from—"

Peggy jumped up and pulled the door open, calling after Maisie to come back. She reentered, looking puzzled. Peggy pointed a finger at the register.

"What new shipments have been brought into the storage rooms since the Ko Feng was stolen?" Peggy asked quickly.

Maisie flipped the pages. "Three that same afternoon," she murmured. We all looked at one another.

"The thief would have wanted to get the Ko Feng into a safe place as quickly as possible," I said. "He could have got it over here right away."

Peggy turned the register to see the names.

"Bloomington Food Specialties, they're a regular customer, have been for years. Who else? Indonesian Spices and Flavors . . . That's their shipment of crocus leaves."

"Crocus?" asked Kay.

"It's one of their secret ingredients, but they come in all the time."

"So who's the third?" Kay asked.

"Manhattan Supply Company," Peggy read out. "Who are they, Maisie?"

"Never heard of them," Maisie said promptly.

"What's their storage number?"

All four of us hurried out of the office and through the aisles of the warehouse. Maisie led the way into the adjacent storage area with its maze of wall and ceiling pipes that controlled the separate environments. Neon strip lights glittered off the shiny white walls and it was chilly and dry. Maisie went to get the storage man.

He was introduced to us as Harry, but it had once been something quite different judging by his Eskimo looks. He seemed very much at home in the cool atmosphere as he looked at the ledger number. He took out a bunch of keys and led us to a large storage locker with a door about seven feet tall.

He opened it and swung the door open.

Maisie squealed. Harry recoiled, gasping something unintelligible. Kay and Peggy stood in horror.

We all looked at the body of a man in a light suit, slumped on the floor. His face was turned toward us and though it was ashen in death, it was instantly recognizable as that of Willard Cartwright.

CHAPTER THIRTY-EIGHT

It was a very long day. The police station where we now found ourselves was not the kind of place anyone would want to spend five minutes even as a witness. Even the most unflattering of television series showing cops in their natural habitat was not sufficient preparation for the harsh reality. I shuddered to think how much worse it would have been had I not had four other witnesses present when the body of Willard Cartwright was found.

As it was, Lieutenant Gaines was decidedly not cordial. He scowled and sneered and looked threatening but at least the King's Balm was working. He didn't chew his lip, his face muscles didn't twitch and he didn't once reach for antacid tablets. I was glad it was an interview and not an interrogation, though it could probably fool some people.

Gaines had arrived at the Spice Warehouse quickly, siren screaming. The place had been sealed off and after taking depositions from all the customers and the other staff, it had been closed for the day and the five of us taken to the station.

"You already have mine," I said when we were told we were being taken to be fingerprinted.

"Yeah, from the last murder," said Gaines sarcastically.

I didn't see any of the others from then on. I told Gaines exactly what had happened. He was rough and edgy but I felt he was entitled.

"Two murders in the same place and you're there both times," he grunted.

"Was Cartwright killed the same way?" I asked, expecting him to snarl but he nodded.

"Seven-millimeter bullet wound and looks like the same weapon."

"Had he been dead long?"

"Death occurred late the previous afternoon. Oh, and there is no Manhattan Supply Company."

He gave me his piercing look. "So . . . we no sooner get a firm line on our man than you find him murdered."

"There are better ways of phrasing it," I said, "but that's what happened."

He continued with his questioning, using that same gritty voice, and I did my best with the answers. He called in a young Hispanic woman, who took me into a cheerless room where I read a magazine interview with the "current" president, George Bush. She came back and took me into a lab where my hands were tested under ultraviolet light, presumably for stains indicating that I had fired a gun recently. I was given a cup of vile coffee and taken back to the room with the magazine, then into an office where Gabriella sat.

"So how was your day?" she asked sardonically.

"Don't ask."

She nodded and there was a trace of sympathy. "Any idea what Cartwright was doing there in the Spice Warehouse?"

"No," I said. "I was astounded to find him there."

She leaned back. "We were still trying to locate him when we got your call. So now it's a double murder case. The pressure's really on and even Hal Gaines agrees that the Ko Feng is the key to both murders."

"I don't see how there can be any doubt about that."

"Hal doesn't either—not really. It's just the idea of a spice that's worth more than a million dollars—he has trouble with that."

"But you're the Unusual Crimes Unit. You must have had a lot weirder cases than this."

"Sure," she agreed readily. "But they didn't involve food."

"You mean if someone murdered the Kentucky Colonel, he'd be right on the case?"

"Fried chicken, he can understand. A million-dollar spice—no way."

"So what's our next move, Sergeant?"

She smiled at my eager question. "You'll see. Now if you'll sign this, you are free to go."

A shower, a couple of hours of mind-numbing television and some heavy reflecting brought me to thoughts of dinner. I decided to go to a sidewalk cafe on nearby Seventy-fifth Street that I had noticed a couple of times in passing. With a name like the Right Bank, it was clearly aiming at a French ambiance but doing it with a sense of humor that avoided pretension.

It had only a fleeting—even hypersonic—resemblance to a Parisian establishment but the management was trying. The tiny tables were crowded close and the steel-tube chairs belonged in a torture museum. An attempt had been made to render them tolerable with small cushions, which kept slipping off. I was lucky to get a table between four elderly matrons who were making unflattering comparisons with their native San Francisco and a German family grimly determined to enjoy it.

At a neighboring table, an unexpected breeze nearly lifted the umbrella into the air. "Hang on," someone called out, "or we'll do a Dorothy and find we're having lunch with the Wizard."

A boy in white plastic clothes with silver ornaments went by, on his shoulder a radio big enough to be heard in Canada. The reverberations crushed all conversation and provoked a barrage of glares. A truck passed, belching out black fumes. An old man waved his cane at it angrily and someone else commented, "Suddenly, my salmon's smoked!"

"I love sidewalk cafés," said one of the matrons from the city on the bay. "They're so French."

Despite the number of customers, the service was fast and I had just made my choice when the waiter came to take my order. I had decided to pass on the French items and have something typically American—something I could not get in London or at least not an authentic version.

But what is typically American? I didn't want a hamburger or a hot dog. Tacos, tamales and enchiladas were on the menu but they are basically Mexican even if they do taste better in America. Similarly, pizza is really Italian even if the American version is far superior. The fact is that American cuisine has taken in, adapted and in most cases surpassed the originals.

I decided that a charcoal-grilled steak came the nearest to what I was searching for. American steaks are the finest in the world although I knew that the unfortunate fact is that most steak houses—especially in New York—use gas-fired briquettes. The Right Bank however offered what they claimed to be real charcoal-broiled steaks in a good variety and I chose a six-ounce filet mignon. It came with a baked Idaho potato with sour cream and chives and, in true American style, no vegetables. A comparable restaurant in Paris would serve at least three vegetables with a steak but I was making no comparisons. Wine by the glass is a rare commodity in Europe but happily a commonplace in the U.S.A., so I ordered from the wine list a glass of Pinot Noir from Santa Cruz.

The waiters were determined not to set precedents for service. "No, we don't have cappuccino," snapped one. "Where do you think you are—Rome?"

When the steak came, it was tender and juicy. It was also done just the way I had ordered it—medium rare. No other country can satisfy a diner's order so accurately. The potato was a little mushy but the wine was rich and vibrant, if a year ahead of its time.

I paid the check and when the waiter returned with my change, with it was a note. I opened it, expecting perhaps some thanks from the management for patronizing them, but it said, "If you want to authenticate the Ko Feng, get into the taxi nearest you."

I looked up in astonishment but could see no one I recognized. Before the waiter could get away, I asked him where he had got the note. He shrugged. "I don't know—some guy."

A taxi stood there at the No Parking sign, engine running. The driver's face was pockmarked and Arab-featured. "Are you waiting for me?" I asked.

"Guess so," he said idly.

I hesitated.

"Gonna get in?" he said impatiently. "It's paid for."

I got in and he drove. No, he told me in response to my questions, he didn't notice who had given him the instructions—just the portrait on the banknote.

The journey was short. Our destination was on the northern edge of the theater district. We passed the Neil Simon Theater on Fifty-second Street, made a couple of turns on one-way streets and stopped in front of a restaurant with a brown-painted front, slightly weathered and chipped, white curtains at the windows and a simple sign, MARTHA'S. The driver jerked an uncaring thumb at it and left me standing there.

It was dark inside. Then I noticed the sign on the door— today was the day it was closed. I leaned on the handle in exasperation . . . and the door opened.

I went in. It was quiet and I was contemplating a strategic retreat, but *no* I told myself sternly. This is the chance I've been waiting for—a step toward recovering the Ko Feng. It had been neatly done so far, giving me no opportunity to phone for support.

The white tablecloths were ghostly shapes in the dim room but then I saw the reservation booth, a small high desk by the door with, of course, a phone behind. I moved to it and a spurt of light flashed across the room. A curtain at the back had been pulled and the silhouette of a figure stood there.

"You the guy that wants to taste this pasta?"

I had hardly expected the thief to show himself. In fact, I didn't know what to expect. The thief had a problem in concealing his identity but then the buyer had a similar problem. All I could do was go along with it.

The man's voice was deep. He came forward, leaving the curtain open behind him. I had a glimpse of several people sitting at a table. Surely it wasn't an open auction?

"Are you Martha?" I asked.

"Marty," he said, coming closer. "This is my place. Martha took off five years ago with one of the waiters." He motioned behind him. "Angie replaced her—in my bed as well as in the restaurant. Those are her folks. It's her birthday."

All these domestic details were confusing me but Marty seemed to be well drilled in what he was supposed to do.

"Siddown," he said, motioning to a table near the front. "The pasta's ready."

He went back through the curtain and returned with a Styrofoam container, carefully sealed with tape, in one hand and a glass of water in the other. He turned on lights overhead.

"There," he said. "That's what he told me to do. Said you'd open it."

I nodded. Voices were raised in the back room and Marty shook his head in despair. "That cousin of hers—she should have stood in Bosnia. Well, *bon appétit,* as they say." He rejoined the birthday party.

I used a knife to cut the tape and lever up the plastic lid. I held my breath as I lifted it. In the bottom of the container lay eight or nine small, blackish pieces.

I sniffed. My memory banks recalled for comparison the fragrances of that day at JFK—cloves then cinnamon but no, more like cardamom. "Anise," Don had said, "and a hint of orange . . ."

I turned the pieces over with a fork, examining their shape. I separated one and chopped it as finely as I could with the knife. I drank some water, waited then tasted the chopped fragments.

Laughter came from the back room in a sudden gust and strident voices argued. More laughter came. I drank some more water and sat for a while. I repeated the process, then put the cut pieces into the container and closed it.

I should know what my decision was, I told myself. I had had plenty of time to prepare it. After all, the choices were simple . . .

Should I declare the Ko Feng phony or genuine?

Should I tell the truth or lie?

Crockery rattled and cutlery clinked in the back as the meal gradually took priority over family disputes. I sat, thinking.

When the phone rang, it jangled every nerve in my body and sounded loud enough to be heard all over Manhattan Island. After the third ring, the curtain pulled open and Marty appeared.

"It's for you," he said.

"How do you know—" I began but he had already closed the curtain.

I went over and picked up the phone.

"Have you examined it?"

The words were measured and deliberate. The speaker was also using some means of disguising his voice—or her voice, for it was an indeterminate huskiness that could have been either. I knew there were easy ways of changing the sound of a voice over the phone.

"Yes."

"We must be absolutely sure what we're referring to. What is it supposed to be?"

"Who are you?" I asked.

"The buyer."

"It's supposed to be Ko Feng."

"All right. You have examined it. Is it really Ko Feng?"

I took a couple of breaths. "No, it isn't."

There was a silence. It was louder than any noise. "Repeat that."

"I said no, it isn't."

Another silence.

"You know what you are saying?" Despite whatever means were being used to disguise the voice, the emotion showed through.

"Yes."

I awaited the inevitable question: *Are you sure?* It didn't come. The voice said, "Your fee is with the container" and the line clicked dead.

Several queries about how the thief had made contact with Marty had passed through my mind and I had intended to ask them before I left but now it didn't seem like a good idea. My instinct was to get out fast.

I looked underneath the Styrofoam container. An opaque plastic envelope was attached. I opened it and found five one-hundred-dollar bills. I put them in my pocket, took the container and shouted to Marty, "Thanks for the service!"

His face appeared through the curtain. "Everything okay? Some kind of new pasta they're trying out, huh? Weird way to do it but hey, this is New York, right?"

"It is," I agreed. "It certainly is."

I departed quickly and walked along the block. The Ziegfeld Theater was on my right and Tom Hanks was appearing in *Hamlet,* but the theater was not uppermost in my mind. I was concerned now only with making sure I was not being watched or followed. At the intersection, I waved for a cab. When one slowed and pulled over in a unique example of lightning service, I stepped back and waved it on. Another came only seconds later and I took it as far as Lincoln Center where I alighted in the middle of the busiest traffic I could find and then took another cab back to the hotel.

I was just getting out of this one when I realized that most of the players in this bizarre game knew where I was staying anyway.

CHAPTER THIRTY-NINE

Here I was again in the home away from home of Lieutenant Gaines and Sergeant Rossini. This visit was more voluntary than the previous ones. I had called Gabriella to tell her of the incident at Martha's Restaurant, she had checked with Hal Gaines and they had agreed that I should come into the station.

It was a different room this time but only one degree less grim than before. The two detectives sat facing me. Gaines looked much better, no chewing, no twitching and no more stress lines than might be expected, considering the pressures of the case. Another triumph for King's Balm. Gabriella looked prim and official, making her even more comely than usual.

"No intonation, no spacing of phrases, nothing to give away the voice?" Gaines was still trying to learn more from my account of the phone call to the restaurant after I had tasted the sample in the box.

"Nothing that struck a chord," I insisted.

"Most people have characteristic bunching of words or ways of breaking up sentences," said Gabriella. "Think back."

"I've tried. I was too caught up in the situation at the time but I've reviewed it in my mind since and no, I just can't pinpoint anything identifiable."

A woman in uniform came in and handed Gaines a folder. He glanced at it, put it down and shook his head.

"We checked the call to the restaurant. It was made from a drugstore phone in midtown." He examined me keenly. "So you told this person that the stuff was phony?"

"Yes."

"And it wasn't?"

"No, it was the real thing right enough."

"You're absolutely—"

"Yes, absolutely sure."

"So we got ourselves two possibilities." He drummed stubby black fingers on the metal table and it hummed softly in response. "One is that the murderer is so monumentally pissed off at you that the only important thing is to knock you off and soon."

I looked from him to Gabriella. She shrugged.

"You screwed up the murderer's chance to sell the spice," she said. "What can you expect?"

"I don't think I like that possibility," I said. "What's the second? Am I going to like it any better?"

"The second," said Gaines, "is that the murderer is more concerned about the money."

"The million or two he can get for the spice," added Gabriella. "Which means that he will concentrate on selling it fast. The question is, will he use you as the authenticator after you've double-crossed him?"

"He or she," grunted Gaines.

"I do like the second possibility better," I admitted.

"But don't rule out a smoldering resentment against you," said Gabriella sweetly, "which may still exist. The person we're talking about has killed two people already and won't hesitate at a third. In fact," she added and quite unnecessarily, I thought, "his motive in your case might be the strongest of all."

Hal Gaines nodded agreement, squinting at me. "Yeah, you're still a vital pawn in the game."

"Hate being a pawn," I said, "but vital—that's not so bad."

"So whichever way our murderer goes, you're in danger."

"He or she might want to eliminate you before the sale of the Ko Feng, afterward—or even at the same time," Gabriella pointed out. I wished she wouldn't be so analytical.

The policewoman came in again with another folder. Through the open door, I could hear a voice being raised in what sounded like protest at police brutality. After what I had heard in the last few minutes, I was prepared to support a significant amount of it.

Gaines skimmed through the folder, nodded and the woman left.

"This charity clambake tomorrow," Gaines said. "Everybody who's anybody in the food business is gonna be there, looks like."

"Yes. I have an invitation and I wouldn't miss it for the world. Aside from that though, I really feel that in some way, the murderer is going to take advantage of it, use it as a screen. Why don't we encourage him? Get them to call it a Ko Feng affair."

Gabriella nodded and Gaines shrugged. "Yeah, we can do that," Gaines aid. "We already leaned on Marvell and New England Assurance to make no deals. That blocks off those two routes."

"And we'll be there too," Gabriella said brightly.

"Both of you?" I asked apprehensively.

"Yeah, undercover," said Gaines, less enthusiastic.

"We'll also have some of our people among the staff," Gabriella said.

"You're really giving me good protection, aren't you?"

"We don't want it to look that way," the Gaines said firmly. "We want you to look really vulnerable."

"We want to tempt the murderer into making his move," Gabriella nodded in confirmation.

"I get the idea," I murmured. "and I'm with you all the way. How many people did you say you're going to have there?"

CHAPTER FORTY

Y ou must think all we do in New York is eat and drink" said Henrietta Winslow. She had just introduced herself to me as a food writer for the *Paragon* magazine chain and she made the comment after observing that I was a visitor from England and asking what did I think of it. I took the question to mean New York and answered it accordingly, deciding to make no mention of murder, theft or Ko Feng.

Henrietta accepted another martini from a waiter and embarked on the expression of opinions that would doubtless be organized into a column at some early date. Another waiter came within reach, carrying a tray of full champagne glasses and I accepted one.

"You know, since the cocktail was first invented in the 1870s, it just grew and grew in popularity until—in the fifties and sixties—it was an integral part of American life."

"With only a hiccup during Prohibition?" I asked.

She was a large lady with silvery hair. She smiled.

"Prohibition made cocktails more popular than ever before. Maybe people didn't drink as many but more people became aware of them. It wasn't until the eighties that they declined."

"And what do you think that decline was due to?"

"Well, for one thing the real drinkers went to straight spirits like the Absoluts, and people who were worried about calories or driving switched to wines."

"You haven't been diverted to either one," I said. "You're still a martini drinker."

"Always have been—always will be. They make a good one here too. Were you here at the opening?"

We were at the Park Avenue Towers, one of the newer hotels in New York and the All-Charities Buffet was being held in the Vespucci Room. The decor was modern but not too severe and the murals depicted scenes from the discovery of the continent, evidently the work of a painter determined to erase the Columbus myth.

"No, I missed it," I told her.

"I didn't," she said. "They had a martini bar where they'd mix it any way you wanted—exact amount of vermouth you asked for, any one of twenty or more gins or vodkas, however many olives you wanted—and you could pick five or six places where the olives came from—stirred, shaken or whisked, and you could even ask for fast or slow, gentle or vigorous . . ." She sighed in glorious reminiscence. "Still, this is a good one too" she said, looking fondly at her glass. I suspected they all were.

"I come to this event every year," she told me. "New York has more charity functions than Los Angeles has tremors. This is one of the best, though. All we seem to lack this year is the mayor and Rollerena." That didn't mean much to me but I decided not to ask.

Lots of other people besides those dignitaries came to the event judging from the crowds now besieging the buffet tables. Corks popped, drinks fizzed, glasses rattled, conversation throbbed and delicious smells were in the air, sizzling meat, pungent cheeses, spices like ginger and curry and coriander.

"I wonder why they're calling this a Ko Feng luncheon," she mused, only half to me.

"It's that spice," I said. "You may have read about it."

"I know what it *is,*" she told me. "I'm wondering why this luncheon is named after it."

I could see the bald head of Alexander Marvell and I nodded in that direction.

"The man who bought it is over there. He may know why."

She regarded him thoughtfully.

"There might be a story in it," I hinted and she promptly wandered over in Marvell's direction, pausing to get another martini on the way. The buffet tables were enjoying a lot of business and I headed in that direction.

Tiny buckwheat crepes heaped with caviar made a fine start and then as I took a tartlet of leeks, cheddar cheese, gruyère cheese and shiitake mushrooms, I found I was being hailed from across the table. It was Professor Willenbroek.

"So the famous spice is back with us at last, is it? They're calling this a Ko Feng luncheon."

"An adventurous spice," I said. "Probably determined to make up for its centuries in Limbo."

"Ah," he said vaguely. "So what's Marvell going to do with it? Auction it off?"

"He's over there. Why don't you ask him?"

"Believe I will."

He paused for a slice of pumpernickel with blue cheese on it then disappeared into the throng. Smoked salmon is one appetizer I find irresistible. Here, it was offered on slices of papaya, which accented the smoked salmon taste.

I was sampling a grilled medallion of moist, rare venison on a toothpick with a square of chanterelle pasta when I heard another voice I recognized. I quickly completed my mental analysis of the pasta—dried chanterelles had been worked into the dough—and looked up.

Abraham Kefalik's bulk strained against the dark suit, no doubt more accustomed to a chef's apron. We shook hands.

"Have you tried these snails?" he asked.

I hadn't but I did so now. They were wrapped in bacon and charbroiled.

"No question about the garlic, the parsley and the bay

leaves in the marinade," I said. "But what else do you suppose is in there?"

"Marcel Dracy at the Ile de France prepares them especially for this occasion," he told me. "So I know how he does it. There's nothing else but white wine and lemon juice."

"They're superb—and surprisingly simple."

"Many of the best dishes are" he said, taking another snail. "Are the rumors true? Have you recovered the legendary Ko Feng?" He frowned. "Is it true that Willard Cartwright was killed? And that he had stolen it?"

"I think all is going to be revealed today," I conceded. "There will probably be a police statement and I understand that Alexander Marvell will make an announcement during this lunch."

Kefalik rubbed his knuckles down his bushy black beard. I couldn't tell whether he was contemplating the future of the Ko Feng or deciding which appetizer to go for next. It could have been both but all I could be certain of was his selection of a couple of baked clams. I chose an oyster in escabeche, a Galician specialty that I hadn't tasted in some time.

"I don't suppose Marvell is going to let us have any Ko Feng," Kefalik said in a disgruntled tone.

By "us," I knew he meant the restaurateurs and I was sure his supposition was right but it wasn't the time for me to say so. I chose the diplomatic approach and said, "We'll soon know what his intentions are." He gave me a glance which showed he was wondering how much more I knew than I was saying, said "See you around" and wandered away.

Two girls who looked like models came to the table, looking longingly at the items. "Dieting is just starving to death so that you can live longer," said one. "It certainly seems longer," agreed the other. They finally selected wild mushrooms rolled in olive oil with garlic and parsley.

An Asian face approached, jovial and underpinned by a rotund body. It was Mr. Singyang. His eyes glinted with merriment as he feasted on a turkey roulade with a wafer-thin slice of prosciutto on it.

"These are excellent," he assured me. "We should make more of the turkey in our Chinese cuisine."

"Some restaurateurs think all they have to do is substitute turkey for chicken," I said. "That's a mistake. The turkey has a much higher fat content and also it needs to weigh more. Young turkeys are tasteless."

"Wild turkeys fed on berries are incomparable," said Mr. Singyang. "They need to have that gamy flavor. Was it not Benjamin Franklin who lamented that the eagle was chosen to be the emblem of America when it should have been the turkey?"

"I believe so, though we must admit that the eagle has more appeal."

"As does turkey for the table."

We laughed together and the social amenities dispensed with, I reminded him of our earlier talk.

"The affair of the birds' nests, yes, I remember. Of course it was five years ago . . ."

"Since we talked, Willard Cartwright, who worked for Alexander Marvell, has been murdered. I was hoping you might have recalled something that might help. Shedding more light on the theft of the birds' nests might lead the way to finding the killer."

"Most regrettable," he murmured. I recalled he had said that before.

"It's more than that. It's downright dangerous for me. As the man most likely to be called on to identify the Ko Feng, I might be next on the murderer's list."

To his credit, he didn't reach for another turkey roulade. He regarded me for a moment, then said, "The rumors are circulating wildly. It is being hinted that Cartwright was responsible for the theft of the Ko Feng."

"What's your opinion, Mr. Singyang? Do you think that's all they are—rumors and hints? From your recollection of the event five years ago, does it seem probable that perhaps they are true?"

"Ah, very possibly so," he purred. "One hesitates to speak ill of the dead, of course, but in this case the welfare of the living has to be considered."

It was as much of an admission that he had bought the birds' nests as I was likely to get but I couldn't resist going a step further as he reached for a slice of grilled portobello mushroom on a slice of dark, grainy Arab bread.

"The living . . . ," I said reflectively. "Yes, that includes not only myself as a potential victim but also Cartwright's accomplice, the murderer." I gave him my steeliest gaze but it bounced off his armor.

"I fear that I cannot offer any clue as to that person's identity."

Maybe he really hadn't known who he was buying the birds' nests from at the time. My guess was that he surmised it now and he was probably telling the truth when he said he had no idea who Cartwright's accomplice was. I had the feeling that even if he knew more, he was not going to divulge anything. We sipped wine as each of us assessed the other's answers.

I think he would have liked another portobello mushroom but he knew when to move and he moved now, gliding away and greeting an old friend effusively.

CHAPTER FORTY-ONE

The room was crowded. I had to shoulder my way through and I almost collided with a serious-looking black man with heavy black-rimmed glasses. I didn't recognize Hal Gaines at first—he could have passed for a college president.

"Brilliant," I told him. "All done with a pair of glasses."

He nodded. "Everybody on our hit list is here."

"I had an idea . . . ," I said.

"Yeah? What?"

"I'd better not tell you, you'd only laugh."

"Then why're you telling me?"

"Just to make sure you're keeping a close eye on me."

He shrugged. "Suit yourself. It's that dangerous?"

"Maybe not much more than being here."

"Then go for it," he grunted. He clearly believed the risk was justified.

"You're looking quite relaxed for such a serious occasion," I said.

"Yeah, Gabriella gave me this stuff that completely cured my stomach. I feel great." He gave me a strange look. "It's some kind of herbal junk. You know anything about that?"

"They're doing wonderful things out there in the jungle," I told him. "Is Gabriella checking the door?" He nodded and I left him to look for my favorite policewoman. I was waylaid, first by some crabcakes that were not as delicious as they looked— too many red peppers overpowered the delicate crab. Then Selim Osman appeared, anxious for news of the Ko Feng.

"The case should be wrapped up very soon," I told him as we shook hands.

The case, in fact, had slipped from news prominence, pushed into near obscurity by the Headhunter, as the press styled him. The bloodthirsty American public gives serial killers the same adulation as baseball stars and soap opera heroes and this one—who cut off the heads of his victims and mailed them via Federal Express to the home of the police commissioner—was getting all the notoriety.

"An arrest is imminent, is it?" Selim Osman murmured.

"And followed by 'The stolen goods were recovered,' " I told him.

"Congratulations." His eyes searched my face as he waited for more.

"When the announcement appears, the police will deserve most of the credit," I said modestly.

I left him sampling thin slices of smoked swordfish on brioche and finally spotted Gabriella disengaging herself from an admiring group of men. It was easy to see why. She was wearing a dress in a shiny material of midnight blue. It was tight around the waist and built up to a plunging neckline and a padded bodice—though on second viewing, maybe it wasn't padded.

"Terrific disguise," I told her.

"The wardrobe department didn't have much else in my size." Her eyes sparkled—she must have been in the makeup department too.

"I hope it has room for a weapon."

"Of course," she said demurely but didn't enlighten me. I studied her again and shook my head.

"Amazing," I said and she laughed.

"Nothing from the main entrance?" I asked her.

In our discussion that morning, Hal Gaines had told me of the equipment they had installed here. It was essentially the same as the device used at airports as a metal detector and this modification was built into the door frame. Every guest entering was asked to sign the register and this enabled the smiling blond receptionist—a police technician—to read the monitor out of sight below her desk and associate it with the name. The meter was set to identify anything with the metal content of a Tokharev automatic—keys, coins and jewelry would be passed.

"Nothing so far," said Gabriella. "Everybody who has come in up to now is clean." She looked around the room. "But there's someone here who is really furious at you for fouling up a sale."

"I think so too. I can't believe whoever it is could resist this occasion."

"Both for a final chance to unload the Ko Feng and to complete your termination."

"Police jargon can be so comforting. It's so impersonal."

She was eyeing the nearest table of food but she said, "See that balcony up there? We have two people scanning the crowd. And two of the waiters are ours."

"Let me get you another glass of champagne. It's the least I can do."

She smiled fetchingly. "No, thanks, I've had enough—besides, it's just ginger ale."

She surveyed the room. "Seen your insurance girlfriend?"

"Kay Grenville? I hardly know her. Anyway she wouldn't even alibi me. What kind of a girlfriend would she make?"

"I'd like to find out what kind of an accomplice she'd make."

It took a few seconds before the full import of her remark sank in. "Accomplice? Her?"

"She *was* at the Spice Warehouse at the time of both murders."

"She left just before Renshaw's murder," I said.

"She left *you*. You can't be sure she left the warehouse."

I said nothing. I was thinking that Key Grenville had also been at that illicit sale of nefarious foodstuffs at the church and by her own admission had also been at the Marvell laboratories in New Jersey though she had neatly dissociated herself from any responsibility in it.

Gabriella was eyeing me suspiciously. She really was getting to know me too well—she must have been having lessons from Dr. Li.

"Is there something you want to tell me?" she asked.

"Well, I just can't think of her as an accomplice."

"Just because she's—"

"No, no, you're right," I assured her. "Investigate her by all means."

"You know that insurance might be our killer's way out—if a deal can be struck."

"Yes, that's true. Carry on, Sergeant."

She gave me one more uncertain glance before sashaying off in search of her victim. I watched her with approval. There was no doubt about it—her entire appearance was a wonderful disguise. But as far as carrying a concealed weapon, I would need a lot of convincing.

It was then that I saw a tall figure towering over those around him. It was the last person I had expected to see here—Dr. Li of the Methuselah Foundation. He saw me at the same time, he excused himself and approached me, hand extended.

"It is gratifying to find you so well," he greeted me and I supposed that by "well" he meant alive. "Rumor has it that you have recovered the Ko Feng," he went on. I gave him my most implacable look. "I rarely attend this function," he continued, "although naturally I am fully in sympathy with its laudable aims."

That confirmed my surprise at seeing him here, though the question that followed was entirely predictable.

"What does Alexander Marvell plan on doing with the Ko Feng now, do you suppose?"

I didn't correct his misapprehension. "I think he intends to enlighten us on that point before this luncheon is over."

Dr. Li nodded gently. His black mustache had the same carefully trained droopy angle as before but it was those jade green eyes that held my attention. As I looked into them, I felt as if I were sinking into a pool of seductively warm water. Then an idea struck me and I looked briefly away to clear my head and avoid that hypnotic gaze so that I could frame my words.

"Dr. Li, I am sure you are still interested in obtaining some Ko Feng."

"Of course." His reply was prompt and he bowed from a great height, emphasizing his words.

What I wanted to say wasn't coming easily and I fumbled for the right way to say it. "When we talked earlier, I was—er, impressed with your ability to—well, sort of see into my mind."

The ends of his long black mustache twitched slightly in what I was sure must be a smile. "I wouldn't say that," he said modestly, though there wasn't a grain of humility in his voice, "but there are some techniques practiced in the East that are not widely known in the West. I am familiar with a number of these."

I took that to be a yes and went on. "There are others here today who, like you, would very much like to get hold of some Ko Feng. I'm sure you know who these people are."

He nodded and I thought I detected a glint forming in those strange green eyes. "I have reason to believe that one of those killed Renshaw and Cartwright and stole the Ko Feng," I continued. "What I was wondering is this—while you're circulating here today, could you probe a few minds and perhaps identify some guilt, you know—some anxiety, apprehension even . . . ?"

It was a clumsy way to put it but surely Dr. Li had been in New York long enough to be able to translate my blunt words into a more subtle form so that he understood what I was saying? Maybe he had, I thought—the glint in his eye was as near to a twinkle as I was likely to see.

I pressed on before those eyes swallowed me up because I had to look at him while I was saying all this. "Your interest is, I realize, mainly in the Celestial Spice. But a double murder is more important and I'm sure you would wish to use your powers in such a—well, laudable aim."

Those twin beams of his eyes were drilling into me. Was he trying to discover if I knew more than I was telling him? More to the point, was he learning anything?

"Don't expect too much," he said blandly and turned off the current.

He walked away with his long stride and I watched him, curious to see whom he approached first but I lost him in the crowd, despite his height. Well, it was worth a try . . .

A woman with masses of blond hair piled high went by with an elderly man who had the honest look of a politician. "But how can it be the best restaurant in New York City when it only has fourteen tables?" the woman was asking loudly. "Because it has fifteen chefs," replied the man patiently and I recognized the place they were talking about. A waiter came, bringing a huge tray piled with new delights and as he unloaded, I studied him briefly, wondering if he was "on our side."

I spotted Professor Willenbroek and Kay Grenville talking together and tried to get close enough to hear their conversation but the sharp-eyed professor saw me and waved me toward them.

We exchanged pleasantries. The professor wore a light linen suit that probably served him well in the Central American jungle while Kay had on a summery, daffodil yellow silk suit and pale gold earrings.

"We were discussing the Ko Feng," said Kay.

"Interesting subject," I agreed.

"Does Marvell have it back?" the professor wanted to know. "There are rumors around that he does but I asked him and he was very evasive."

"Evasive?" said a new voice. "Must be talking about politicians."

A smiling, diminutive man with a German accent stood there and the professor introduced him as an eminent New York restaurateur. Kay Grenville knew him already, it seemed. We chatted for a few moments. The man wanted Professor Willenbroek to appear on his weekly television show but his words were not persuasive enough.

Still smiling, he took the arm of the professor and steered him away. As they left, Nelson Keyhoe of Keyhoe Chemicals, the man with eight thousand products and a place in the Fortune 500, came up, greeting Kay and then me with handshakes.

"Rumors say that Marvell has recovered the Ko Feng." Keyhoe looked from one to the other of us, his military manner demanding answers.

"Miss Grenville can probably tell you more," I suggested. "She has her finger on the insurance pulse."

"Nothing to report," she said sweetly.

"Tell me," Keyhoe said, "is is true that in most cases like this, the insurer is found to have stolen his own goods?"

Kay turned her most innocent gaze on him. "Why, Nelson, that sounds like an accusation!"

"Not at all," he said gruffly. "Just talking in statistical terms."

"Well . . . it does happen," Kay said cautiously. She waited until Keyhoe had neatly swept a couple of glasses of champagne from a passing tray and handed them to us. "Nothing specific?" she asked archly. "Just statistical?"

He adroitly scooped a third glass from the tray and studied the rising bubbles. "I found it strange . . ."

"Found what strange?" Kay asked when neither she nor I could wait any longer.

"At JFK. It was Willard Cartwright who came out to collect the Ko Feng." Keyhoe edged nearer a table where an array of Indonesian satays had caught his eye. He selected one—it looked like a pork cube, probably marinated in soy sauce and spices then grilled and offered with peanut sauce as a dip. I took a chorizo sausage wrapped in a corn crepe. Kay declined.

"Go on," she urged.

"What I mean is—we have this romantic story of Marvell discovering the field of Ko Feng, all mystical aura and the wonder of the East. So is he burning with impatience to get hold of it? No, he sends Cartwright to get it."

There was a silence in our group. It contrasted with the hubbub of voices around us. Keyhoe had a point . . . and it hinted at Marvell as engineering the theft with Cartwright as his accomplice. Gabriella's suspicion of Kay came to mind and there was a reasonable fit between the two theories—Marvell could collect the insurance and sell the Ko Feng too. He no longer had to split it with Cartwright—what were his plans for Kay? Or was she involved?

CHAPTER FORTY-TWO

W hat are those?" Kay asked. She indicated a display of puff pastries.

"They're different kinds of cheese. There's mozzarella, that's bel paese, then feta, can't mistake that one—it's Norwegian mysost—and those on the end are probably goat cheese."

She certainly wasn't worrying about Marvell's plans or whether they included her. All I could see was a very attractive woman eating puff pastries. A man with an Italian accent descended upon her in midbite and they exchanged pleasantries. Keyhoe was nodding to a couple he recognized and I chose the moment to disengage.

A platoon of waiters swept in, carrying aloft trays exuding a delicious aroma of ginger and garlic. The buzz of conversation had risen several decibels—perhaps in direct proportion to the amount of alcohol consumed.

"I heard somebody say Daniel Boulud was here," commented a tall woman with spiky hair.

"I thought I saw David Bowie," said her companion, an ample redhead clad most unsuitably in a clashing red dress. "Are you sure that's not who you mean?"

Another group was discussing restaurant reviews. "I gave up reading them when Ed Koch started writing them," said a bearded man. A large woman in canary yellow was asking a waiter if there were any mussels. He indicated a table. "I had some of those," she said. "They're too salty." She looked around. "What about shrimp?" Again he pointed but she shook her head.

"I can't eat them with heads and tails on. What about oysters?"

"With or without pearls, madam?" he inquired, deadpan.

I strolled by a sextet arguing about chicken farming and the conditions therein but none of them looked as if they had ever seen a chicken farm. Raised voices caught my attention and I closed in to investigate. A small bustling lady in an unsuitable flowery dress, a glittering necklace and a loud voice was speaking.

"They really shouldn't serve those at affairs like this," she protested.

"Which?" I asked.

She pointed to strips of sirloin steak, probably marinated in soy sauce, sesame and garlic.

"And those," she said accusingly, indicating an array of meatballs which appeared to represent the cuisines of half a dozen nations. Some looked Persian with a curry sauce while others looked like Danish frikadeller. Those in a tomato sauce were most likely Turkish *koftesi,* then there were Greek *kefthetakia* flavored with fresh mint, Moroccan *kefta* with marjoram, cumin and coriander, and Indian *kofte* in a rich *korma* sauce, Kashmiri style. The similarity in the names was interesting and someday I intended to track back and see which came first.

"We objected last year but they ignored us," said the lady.

" We' being who?" I asked.

"The New England Vegans," she explained. "We tried again this year but they didn't listen. Have you seen our T-shirts?" she asked.

I was obliged to admit that I didn't think I had but to be on the safe side I asked her what they said.

"They say ANIMALS ARE OUR FRIENDS—DON'T EAT THEM," she told me. "We wear them every time we go to the supermarket."

A tall skinny man with thinning white hair spoke up in a loud voice. "You should be a lot more concerned on health grounds," he proclaimed. "Beef is a killer—worse than AIDS, Oprah says so."

"What does she know from beef?" another equally strong voice demanded.

"She's writing a book on it," said a tiny woman support-ively. "Must know a lot about it."

I tore myself away before that party got rough. I listened to one group debating the conditions under which snails were raised, another where a tariff on rice was being proposed, the argument being that the United States could easily produce all the rice the country could eat and much cheaper and better quality than the imported product. Irradiation of food was rearing its ugly head again but I was determined not to get involved in that.

I scanned the room. I couldn't see either Hal Gaines or Gabriella. It was just as well. I would probably hear some earthy New York epithets if I said, "Oh, by the way, I've just enlisted the help of a Chinese hypnotist."

A figure materialized by my elbow. I turned to see Alexander Marvell.

He looked as if he needed a truckload of good cheer more than my conventional greeting. His face was grim and uncompromising and I prepared myself for some harsh words but he was remarkably civil. He even asked my opinion.

"Are we going to have some resolution of this dreadful business at last?"

"I really think so," I told him sincerely. "In fact, I could almost say I'm betting my life on it."

He grunted. It was hard to distinguish whether it was skepticism or sympathy for my vulnerable position.

"Something I've always wanted to ask you," I said. "Why did you send Cartwright to JFK that day? I would have thought you couldn't resist being there yourself when flight 227 touched down."

He glanced at me briefly then looked away. "I had urgent personal business," he said.

"Oh," I said as if I understood. "But then you had every reason to trust Cartwright, didn't you?"

He nodded. "Misplaced trust as it turned out."

I wondered if Gabriella had checked out the alibis of the key people at the time of the theft. It was unlikely she hadn't . . . but Marvell was looking at me with what amounted to suspicion in his eye.

"I want to ask *you* a question," he said in a voice that hardened suddenly.

"Go ahead."

"Why did you phone the Mecklenburg Botanical Institute?"

"In San Francisco?" It was a silly response. I knew quite well where they were but I was puzzled.

"Yes."

"I didn't."

"They say you did."

I was still puzzled. "You've talked to them? They told you this?"

"I had to call them on another matter and they mentioned it."

I shook my head firmly. "I haven't called them."

He was unconvinced. "They told me you did."

"It wasn't me—they're mistaken."

He gave me a glare of incredulity and stalked away.

When I caught sight of Gloria Branson, I had the distinct impression that she saw me and turned her back, but I approached her anyway. Her back view was almost as good as the front. She wore a white dress with a sort of crimson sash and looked spectacular, but her handshake was cold.

"I heard you had gone back to London."

"An exaggerated report, premature," I said, wondering why

the frosty reception. "I have some unfinished business here that hopefully will be taken care of today."

"Do you?" Her tone was uninterested and her face like alabaster—and just as immobile. Then it struck me why she was behaving like this.

I was at a loss to know what to say but it didn't matter because she turned back to the people around her, ignoring me completely. One of them, a woman with gold-rimmed glasses that must have consumed a couple of nuggets, gave me a look of sympathy just as I heard a familiar voice behind me.

"Still investigating and authenticating?" It was Tom Eck. I shook his hand; in the other he held a floweret of broccoli. "Have you tried these? They are really superb." He nodded to a nearby table and I took one. I didn't notice any taste.

"I'm still on the case, yes."

"Any luck?"

"Some," I admitted. I looked around. "I need another glass of wine—ah, over there." He strolled with me and I took a glass from the table. Eck looked over the foods adjacent and took a slice of avocado with Parma ham and curried mayonnaise on it.

"I was talking to Kay Grenville just now," I said. He nodded with casual interest.

"Going to pay out, is she?"

"I doubt it. It's still very early anyway." I took a slice of the avocado too. "What's your experience of insurance companies paying on claims like this?"

"They pay out millions every year."

"Do you think their own investigations turn up anything that the police haven't?"

"Some things, I suppose, but nothing major."

A face behind me caught Eck's attention and he introduced me.

"Bengt Johannson, BJ Vitamins." He was a blond, blue-eyed sturdy Viking type and promptly launched into a discussion on the vitamin content of the foodstuffs on display, although I was trying to get away.

"You could eat here all day and not get enough vitamins," he stated solemnly. "Vitamin additives are essential—and don't be misled by people who tell you to avoid synthetic vitamins, they're just as good as . . ."

I finally managed to break away and went in search of Hal Gaines or Gabriella. They had said they were undercover and at the moment they certainly were. I couldn't see them but seemed to have no trouble finding others. I saw Ayesha but got only a wave. At least that made up for the withering stare from Lennie Rifkin, who was close by her side. Mr. Koo was eating artichoke mousse on toasted Syrian bread and declaring his intention of giving it a Chinese twist. I thought I saw Salman Rushdie with Cher but it seemed unlikely. The vegan lady intercepted me and initiated a discussion on Buddha and whether or not he was a vegetarian.

I would have enjoyed that at any other time but I was desperately anxious to find Hal Gaines or Gabriella and tell them that I knew the identity of the killer of Renshaw and Cartwright and the thief of the Ko Feng.

CHAPTER FORTY-THREE

The two of them were hard to find. I was still searching when a waiter stopped me. "The lieutenant's looking for you," he said and pointed to the balcony. "The Atlantic Room up there."

I hurried up the stairs. The Atlantic Room was a large conference and lecture room, one of a dozen or so. I went in. The room was in near darkness and I stopped abruptly as the door was pulled out of my hand and closed behind me.

There was just enough light to make out Tom Eck.

"Was it something I said?" he asked softly.

It was a perfect time to come out with a Nick Charles quip but I missed my cue. Instead I found out what it means to have a sinking heart.

"You know, don't you?" he asked, in a voice that was still soft.

I hoped he couldn't hear my brain working—inside my head, it sounded like a demented chain-saw. Suddenly, I saw a glimmer of what might be a way out . . .

"The buyer had to be you or Keyhoe or Gloria Branson," I said, though my voice wasn't as steady as I would have liked. "I had a second string of suspects but of them, Professor Willenbroek seemed too true-blue and it didn't seem like Dr. Li's style. But one of you five had to be the buyer—" I paused, not just for dramatic effect but because I was still ad-libbing.

"—and I know now that it's you."

My eyes were adjusting to the gloom. The lights were on at the far end only. At this end was a platform with a speaker's dais and microphone, and behind it a large screen. We stood inside the door, near the edge of the platform.

"When you're a food broker, people come to you," Eck was saying in a chatty tone. "Some want to sell, some want to buy. There's an awful lot of people who would love to get their hands on some Ko Feng. It's natural they should come to me."

I nodded, trying to look understanding and compassionate.

"So someone came and wanted to sell the Ko Feng to you?"

"Right."

"Why not directly to one of the research outfits?"

"I'm sure that was the initial idea. It was made more complicated and difficult due to your interference. None of the likely buyers wanted to risk being identified and the problem of authenticating the spice made it even trickier."

"So you were approached as a middle man?"

"Right again."

"And that one person was a murderer."

"Catching murderers is a job for the police," Eck said with a shrug. "I'm just a food broker."

"You're a buyer of stolen goods too," I said in a firm accusatory tone.

There were voices outside. They had to be loud as this room was surely sound-insulated. But we were near the door and though the words were unintelligible, it sounded like the staff disagreeing over some problem. The voices faded away.

"All right, let's get it over with," I said resignedly.

Eck regarded me with a noticeable lack of interest. "Get what over with?"

"You want me to authenticate the Ko Feng for you. Well, where is it?"

He shook his head with an amused tolerance. "I don't want you to do anything of the kind."

"But—" I stammered, "you're surely not going to buy the Ko Feng without establishing that it's genuine."

"That's all been done," Eck said dismissively.

I had the nasty feeling that the situation was slipping away from me.

"So your role in all this is finished," he added.

His words had a ring of finality that I didn't like at all but I put as much joviality as I could into it as I said, "Then I'd better see when the next flight to London leaves."

Eck didn't move. "Not just yet," he said. "let's settle a few details first."

"What details?"

He kept looking at me. There was something he wasn't certain about—something he had to know. Finally he said it. Again.

"You know, don't you?"

CHAPTER FORTY-FOUR

It was quiet. No voices could be heard from the balcony. The gloom in the partly lit conference room made the silence all the more foreboding. Eck had put one hand into his pocket. At least there couldn't be a Tokharev automatic there, I thought. But where were Lieutenant Gaines and Gabriella? Why weren't they keeping an eye on me? Didn't they know yet about the fake message that had brought me up here?

"Tell me," urged Eck and his hand moved in his pocket.

"All right," I said quickly. "It's Marvell, isn't it?" I said. "He got Cartwright to help him steal the Ko Feng. Renshaw saw the similarity with the earlier theft of the birds' nests and one or the other killed him. Then Cartwright tried to double-cross Marvell—who killed him. Marvell's background had led him to believe that he could easily sell Ko Feng to someone in the restaurant business but he miscalculated. It was Cartwright who had gotten him to switch to the research lab people as a much more lucrative market. Even that was tricky because, as you said, they couldn't get the Ko Feng authenticated and sell it while still concealing their identity."

I paused on a how'm-I-doing note. Eck said nothing so I went on.

"The point I'm not clear on is to what extent that insurance woman is mixed up in this. Maybe she knows, maybe she doesn't, maybe she only suspects. Regardless, Marvell having disposed of Cartwright decided to sell the Ko Feng and collect on the insurance as well. You were an ideal choice to sell it to—

you know everybody in the business, you could find the highest bidder."

We were standing near the edge of the speaker's platform. It was about a foot high and now that my vision was adjusted to the gloom, I had seen the cord from the microphone. It ran from the bottom of the speaker's dais and passed within about three feet of where I was standing.

While I was talking, I was edging closer to it. I did some hand gesturing and waving to emphasize my words—not nearly as much as an average New Yorker but more than I usually do. I hoped it would distract Eck enough. I thought he was frowning but I couldn't tell if it was because he was thinking about what I was saying or if he was puzzled at my untypical ebullience.

"I thought for a while the Ko Feng might be shipped out of the country but I'm sure that meant too many risks."

"The thief had to be someone right here," agreed Eck.

"You say 'the thief' but if you bought the Ko Feng from him, you must know it's Marvell."

He looked at me strangely.

"Neither the thief nor the buyer wanted to be seen," he said. "Bringing another authenticator into it too made it even more complicated."

A bell rang in my head. "Another authenticator! You brought in someone from the Mecklenburg Institute . . ."

"Actually you did."

"Me? How could I—ah, I see. You used my name, pretended to be me."

I edged another couple of inches nearer to the cord.

"Yes." He took his hand out of his pocket. It held a gray automatic pistol that looked as if it was made of plastic.

He waved it menacingly. "It's real—don't be fooled by its appearance. It's high-impact ABS plastic with a titanium tube barrel. Up to ten feet, it's as dangerous as any other weapon but it doesn't set off metal detecting devices."

He must have spotted a change in my expression. "Yes," he said, "I was just about to walk in here today when I saw the woman at the desk looking down at something so I waited a while. She did it every time a guest came in. I figured she had a metal detector there so I went back to the car where I keep this." He waved it again. "You can't be too careful on the highway."

He jabbed the gun in my direction. I hate guns and refuse to carry one even when an investigation in the food business seems to be turning dangerous. This one of Eck's might be plastic but it was just as terrifying. I noticed something else—it had what looked like a small cork on the end of the barrel, probably a silencer.

I slid one foot under the microphone cord.

"You can cut out the play-acting" he said, and his voice had hardened. "We had enough of that with that cute trick you pulled at Martha's. Now, I'm only going to say it one last time. You know, don't you? But how do you know?"

So that was what was worrying him. It may have been why he hadn't shot me already. He had to know how I knew—and more important, it wasn't ego or curiosity. He had to know if anyone else could know.

I was determined to drag this out a little longer. He wasn't going to shoot me until I had answered his question and anyway, that confounded cord was slack. I pulled it a little more, trying to get it tight.

"All right," I agreed. "I did think that a partnership of Marvell and Cartwright was responsible—until now. But I tried something. I shook everybody's hand and when I shook yours I knew it was you and Cartwright. You killed Renshaw and then Cartwright. One of you was trying to double-cross the other and take the sack of Ko Feng."

"I'm not going to ask you again." His voice was bleak and if I had thought of him as a nuclear sub commander, he was now ready to push the red button.

"Your hand smelled of Ko Feng," I told him.

His square jaw no longer appeared determined, now it was threatening. The eyes that had been cool and gray before were now metallic and menacing. I fancied I could see his knuckle tightening on the trigger.

"Nonsense."

"It's the truth. Besides its unique taste, Ko Feng has a powerful and extremely pervasive aroma. I noticed it on my hands the day after the theft—they still smelled of it. I went round this afternoon shaking hands with everyone—as soon as I shook yours, I knew."

He was eyeing me uncertainly but it didn't make him any less threatening.

"You had to have handled it," I said, still twisting one foot but trying to keep his gaze locked with mine. "No one could resist—a legendary spice, lost for centuries—how could you have the sack in your possession and not open it, feel it, smell it . . ."

It was an involuntary reaction. Without deviating his aim, he raised the weapon so as to sniff the back of his hand. Our eyes met and I tried to suppress a smile of satisfaction. We both knew he had given himself away.

He lowered the gun to realign it at my stomach and the mild nausea that immediately resulted had nothing to do with the avocado or the mayonnaise or the crab cakes. I gave one more twist of my foot, heedless now as to whether he saw me.

The microphone cord tightened and I kicked frantically sideways. The cord yanked the microphone clear off the dais and Eck's head spun in that direction, but instead of the dais crashing too, it stayed there, unmoving. It was only the microphone that came clattering onto the wooden platform. It bounced twice and the two of us watched it come to rest.

An interruption startled us both. A loud voice shouted something and the lights came on, all of them together. It was dazzling after the semidarkness. I groped for the microphone and threw it in Eck's general direction, then I bolted to the nearest door. As I crashed through it, there was a pop from Eck's silenced automatic and a bullet crunched into the wall.

Out in the corridor, I raced for the nearest stairway, took the stairs three at a time and rammed my way through swinging doors. The large entrance ahead of me was marked as being the Vespucci Room and "safety in numbers" came into my mind. I knew it wasn't always true but my pounding pulse wouldn't allow me time to think of a more appropriate proverb. I went storming in.

An enormous room, crowded with people, noisy, jostling, the din of conversation, the rattle of plates and glasses . . .

No.

Oh, the people were there but all were still and silent as statues. As I made my noisy entrance, over a thousand eyes turned in my direction.

CHAPTER FORTY-FIVE

I stared back, not out of insolence but bewilderment. Why was the room so still and quiet? Then, over the heads of all the others, I saw Alexander Marvell. He was at a front table. On one side of him was a large lady in a Marie Antoinette coiffure and a lot of jewelry, and there was an immaculately dressed elderly man on the other.

Marvell had apparently been speaking. Moreover, the smoldering glare that burned in my direction suggested he had been rudely interrupted. He glanced back at his notes and resumed, speaking of the fine work being performed by the committee and naming the various charities that were benefiting from this gala affair.

Eyes were now swiveling back in Marvell's direction, a few at a time, then more and more. I had felt a brief period of safety while everyone's eyes were on me but now I was exposed and isolated again. I moved quietly around the back of the room, looking for police help. My boisterous entry had fortunately attracted official attention, for a vision in blue came toward me.

"Where have you been?" hissed Gabriella. "We've been looking all over for you."

"First," I said urgently, "find out which car in the hotel garage belongs to Tom Eck. Don't let him near it—he's our man and the murder gun is in the car. I think he's still in the hotel, so block all the exits."

She had her phone in her hand and was rapping out instructions before I had even finished. Then I told her what had happened. Before I had completed my account, Hal Gaines had emerged from the assembly and I brought him up to date. He told Gabriella to alert additional men outside and bring some of them in.

"You haven't checked in here yet?" he asked. "He could have come in a little more quietly than you did."

"I haven't looked yet. He might find me before I find him."

"Which is more important to him?" asked Gabriella. "Killing you—which is, after all, nothing more than revenge at this stage—or getting out?"

"Yeah," said Gaines. "If he's done the deal and gotten the money, he ought to be taking off—in fact, he shouldn't even be here at this lunch."

"I can see why he is," Gabriella said. "I interviewed him twice. He's an egotist. He wouldn't be able to resist the chance to come here and gloat—to talk to all these people, knowing something they don't."

"Regardless," said Gaines, ever the pragmatist, "let's find him. We'll stay behind the crowd. You two better stay together, start at that end. I'll take this end."

Five minutes later when we met, head shakes were exchanged. Eck wasn't in the room. Then for a moment he was forgotten—by me, at least—as, with the introduction of various dignitaries and the thanks to numerous fund-raisers over, Marvell resumed speaking.

"Many are asking why we have referred to this as the Ko Feng lunch. Well, the police are on the verge of recovering it and I wanted to take advantage of this opportunity to tell you what's going to happen to it.

"The Celestial Spice has had a bloodstained welcome to the United States. Two men have died because of it and, sadly, greed and cupidity have been aroused in many. Consequently, I have made arrangements for the spice to be placed under the mandate of the Globus Group, who are widely known for their impartiality and independence from all commercial influences. It will be their decision where and how to allocate Ko Feng for testing for its various—and hopefully highly beneficial—characteristics."

So, if I had needed any proof that Alexander Marvell wasn't involved in the theft or the murders, that was good enough for me. Giving away the spice took away his motive. Not that I had suspected him—it had been a convenient stall to use with Eck before I had finally had to tell him the truth.

To resounding applause, Marvell sat down and the lady with all the jewelry invited the assembly to return to the food and drink. Lieutenant Gaines turned to Gabriella and me. "Let's check all the entrances and exits from this room."

We did so but when we met, it was again with a shaking of heads. Police on all the doors reported no one had left. A few guests had complained at not being allowed to leave, some pleading all manner of vital engagements but a quick check of their appearance told us that none of them was Eck.

The gala event was once more in full swing. The babble of voices was loud despite the excellent acoustics, the smell of food was pungent, sweet, cloying, tangy and piquant in turns. Champagne flowed as if there were a pipeline all the way from Reims.

We were standing near one of the batteries of dumbwaiters, bringing food up from the kitchens in the basement. A row of screens separated us from the throng. One of the waiters stated his opinion in a resounding Brooklyn accent. "Jeez! What's the matter with those guys down there! Haven't they ever worked in a kitchen before?"

Something in the framing of the rhetorical question struck me, but it was something that their framer hadn't intended. Hal Gaines turned at the same moment and his eyes met mine. We looked at the dumbwaiter the man was pointing to and saw several large loaves of uncut bread. I knew that Hal Gaines was thinking the same thing I was—someone in the kitchen was under duress and rather than be seen doing nothing, had made himself busy doing the first thing that came to hand.

"We have people blocking the exits from the kitchen," snapped Gaines, "but there'd be nothing to stop him going in! Let's go!"

The three of us raced out, pausing only for Gaines to shout at the officer on the door, "Which stairs lead to the kitchen?" and then following his pointing finger.

Glistening stainless steel and warm, mellow copper reflected the high-intensity lighting and shadows swam mistily in the white-tiled floors. A few pots steamed, probably in preparation for the evening meal, but the kitchen was quiet as most of the buffet had been prepared ahead. Only four or five white-clad figures moved, ghostlike, and only the clatter of an automatic dishwasher made any significant noise.

We scanned the faces that turned inquiringly toward us. None of them was Tom Eck.

Gabriella suddenly said, "Look!" and a swing door, recently set in motion, was just juddering to a stop. With a quick look to make sure that there was no crouching figure behind a cabinet or workbench, we headed for the door with Gabriella in the lead.

She had barely reached it when without warning, it was flung open. Gaines gasped something and grabbed for his gun. Gabriella already had hers out but she had been so fast, I didn't see where it came from. As the unarmed member of the trio, I was naturally last. All three of us froze.

Through the door and into the kitchen marched Tom Eck. He was on tiptoe and his face was red, his expression apoplectic. He moved like a rag doll, limbs seeming uncoordinated. The reason for his bizarre appearance was promptly evident. Behind him came a giant of a man.

He was black—blacker than the proverbial ace of spades and

certainly as black as the deepest midnight. Only one man was that huge and that black—it was Yaruba Da.

The wide grin on his face suggested that he was having a good time and the twin rows of teeth gleamed like a TV ad. He had one hand the size of a pineapple grasping Eck firmly by the back of the neck. It was with no visible effort that he held Eck almost clear of the ground in a manner that hinted he could snap that neck with a flick of his wrist.

"This man tried to rush past me. He had this in his hand." He held out a black palm so massive that it made the gray automatic look like a toy. "I didn't know what it was all about but I decided that he could be up to no good." He glared at the hapless Eck as if he were a schoolteacher scolding an errant pupil. "So I disarmed him." He beamed at us. "I'd read him his rights if I knew what to say, although any man who runs around with a gun in his hand shouldn't have any rights, don't you agree?"

Two uniformed men came rushing in from another door and Hal Gaines told them to take charge of the culprit.

"What were you doing here?" asked Gabriella.

The giant from the Congo grinned sheepishly. "A few of those hors d'oeuvres upstairs were so good, I decided to come down here and do a little spying, find out how they made them."

"So that's why I didn't see you up there," I said.

"I am not an unsociable man," he said quickly, "but I am very fond of my work."

His handling of Eck had left the latter without speech and the two police took him out without resistance. Gaines's admonition to Eck that he had the right to remain silent seemed almost unnecessary.

CHAPTER FORTY-SIX

We were back up on the main floor where the festivities were still in full swing. Hal Gaines had offered to let me tell Marvell that Eck was under arrest but I said he should do it—after all, arrest was a police matter.

"There's one thing I have to do, though" I told the lieutenant. "Can you hold off opening the doors and releasing everybody for just a couple of minutes?"

He looked puzzled but agreed.

Dr. Li was again easy to locate. He towered over the two Australians he was in conversation with when I found him. He excused himself and took me aside.

"Any luck?" I asked eagerly.

His green eyes had a hooded look, which was a relief. I felt too weak to have any resistance if he turned up his voltage all the way.

"Possibly," he said. "Concerning Mr. Eck, I can tell you nothing—I have not been able to trace him, though I know he is here."

"That's all right," I said. "We'll come back to him in a minute. What else?"

"Both Ms. Branson and Mr. Keyhoe exhibited signs of considerable mental unease when I discussed Ko Feng with them. Ms. Branson was, in addition, perturbed for some other reason."

"Guilt, either of them?"

"They both have something to hide. Guilt is for the authorities to determine."

He continued to regard me from behind those hooded eyes but I couldn't tell if he was debating if he should say more or waiting for me to make a contribution.

"Thanks," I said. "Thanks for your help. Er—is there something else?"

"Did you consider the possibility that I myself was involved in a Ko Feng transaction?"

"I did," I told him. "I took a chance that you weren't."

He bowed his head an inch in acknowledgment. "I thank you for your trust."

"Not at all." I could be just as polite. "And in return for your help, you can be almost the first to know—Eck has just been arrested for the theft of the Ko Feng and the murders of Renshaw and Cartwright."

A glow flickered briefly in the green eyes and then was gone.

"And the Ko Feng?" he asked.

"Well, after Marvell's announcement, you can be sure of getting some of it for your research."

"That is true," he agreed. "Let us hope that the Celestial Spice lives up to its reputation."

"I hope so too—and now if you'll excuse me I must have a few words with a couple of people."

I went through the crowd looking for the two suspects fingered by the occult wisdom of the East.

Near the platform where Marvell still stood, Gaines had apparently broken the news. When Hal saw me, he raised his eyebrows and moved his hands in a pressuring movement. I responded with a wait-a-minute wave.

Gloria Branson looked as stunning as ever. I found her in conversation with a Rudolph Valentino look-alike but when she saw me, she broke off and I joined her.

"I understand why you were so arctic a while ago," I said. "I fouled up your purchase, didn't I?"

"I don't know what you mean," she replied without emotion.

"I think you do. Eck has been arrested for the theft and the murders. The Ko Feng is about to be recovered, you'll be able to get some of it and you may be able to do some research on it after all."

Her eyes widened at the news, then she shook her head sadly. "I'm afraid that may no longer be possible."

"Why not?"

"Paramount Pharmaceuticals is having a reorganization. There won't be a place for me in it."

"You're losing your job?"

"Yes."

"Owing to Ko Feng?"

"Of course."

"But you just heard Marvell's statement—he's going to have the Globus Group distribute it. That means it'll be available for research in vitamins, pharamaceuticals, foods—all kinds of things."

"That's wonderful," she said with just a hint of sarcasm. "All mankind will benefit, but in the meantime the juggernaut of business roars on. And it rolls right over losers. I'm a loser because we didn't get the Ko Feng at Paramount—us exclusively, that is."

"Don't blame yourself too much," I consoled her. "After all," I added carefully, "you tried."

There was a flicker in those beautiful eyes.

"Not hard enough," was all she said, though.

"Tell me something," I said, "now that it's all over. When you phoned that number at that restaurant at that precise time and asked me if the Ko Feng was genuine—were you really prepared to buy it?"

"You mean you went to a restaurant to authenticate some Ko Feng and someone phoned you there?" Her eyes were round. "All part of the secrecy, I suppose?"

"That's right. I tasted the Ko Feng and was asked if it was genuine."

"And was it?"

"I said it was a substitute—a phony."

"And that was the truth?"

"No. It was a lie."

"I'm surprised at you, the honest English detective."

The words were a quick attempt at covering her lapse but we both knew it was too late. The expression that passed across her face was unmistakable, though it was gone in a flash. That and her statement that she had been fired meant she didn't have the spice.

"Actually, I'm not a detective really. I have no authority of any kind so there'll be no official mention of this."

She nodded but turned away as I wished her good luck in finding a new job.

Gaines was waiting impatiently where I had left him.

"Keyhoe has the Ko Feng," I told him. "He must have bought it yesterday so he can't have had time to do much with it."

He opened his mouth to ask me if I was sure. Luckily, he closed it, nodded and hurried off. I was glad of that. I didn't want to have to explain . . .

CHAPTER FORTY-SEVEN

La Perla di Napoli was on the edge of Greenwich Village between a grocery store and a tiny office that published what appeared to be a highly subversive newspaper. The dark green paint on the outside would need some work soon and the green and white striped awning was only good for perhaps a couple more years, but inside the friendly welcome and the rustic Italian atmosphere made up for everything.

Of course, I was greeted in a friendly manner because I was with Gabriella but I watched couples and families coming in after us and every one was known to Giovanni and Elsa Rossini. The restaurant was small with only a dozen tables squeezed close together. On the walls were oil paintings, probably by some local artist, depicting familiar Italian scenes from pigeon-laden St. Mark's Square to a certain tower with a very pronounced tilt. Between them hung wicker-covered Chianti bottles, banners declaring undying support for the Intra-Milan soccer team and photographs of prominent Italians from Tony Bennett and Dean Martin to Pavarotti and the Pope.

The scent of basil hung heavy in the small room but it was losing the unequal struggle against waves of garlic. I fancied I could discern the smells of sage and rosemary but against such powerful competition, that was probably imagination. If pasta had a smell, though, it would have dominated all others, for the steaming plates sailed by continuously, carried aloft by Gabriella's perspiring father, a small wiry man with a happy grin and a non-stop line of chatter in both Italian and English.

"Does your father cook too?" I asked Gabriella. She was wearing a black sweater with tiny sparkles in it and a skirt in a sort of cobalt color. Her hair was lustrous black—I tried to push the overused "raven's wing" description away, apt as it was.

"Oh yes. He's a bit lighter on his feet than mamma so he spends more time here up front. But he's up every morning by six, making the pasta."

"Seldom had better," I told her.

We had started with a tray of antipasti—mortadella, Parma ham, *margottini* (small domes of polenta sprinkled with gruyère), salami, smoked salmon with sliced mushrooms (Gabriella's eyes had widened—"Everybody doesn't get this," she confided), *ceci* (chickpeas), eggplant slices rolled around *caciocavallo* cheese, marinated mussels, a slice of *scarpazzone* (spinach pie) . . . It was a feast in itself and the accompanying garlic bread had been carefully soaked in olive oil but not allowed to become soggy.

We had finished the pasta course. It was readily identifiable as having been made from semolina but Gabriella explained that it was known as *cavatieddi,* a specialty of Apulia. Pieces of dough the size of a thumbnail had been pressed out with the tip of a butter knife to produce a shape like a seashell but smaller than the similar and better-known *orrechietti* that resemble the lobe of an ear.

Giovanni came and poured more of a luscious ruby-red Amarone, then hurried off, calling "Pronto, pronto" to a loud demand for more bread. "He usually serves a Chianti Classico to special customers," said Gabriella. "He must think you're running for mayor."

"Not even chief of police," I told her.

We sipped the wine. It was rich and smooth. A wine taster would describe it as having raisin and chocolate flavors but such descriptions should be confined to the trade—they merely confuse the average wine drinker.

"So the case is all wrapped up now," I mused. "You found

the gun in Eck's car and it fired the bullets that killed both men."

Gabriella sipped a little more of her wine. "As wrapped up as they ever are. We've leaned on Mr. Singyang too. He most likely did buy the birds' nests, though we'll never prove it, but it looks as if the sale was done so carefully that he really didn't know the identity of the seller."

"Have you found out how Keyhoe paid Eck? I mean, was it twenty thousand fifty-dollar bills or what?"

"No trace yet but it won't take long. Might have been diamonds—that's a popular way to pay large sums using a small package."

"Then the seller has to be able to tell real from phony too. Does *he* have to get an authenticator as well?"

"Hopefully," said Gabriella. "Anything to make things tougher for the bad guys."

"Another thing—I hadn't realized that you had probed into Marvell's movements so closely."

"Oh, of course we did. And we found out that Marvell had to fly to Boston to be there when his daughter had a critical brain operation."

"He could have told me that."

"He's a very private man. Doesn't like to give anything of himself. He knew this two weeks earlier—which was when he told Cartwright that he was to meet the delivery, giving Cartwright time to plan the theft with Eck. That also prompted Eck to spread suspicion on Marvell—spread further by Keyhoe."

"So Keyhoe caved in and Marvell has the Ko Feng back."

Gabriella nodded agreement.

"I'm still uncertain about the motive for killing Don Renshaw," I said.

"We expect to get confirmation from the interrogation of Eck but we know that Renshaw spotted the similarity in the two thefts. The obvious man for him to call was Cartwright, who told Eck, and both of them evidently thought that Renshaw knew more than he did. Incidentally, we had already had word that Eck's desk was heavily in debt."

In a casual voice, she went on, "I had a half hour with the vice-president of Paramount Pharmaceuticals this morning. You hadn't mentioned she was a woman."

"Didn't I?" I frowned, tapping my forehead. "I suppose it wasn't important. I just saw her as a vice-president."

"I was wondering," Gabriella said, still casual, "why you thought she was telling the truth when she told you she was losing her job because she hadn't been able to buy the Ko Feng."

"It wasn't the truth? You mean she's not losing her job?"

"Oh, that's true enough. I confirmed it before I talked to her. I just wondered how you were so sure."

"Oh, experience," I said loftily. "From years of talking to witnesses."

"Witnesses to who put the copper wire into the gorgonzola, for instance?"

"I know that's not like grilling murderers," I protested. "But I could tell she hadn't bought the Celestial Spice."

"Too good-looking?"

"Not at all."

"You mean you don't think she is?"

"Oh, in a—a blond sort of way, I suppose she is, yes. But that's not why I thought she hadn't bought the spice."

"Hm." She sounded unimpressed but I supposed she was used to much sterner interrogation techniques at the NYPD. "You know, you still haven't explained how you learned that Keyhoe had bought the spice."

"I—er, didn't exactly learn it, well, not in a direct manner . . ."

"Because it could have turned out to be somebody who hadn't previously shown up in inquiries."

"I didn't think so. I was counting on the pressure we had put on the thief. After all, I had declared a sample a phony when

I knew it was the real thing and that had queered that sale. We discussed the likelihood of killing me as revenge but I was betting on the thief continuing to act in the same rational, logical pattern as before and not react emotionally.

"So rather than go further afield," I went on, "which would take longer, he did the smart thing. He got another authenticator—one from three thousand miles away—and got the best deal he could from one of the willing buyers on hand."

"The testing you went through at Martha's should have sewed it up," said Gabriella. "Which willing buyer was that?"

"It was Gloria Branson."

She darted me a sharp look. "It was? You didn't recognize her voice . . . well, no reason why you should. Any security store sells devices for $19.95 that will disguise your voice so that your own mother wouldn't know it."

"She may have been a good first choice. With her job on the line, she was anxious to buy. Eck probably approached Keyhoe next."

"I think so. He was almost as anxious."

"Gloria Branson talked too about some research you were going to help her with?"

"Whenever I can, I like to help expand the database," I said virtuously.

"I talked to Kay Grenville at New England Assurance also," she continued. "She received a phone call inviting her to discuss a deal for returning the Ko Feng."

"Yes, we talked about that possibility, didn't we? Eck would have been exploring that possibility when he found he was having problems selling the Ko Feng. What did she tell him?"

"She turned him down, although she didn't know who he was. Told him two murders made any deal out of the question."

A beaming Giovanni Rossini appeared with two plates of *fritto misto* and set them down before us with a flourish. He poured us more Amarone—in true Italian style, he wasn't fussy about when to serve white and when to serve red.

Gabriella went on. "We were having another round of interviews with the restaurant people too, just in case the thief had any idea of trying some different approach with them. I talked to Mrs. Rifkin first."

"Who?" I had asked the question before it struck me but Gabriella was already saying, "Well, I suppose you know her only as Ayesha . . ."

"How do you decide on your interviewing technique?" I asked, savoring the crispy, crackly little fish. "Start with all the women?"

She smiled. "Hal thought I might get more out of them. You know—woman to woman . . . Why, what's the matter?" she asked slyly, "afraid your girlfriends might blurt out some indiscretion?"

"I'm sure any of them might," I said, "but as long as it concerned the case, it wouldn't matter." I motioned to the *fritto misto*. "This is excellent. Cooked just right. Your mother has a magic touch."

She chuckled delightfully, attacking the fish with gusto. "Okay, I won't tease you anymore. This is good, isn't it? It's one of my mother's favorites, she can make a meal of it."

With every table filled, Gabriella's father was kept busy. "He has a waitress help him on Friday and Saturday nights," Gabriella said. "Other nights, he manages alone."

Tiny fish fried that way are always salty and Giovanni thoughtfully brought us a large bottle of San Pellegrino.

"It's almost ready," he said and Gabriella and I exchanged excited glances.

The previous day, as soon as I told Hal Gaines that Keyhoe was the buyer of the Ko Feng, he had promptly placed him under arrest. Leading him to believe that Eck had admitted who the Ko Feng had been sold to had resulted in Keyhoe caving in completely. The precious sack had been recovered and—for the last time, I hoped—I was called upon to authenticate it.

I had been tempted to turn a disappointed face to Hal Gaines and say that it wasn't Ko Feng but I was doubtful if he had either the patience or the sense of humor at that moment so I gave him a thumbs-up sign.

"I'll tell Marvell," he had said. "He can make arrangements to come and collect it."

I had held out a hand—it had two stamens in it. "My fee for the authentication," I said and Gaines rolled his eyes and gave me a to-each-his-own kind of shrug as he went out.

Those same two stamens, carefully chopped, had been added to the seasoning of the *osso buco* that Mamma Rossini was now cooking as the main course. Little wonder that our mouths were watering.

"Speaking of fees for authentication," said Gabriella, "I hear you donated the five bills you got at Martha's Restaurant to the charities fund yesterday."

"How'd you hear that?"

"We have our ways."

"Evidently. Well, in our first meeting, Marvell cut me off completely but now he's come through in style and is paying all my expenses and my originally agreed fee."

"You could have kept the other five too."

"No. That was blood money—bloodstained money."

Giovanni went by, both arms laden with plates of pasta, then he was back at once with another bottle of Amarone. He pulled the cork, then as he poured, he looked back in surprise. "Hey, here's Mamma!"

Beaming, perspiring, Mamma bustled out with a plate in each hand and set them before us.

"Have you tasted it, Mamma?" asked Gabriella, eyes alight.

Mamma touched fingers to her mouth and raised them in a salute.

"Buon appetito!" she wished us. "It's *magnifico!"*

She left us. Gabriella and I tasted . . . our eyes met. Perhaps the opportunity for research into one of Ko Feng's fabled characteristics hadn't slipped by after all.